UNFINISHED LIVES

WHAT IF...?

UNFINISHED LIVES

WHAT IF...?

CONCEPT BY MICHAEL VINER

DOVE
BOOKS

Acknowledgments:
Anne Frank: The Diary of a Young Girl. Copyright © 1967 by Doubleday, a division of Bantam Doubleday Dell Publishing Group, Inc.
"Heartbreak Hotel" (M.B. Axton, Tommy Durden, Elvis Presley), Copyright © 1956 by Tree Publishing Co., Inc. Copyright Renewed.
"Over the Rainbow" (Harold Arlen and E.Y. Harburg), Copyright © 1938, 1939 (renewed 1966, 1967) Metro-Goldwyn-Mayer, Inc.

ISBN 0-7871-0299-7

Printed in the United States of America

Dove Books
301 North Cañon Drive
Beverly Hills, CA 90210

Distributed by Penguin USA

Text design and layout by Michele Lanci-Altomare
Jacket design by Rick Penn-Kraus
Photos of James Dean, John F. Kennedy, and Marilyn Monroe © Phil Stern Photo
Digital Services by 360°—Mik Lennartson

First Printing: September, 1995

10 9 8 7 6 5 4 3 2 1

TABLE OF CONTENTS

MARILYN
MONROE

BY VERNON SCOTT

*I*t was on the morning of August 5, 1962 when Dr. Ralph Greenson, Marilyn Monroe's psychiatrist, broke the actress' bedroom window with a fireplace poker given to him by her housekeeper, Eunice Murray.

With difficulty, Greenson climbed through the window and rushed to Marilyn, lying nude on her rumpled queen-sized bed, a white telephone clutched in her hand. The physician felt for the actress' pulse and was relieved to find a feeble beat. He lifted her right eyelid. The iris was unusually dilated. Beside the bed, Greenson found two empty vials. One had contained Nembutal and the other chloral hydrate. Greenson moved Marilyn from her prone position to a supine one, resting her head on a pillow and noting her pallid skin was clammy and cool. He speculated on how close she was to death.

He unlocked the bedroom door, allowing Eunice Murray into the room before replacing the telephone on its cradle.

"It's a good thing you called, Mrs. Murray," the graying, bearded psychiatrist said in his authoritative Teutonic accent. "She's still alive. Warm some water. Quickly, now!"

Greenson dialed Dr. Hyman Engelberg. They had consulted many times on their mutual patient. The clock on Marilyn's bedside table read 3:40 A.M. Warm, cloying air swept into the room through the broken window as Greenson waited for Engelberg to answer the telephone.

When he heard Engelberg's voice, Greenson said, "Hyman, it's Ralph Greenson. I'm with Marilyn. You'd better get here quickly. She's done it again."

"How bad is she?"

"Comatose. She apparently overdosed on prescribed medication. There are a couple of empty bottles by the bed."

"I don't recall renewing her prescription. Any other signs of drugs?"

"Not that I can see. But I haven't looked around thoroughly."

Engelberg was silent for a moment. "See if you can bring her around. Stimulate her if you can. Try to get an emetic into her, a purge of some sort. And you'd better call a private ambulance company, just in case. I'll be there in twenty minutes."

Greenson replaced the instrument, then picked it up and called the Goodhew Ambulance service. He proceeded to search Marilyn's bedroom with care. Her clothes: blue jeans, a white silk blouse, cotton brassiere, and white bikini panties were tossed in a jumble near the door. Cosmetics were strewn messily around a vanity that was against a wall near the entrance to her bathroom. A motion picture script was thrown carelessly on the floor, its pages splayed. There was a jagged rip where a page had been torn from the rest of the manuscript. Greenson's eyes probed the disorder until he found the missing page lying on the carpet on the far side of the actress' bed.

He bent to pick it up, straightening with some surprise.

In Marilyn's curious, almost illegible hand was scribbled:

Bobby:
You had no right to walk out on me tonight. You promised!
I believed you. You're using me like Jack did. I can't take
any more of you Kennedies [sic]. This is the last time. But I
love you. I still love you.

—M.

Greenson pocketed the note. He was sure the message was addressed to Robert Kennedy, and he knew the inflammatory consequences its contents would ignite if it were made public. With John F. Kennedy in the White House, the scandal would be incalculable. During recent months in therapy, Marilyn had confided her love affair with Bobby Kennedy as well as her fling with the president. She wept, expressing fears that the celebrated brothers had passed her back and forth like a prostitute while she had given both men her love as well as her body. On her last visit to his office, Marilyn told Greenson that Bobby had seriously discussed leaving his wife, Ethel, to marry her.

The psychiatrist decided against showing the note to Engelberg.

He slapped Marilyn's face sharply on each cheek. She failed to respond to the blows except to emit a barely perceptible groan. Greenson hurried into the bathroom, which was in greater disarray than the bedroom. Drugs, cosmetics, underwear, towels, and toilet articles littered the pink-and-white room, spilling into the bathtub and over the marble counters. Greenson located a bottle of Ipecac in the medicine cabinet. He diluted a capful in a glass of water and returned to Marilyn.

The psychiatrist lifted her head and poured the liquid between her lips. Some of the mixture dribbled from the sides of her mouth, trickled down her chin, and fell on her chest, running down her large, flattened breasts. Greenson set down the glass, retrieved a towel, and dried off his patient. He then pulled the sheet up under her chin, noting that Marilyn's skin was almost as white as the sheet itself.

The telephone rang, startling the doctor. Thinking perhaps it was Engelberg, he lifted the receiver.

A distraught English-accented voice demanded, "Who is this?"

Greenson replied, "May I ask who's calling?"

"Is this the Monroe residence?"

"Yes, it is. This is Doctor Ralph Greenson."

"The phone's been busy for hours. Is Marilyn okay, or what?"

"It is almost four o'clock in the morning. Who is calling, please?" Greenson said.

"Hello, Doctor. It's Peter Lawford. We've met. I talked to Marilyn about midnight, and she was in pretty rough shape. Is she okay now?"

Greenson was relieved it was Lawford. Marilyn had told him the actor was her principal contact with Robert Kennedy, as he had been in her relationship with the president.

"She is very ill. Doctor Engelberg is on his way here."

"Is she going to make it?"

"I don't know, Peter."

"Has she said anything?"

"No."

"Did she, er . . . well, did she leave any messages or anything?"

"Yes, a note."

"Christ! What does it say?"

Greenson hesitated. He told himself the note constituted a confidence between patient and doctor.

"I am not certain Marilyn would want me to divulge its contents," Greenson said. "I will wait until she recovers and then return it to her."

"Just one question, Doctor. Is it addressed to anyone specifically? To me, for instance?"

"Not to you, Peter. But, yes, it is a note to someone of prominence."

Lawford was silent, thinking. Earlier he had driven Bobby Kennedy from Marilyn's Brentwood home to catch a private Lear jet at an almost deserted Clover Field, Santa Monica's small airport. The plane would have delivered Bobby to his San Francisco destination two hours ago. It would be difficult to prove Bobby had interrupted his attendance at the American Bar Association conference that weekend to secretly fly to Los Angeles. After all, he had been accompanied on the trip by his wife and children, although he had left them at the ranch of a friend in Gilroy, California.

"Doctor, if I came up there right now, do you suppose you could give me that note?"

Greenson didn't hesitate. "I think not."

"Tell Marilyn that if she needs me, I'll be right here," Lawford said.

Greenson hung up. Marilyn's face had gained a little color. She was, however, still unconscious when she began to retch. The Ipecac was doing its work.

The first thing Marilyn saw when she opened her eyes was the white ceiling and its hard, cold aluminum light fixture. Her aching head felt as if it were in a vise. She was unable to move it, but peripherally she could see the glucose IV bottle on its stand to her right and another bottle dripping liquid into a tube on her left. She attempted, without success, to move her arms, but they were held fast by restraints. Even her legs were immobilized by straps. She could feel a catheter tube pressing into her.

Her throat was dry and constricted, and she had a bitter taste in her mouth.

"Where am I?" she cried in little more than a whisper.

A black nurse in a crisp white uniform hurried from her chair in the closed room. She stood by the side of the bed.

Marilyn slid her eyes in the nurse's direction and repeated her question.

"You are in Cedars of Lebanon Hospital, Miss Thomas."

"Thomas? Get me a telephone," Marilyn ordered.

"I'm sorry. It's against regulations in the psychiatric wing."

"The *what?*" Marilyn was horrified.

"I'll call your doctor."

The nurse disappeared as Marilyn struggled weakly against her bonds. *Jesus, the psychiatric floor. Who knows I'm here? What will the newspapers say? I have to talk to Bobby.*

Marilyn sank back into a troubled sleep. She was wakened an hour later by Ralph Greenson gently shaking her arm.

"Marilyn," he said.

"Ralph, what the hell am I doing in the crazy ward? Are you responsible for this?"

"Marilyn. Marilyn. We're trying to save your life."

"Don't give me that shit! You cocksuckers are just trying to protect the fucking Kennedys like everyone else. I know what you're doing."

"Please, Marilyn. You've got to pull yourself together. You almost did it this time. Hyman Engelberg barely pulled you through. You'd taken enough drugs to kill a person twice your size."

"Get me the hell out of here, you bastard. Now! I mean it!"

"I cannot do that, Marilyn. You are a very sick woman. No one knows you are here except Mrs. Murray, your agent, and your publicity lady. This must not get out to the media. It would be very destructive to you in every way. You'll have to spend a few days here until you regain your strength, then perhaps a month or two in the country someplace to pull yourself together. I'll . . . "

"Bullshit! Get me a telephone."

"I'm sorry, Marilyn. I . . . "

"I'm going to call the president of the United States. Jack will take my call. That's what I'm going to do. You can't keep me here against my will. It's against the law."

Greenson stroked Marilyn's forehead. She was wan and perspiring. Her face was strangely bald. Without makeup, her eyebrows disappeared, and she was almost unrecognizable as the world's most photographed woman. It had been more than forty-eight hours since Greenson had admitted her to the hospital under the name of Beverly Thomas, but it would take at least an additional week for the toxins to leach from her ravaged system. Several days would pass before Marilyn would be well enough to think and behave rationally.

The psychiatrist's silence annoyed her. "Am I going to get a telephone or not?"

"No."

"You asshole. At least untie my arms."

"We must leave them as they are for a time, Marilyn. It's important that you get the nutrients intravenously. You'll have to follow orders this time. It was a very close call."

"I want to talk to Peter Lawford. Can he visit me here?"

"Later, Marilyn. You are not to see or talk to anyone except your nurses, myself, and Doctor Engelberg."

"You prick, Ralph. You've done this to me. You and Jack and Bobby and all the other goddamn men in my life. You'll pay for this. You—"

"Marilyn, Marilyn," Greenson soothed. "Just for a few days, until you're free of all the poison in your system."

"Fuck you, Ralph Greenson. Fuck you! I'm not your patient anymore. You're fired. Now get out."

Marilyn closed her eyes and sank back into nightmarish sleep.

<hr />

Eunice Murray had put Marilyn's house in sparkling order. There were fresh flowers in every room when the actress returned from Cedars of Lebanon accompanied by Greenson and Engelberg.

For once, the network of hospital tipsters had been frustrated. Her presence in Cedars had gone undiscovered. More than a week had passed in the life of Marilyn Monroe without her whereabouts being known. Pat Newcomb, her publicist, awaited Marilyn at the front door.

"You look marvelous," Pat said, embracing her long-time client and personal friend.

Marilyn gave the publicist a peck on the cheek. "I'm wrung out, Pat. I've got to get to a telephone."

She turned to the doctors as she entered her home. "Thanks, Ralph. Thanks, Hy. I promise, I'll be a good girl."

Greenson was not amused. "I'll stop by tomorrow."

"You okay?" Pat asked.

"What do you think? Ten days in the fucking hospital without a telephone or visitor!"

"Well, I've got good news," Pat said with false cheerfulness. "Twentieth called last week. There's some interest in reviving *Something's Got to Give*. Dean Martin said he was ready to go ahead with it and— "

"The bastards fired me."

"But George Cukor and Harry Brand and the others at the studio think the picture can be salvaged if you're well enough," Pat said hurriedly. "They didn't know you were so ill, Marilyn."

"I can't work now, the doctors say I need to rest. Anyhow, I've got some personal things to take care of this minute."

Pat stopped as Marilyn entered her home. "What do you want me to tell them?"

"Nothing. Call me tomorrow."

Pat turned reluctantly and walked toward her car, promising to telephone later in the day.

Marilyn's blunt, unmanicured finger dialed the familiar number.

"You have reached the White House switchboard."

"I'm making a personal call to the president," Marilyn announced, her tone far from the breathy, little-girl voice so familiar to millions.

"This is Norma Mortenson," she added. The name was one she and Jack Kennedy had agreed upon almost a year earlier. In the past she would be switched directly to the president except on those occasions when he was genuinely unavailable. At those times she was courteously informed the president would return her call.

"One moment, please," the male operator said.

He was off the line for a full minute. When he spoke again, the Secret Service man said, "I'm sorry. The president's office says there is no clearance for anyone by the name of Norma Mortenson."

Marilyn knew instantly her access to the president of the United States had been withdrawn forever. She was stunned by the sudden sense of isolation that swept over her, a deflating feeling of loss of power. She depressed the telephone cradle and dialed another Washington, D.C. number.

"Mr. Kennedy's office," a voice responded.

"May I speak to Mr. Robert Kennedy, please? This is Norma Mortenson."

"I'm sorry, Mr. Kennedy is in conference. Do you care to leave a message?"

"Would you ask him to call me, please. He has my number. Thank you."

Again Marilyn dialed, this time to a Santa Monica beach number.

"Hello," Peter Lawford said.

"Peter, it's Marilyn."

"Thank God, Marilyn. Where have you been? How are you feeling?"

"At Cedars, Peter," Marilyn said in a tired voice. "I accidentally overdosed on amphetamines."

"God, honey, I'm sorry. Are you going to be okay?"

"Yes. Don't worry about it. You've got to help me, Peter. I can't get Jack or Bobby on the phone. I know you have their personal numbers. . . ."

Lawford was silent for a beat, his voice falsely lighthearted. He said, "Well, I don't think that's such an awfully good idea right now, Marilyn. Ah, you know, they're both involved in all that . . . "

"Peter, you're stalling. They don't want to talk to me, do they?"

"No. That's not it at all, Marilyn. They're just busy."

"Bullshit, Peter. Why have they slammed the door in my face?"

"Well, we all heard about your, er, illness, honey. I talked to Ralph Greenson at your house the night you, ah, were under the weather. He said you were in pretty bad shape."

"So?"

"Well, some of us thought you might have been, you know, on the brink."

Marilyn's voice trembled. "You think I tried to commit suicide?"

"Ralph said something about a note."

"What about it, Peter?"

"Ralph gave it back to you, didn't he? You've destroyed it, haven't you?" Lawford's question held an edge of fear.

"You can tell Bobby and Jack there isn't any note. They're both perfectly safe in their perfect little marriages with their perfect little wives. And you can tell them both for me to go fuck themselves."

Lawford, relieved, said, "Come on now, Marilyn, we'll all be getting together again."

"And fuck you, too, Peter. I never want to talk to any of you for the rest of my life."

It was the last contact Marilyn Monroe would ever have with a member of the Kennedy family. Nor would she mention the Kennedy name again. Not in the shock after Jack's assassination in Dallas, not when Bobby was cut down during his presidential campaign in Los Angeles five years later.

Marilyn heeded Greenson's advice. She spent a month with Pat Newcomb, Eunice Murray, and her masseur, Ralph Roberts, in a private rented residence in Maui, Hawaii.

The world-famous glamour girl strove religiously to regain her health. Adjusting her sleeping schedules, she cut her intake of Nembutal to virtually nothing. For the first time since her marriage to Arthur Miller, she watched her diet, refusing sweets and liquor. Marilyn allowed her hair to return to its natural brown and wore no makeup. The retreat, entirely hidden from the public eye, reconstituted the actress.

"The best thing is isolating myself from the men," she confided to Pat.

Marilyn remained out of contact with her former husbands and recent lovers. She managed to convince herself that men had always been the cause of her psychological breakdowns and she no longer needed to rely on them emotionally.

At the end of her Hawaiian rest cure, Marilyn agreed to return to 20th Century-Fox studios to finish *Something's Got to Give*. Her agents assured the thirty-six-year-old actress that she would never again work in Hollywood unless she fulfilled her contract to the studio and completed the movie. The insurance company would underwrite her health.

Marilyn returned to the mainland and faced a carnival-like news conference at Los Angeles International Airport as she stepped off the airplane looking better than she had in years. Her hair, platinum again, sparkled in the sunshine. She looked slender, refreshed, and beautiful. And she knew it.

At six o'clock the following Monday morning, she bathed and toweled off in front of her full-length bathroom mirror. It was to be her first day back at work on *Something's Got to Give*. She studied her body objectively. There was a clear suggestion of sagging in her breasts and stretch marks at the point of her hips. Turning sideways, Marilyn noted unhappily a thickening in her upper thighs. There were small dimples in her buttocks.

She dreaded having to play a nude swimming pool scene later in the picture and felt a slight panic. Marilyn threw open her medicine chest to withdraw a bottle of Benzedrine. Swallowing two capsules, she felt the rush almost immediately, and knew she would be able to face the cameras again.

Something's Got to Give went two weeks over schedule and two million dollars over budget. Marilyn was chronically late, sometimes not appearing on the set at all. Director George Cukor was frequently forced to eliminate close-ups of his star, because her glazed, unfocused eyes would have shocked the audience.

Marilyn found herself in the old familiar cycle of amphetamines and other uppers every morning in order to work, and Nembutals and other downers to sleep. Facing the camera every day was as harrowing for her as it had been during her last picture, *The Misfits*. Each day Marilyn's insecurities grew, and she quickly reverted to the habit established in her recent films, drinking herself almost insensible upon returning home from the set.

Paula Strasberg, Marilyn's acting guru, was at her side every day at the studio doing what she could to protect her charge. But it was no good. Studio executives viewed the daily rushes in growing alarm. They had no choice, however, but to bring the picture in as expeditiously as possible, hoping to salvage what they could at the box office.

"My God," Marilyn told Paula on the last day of work on the set, "I'm getting *old*. I killed every one of the still shots. The lines on my face are getting so deep."

"It's all right, darling," Paula comforted in her curious European accent. "You are an actress. The lines to worry about are in the script, not in your pretty face."

"What am I going to do? How many thirty-six-year-old sex symbols are there, anyhow? They keep signing new girls, and they're giving them the same buildup they gave me. They're so young."

"Not to worry, darling. There is only one Marilyn."

"I'm not so sure. Look at me." Marilyn peered into her dressing room mirror. The heavy eyeshadow, thick pancake, and glistening lipstick failed to conceal the toll the drugs and alcohol were taking. Her face was puffy and sallow. "Christ. George has even cut my close-ups."

Something's Got to Give was released in the spring of 1963 after many delays and changes in the script, and the padding of Dean Martin's role. Marilyn, although given top billing, appeared in surprisingly few scenes. The critics cruelly commented on her haggard appearance and listless performance.

The picture failed spectacularly, and 20th Century-Fox would not recoup its negative costs. Marilyn's unreliability and sudden physical debilitation combined to convince executives at Hollywood's major studios that her career was finished. She had cost 20th Century-Fox five million dollars. MGM, Warner Bros., Paramount, and Columbia were not about to gamble on the fading star.

Marilyn, infuriated by reaction to the picture, became more reclusive. She manipulated friends to contact discredited doctors who kept her supplied with drugs. Her agents beseeched her in vain to accept inferior scripts from marginal producers.

As her physical and emotional condition continued to deteriorate, Ralph Greenson pleaded with the actress to return to the hospital for treatment.

"We cannot force you," the psychiatrist told her late in the summer. "But you are in danger of another overdose. You must get treatment or you will die."

Marilyn was unresponsive. She lost track of the days, then weeks, lost in a haze of drugs. For the first time in her life she became indifferent to her appearance, moving around her home trance-like in a bathrobe. She slept during the day, vacantly watching television far into the night. Eunice Murray was unable to do more than prepare her meals and answer the telephone, telling callers the actress was out of the city.

<hr />

Marilyn awoke late one chilly October night after sleeping thirty-two hours. Disoriented, she staggered from her bed and walked unsteadily into the kitchen to take a bottle of Dom

Perignon from the refrigerator. Unaccountably, her head was clearer than it had been in many weeks. She tuned the set to Channel 4. Johnny Carson swam into focus sitting behind his desk on *The Tonight Show*.

"What was it like playing a love scene with Marilyn Monroe?" Carson asked his guest.

The camera panned to Dean Martin, slouched in a chair beside Johnny's desk.

Martin exhaled a cloud of cigarette smoke. "Terrific," he replied easily. "She's the most beautiful dame in the world. In some ways she's like a little kid."

Carson cocked his head and said, "Some kid! Did you get to know her very well?"

"Naw," Martin answered. "But she did tell me she wanted a child of her own someday. It was kind of touching."

Martin's offhand remark electrified Marilyn. Somewhere within the actress an alarm bell sounded. Even in the aftermath of her hangover, she felt a tingle of life, a vague remembrance of a long-cherished dream.

Marilyn rose, turned off the TV set, returned to her bedroom and sat on the edge of the rumpled bed. She picked up her small personal telephone book, found the New York number she was looking for, and dialed. The telephone was picked up on the fourth ring.

Joe DiMaggio answered with a sleepy, laconic "Hello."

"Joe?"

He recognized her voice at once. "Marilyn. It's been a long, long time. Are you all right?"

"Joe, I need your help."

17

There was a pause and a quiet laugh. "You always say that when you call. And it's always in the middle of the night. What time is it?"

"I don't know. I'm sorry. But I do need you, Joe."

"What can I do for you this time, baby?"

"I've got to get out of Southern California, Joe. I have to get away from the movies and these horrible people out here. I'm afraid. I'm afraid I'm losing my mind."

"Now, baby, you're just having one of your bad nights. You'll . . ."

"No. I mean it this time. I don't want to be a star anymore. Honest. I don't want to act anymore, Joe. I want a family."

"We used to talk about having kids, remember?"

"You and Joe Junior are the nearest thing I have to a family. There isn't even a man in my life."

Joe was silent.

"I don't mean you and I should . . . I don't mean us together," Marilyn said. "I really do want a child. A real home, and everything. Somebody real. Someplace where I can be me."

"Marilyn, it's late. Can we talk tomorrow?"

"Joe, please. I want to stop being Marilyn Monroe. There is no Marilyn left. I want to be Norma Jean again. I swear to God I do. They're letting unmarried women adopt children now. I could go to some other city. I could change my name. I'm serious, Joe."

Joe said nothing.

Marilyn interpreted his silence as reproach. "I haven't had a drink in a couple of days," she went on, her voice rising near hysteria. "I haven't even taken a pill. Please, Joe, listen to me. I'm alone. I'm dying, I know I am."

"Honey, take it easy. Are you serious? Do you mean what you're saying?"

"Yes. Yes. Yes. Please help me."

Five weeks after her conversation with DiMaggio, Marilyn walked unrecognized through the Columbus, Ohio airport. Her hair was tinted dark brown, several shades deeper than her own natural color. She wore slacks, a shapeless sweater, and a bulky coat that failed to conceal the fact that the woman beneath was clearly overweight. Her face bore little makeup.

Marilyn shivered as she stepped out into the brisk midwestern weather to hail a taxi. She told the driver to take her to the Neal House Hotel in the center of the city facing the Ohio State Capitol building. She registered as Norma Johnson.

Safely in her own room, she asked the hotel operator to connect her with the room of another guest.

"I'm here," she said.

In a few minutes she opened the door to welcome Joe DiMaggio, who gently took her in his arms and kissed her forehead.

"Oh, Joe, thank you. Thank you."

Joe found it difficult to speak. He would not have recognized his former wife had he passed her on the street. Marilyn looked bloated, exhausted, and astoundingly frumpy.

He was unable to hide his surprised reaction.

"Nobody on the plane recognized me," she said, touching her hair self-consciously with her hand. "I flew tourist. I look terrible, I know."

"No, baby. You just look different. You even sound different."

"I am. I really am. I don't have to look in mirrors anymore and worry if there's a hair out of place. And you look wonderful. The gray in your hair is really attractive. Distinguished."

"Old ballplayers never die, they just gray away."

"Joe, did you get the house?"

"My friend Bill Murphy has taken care of just about everything. He found a small rental out in Upper Arlington. I didn't tell him who the house was for. But it's all settled."

"When can I see it?"

"Tomorrow."

"What about the adoption agency?"

Joe sighed. "That's going to take some time. His wife, Gloria, works with some people at a private foundling home. They're trying to work things out."

Marilyn touched the sleeve of Joe's blue pinstriped suit. "You're wonderful to do all this for me, Joe. God, I wish I'd known what I was doing when we were married."

Her words made DiMaggio uncomfortable. "Water over the dam, baby."

"Joe?"

"Uh-huh."

"I haven't had a drink or a pill in more than a month. It's been awful. Cold turkey. My nerves are gone. It almost killed me flying here alone like this. But I made it."

"Does anyone know where you are?"

"Not a soul. I gave Mrs. Murray her notice. I just left the house as it was and I only brought two suitcases."

"Did you tell your agents?"

"Nobody."

DiMaggio walked to the window to look out at the State Capitol lawn and the changing leaves of the trees.

"All hell is going to break loose in the press when they find out Marilyn Monroe is missing," he said.

"She's dead, Joe. She didn't want to live anymore. I don't miss her."

Joe was uncomfortable again. He changed the subject. "You're going to be lonely here. You don't know a soul."

"I'll make it work. You'll see. Once I get the baby, it will be all right."

Joe explained as he had on the telephone ten days earlier. The adoption would not be legal. He was careful not to use the term black market baby. Gloria Murphy's association with a home for unwed mothers would enable Marilyn to pay for the natural mother's medical, prenatal, and delivery care in exchange for the child. There would be no official documents or records. Should there be any inquiries, Norma Johnson was a widow who gave birth to her child after her husband's death in a car accident.

"I understand," Marilyn said, nodding thoughtfully.

"I told the Murphys you were a widow from Chicago and that you were moving here. But, Marilyn, are you positive this is what you want?"

Marilyn's eyes glistened with tears. "I've never been so sure of anything in my life."

"What about finances?"

"We went over all that, Joe. I cleaned out my safe deposit boxes and got cashier's checks for my savings accounts. God, it was complicated. I never did stuff like this before."

Joe grinned and turned to face his ex-wife.

"Welcome to the real world. You're learning how the other half lives."

"It was sort of fun. But it's scary, too."

"I won't be able to come here often," Joe said softly. "People still recognize this old ballplayer. And it could tip off the press."

Marilyn was pensive. "But they don't even know I've disappeared yet."

"Don't worry," Joe said. "They will."

The December sixth front-page banner headline of the *Los Angeles Times* ran for eight columns in black block letters: MARILYN MONROE DISAPPEARS.

The wire services picked up the story, which blossomed into print throughout the United States and in most cities of the world. The mysterious disappearance of the actress electrified the media. Rumors of foul play, suicide, and kidnapping were printed and broadcast. Marilyn Monroe's disappearance was second only to the assassination of John F. Kennedy as the story of the year for 1963. Old friends, costars, and associates were questioned by police. Many gave interviews speculating on the fate of Marilyn Monroe. Ralph Greenson appeared on national television, ending his interview with an appeal to Marilyn to reveal her whereabouts.

Many cynics suspected a publicity stunt. The Los Angeles Police Department issued a search warrant to enter her home.

They reported the premises looked as though the actress had left for the day and would return any minute. Her automobile was in the garage. The post office revealed that Marilyn had asked that her mail be stopped with no forwarding address. Utility companies and the telephone company had been asked to discontinue service. Her agents were dumbfounded, as was Pat Newcomb.

Marilyn Monroe, the world's premier glamour girl, had disappeared without a trace. It was the stuff of novels and motion pictures. A New York publisher announced that Norman Mailer would write a biography of the actress. 20th Century-Fox said they would re-release *Something's Got to Give*.

Chief Thomas Parker of the Los Angeles Police Department assigned a special squad of detectives to comb the city for Marilyn's body. False Marilyn-sighting reports came from all over the world.

President Lyndon Johnson gave the Federal Bureau of Investigation permission to enter the case. DiMaggio and Arthur Miller were questioned but were unable to help authorities in their search for leads in the mystery.

Marilyn Monroe had vanished as if she never existed.

◆

The fieldstone-and-frame house on Coventry road in Upper Arlington was comfortably furnished and cozy, an inconspicuous dwelling in the upper-middle-class community.

It was Christmas Day, 1963. Marilyn was dressed in powder-blue pants, a knobby white wool sweater, and comfortable low-heeled shoes. She paced through the living room with its maple tables and overstuffed matching chairs that sat facing each other on either side of the fireplace, where a cheery fire crackled. She walked into the kitchen, which she had made gleam, to open the refrigerator for the eighth time to reassure herself it remained stocked with the proper baby formula. A sideboard held two dozen glass nursing bottles and nipples beside a shining new sterilizer.

Then she went upstairs to her own bedroom, approving its neat and spare appearance. She opened her closet door to hang up the robe she had discarded on the bed earlier. It amused her to see how few clothes she had needed in the past month: earth-toned dresses and jackets, plain pants, and a half-dozen pairs of shoes. It was no longer necessary for her to spend hours worrying about her wardrobe. She relied on her own essentially simple tastes, choosing conservative fabrics and styles, nothing that would draw attention.

She walked almost timidly into the nursery with its pink-and-blue decor.

It's perfect, she thought. She had taken loving pains buying every item in the room. The flounce around the crib was bright and colorful. She had bought prints of clowns and puppies and kittens for the walls. There was a mobile, too, with multicolored plastic birds, twirling lazily beside the crib. A bassinet stood in one corner and a padded rocking chair in another. A changing table was stacked with a generous stock of diapers. *This is where my baby will live,* Marilyn thought.

She glanced into the only mirror in the room. "Ugh!" she groaned. "God, have you gained weight, Norma Jean."

Her hair was darker by a tone since her arrival in Columbus more than seven weeks earlier. Her hips were broader, her breasts heavier, and there was no denying the beginnings of what would become a substantial double chin. But her skin was pink and glowing. She had not had a drop of alcohol nor taken drugs for almost two months. Food, not chemicals, had become her refuge.

Anyone searching her face for a trace of Marilyn Monroe would have discovered she was indeed the actress. But the absence of makeup, the darkened hair and brows, the added weight, and monotone voice served to conceal the woman who had been the star that spring in *Something's Got to Give.* The uproar over her disappearance had abated somewhat, with the investigation diminishing as the holiday season approached. Marilyn dispassionately followed the story in *The Columbus Dispatch* and on the television news shows. It was as if she were hearing about a woman she never knew.

Her neighbors paid her little heed. At the Upper Arlington shopping center, the pretty but overweight newcomer was accepted as just another housewife. It pleased Marilyn that she did not draw a second glance from the other shoppers. In the evenings, she contented herself watching TV, reading light fiction, and anticipating the first glimpse of her child.

Today was Christmas, after all. Gloria Murphy would be bringing the baby, a week-old girl, at any moment.

After what seemed an eternity, the door chimes brought Marilyn scurrying down the carpeted staircase. She threw open the door in the small entry hall to find Gloria, accompanied by her husband, Bill, standing in the snow that had accumulated on her front porch. They wore huge smiles, but Marilyn could only see the tiny bundle in Gloria's arms. Instinctively, she reached for the child and pressed the blanketed baby to her.

"Merry Christmas, Norma," Gloria said, suppressing a desire to weep.

"I feel like Santa Claus today," Bill said, laughing.

Marilyn's blue eyes filled with tears. The warmth of the baby radiated to her core.

"She's all yours," Bill said. "And she's a real little beauty."

The three adults stood motionless for a moment in the bright, clear sunlight shimmering off the snow.

Marilyn was the first to speak again. "Please, do come in." She turned toward the open door, a cold breeze wafting into the small house.

The Murphys looked at one another knowingly. "We have to run along," Gloria said. "I think you'd like this special moment to yourself."

Bill nodded, his own throat tight with emotion.

Marilyn turned in their direction and, the baby clutched to her possessively, kissed them each on the cheek.

"God bless you," she said, tears flowing freely now. "A merry, merry Christmas to you."

She closed the door and walked quickly to the divan in the living room, where she sat down, hugging the child. With deliberate care and tenderness, she pulled back the lightweight receiving blanket to reveal a delicate pink face and a pair of bewildered blinking blue eyes.

Marilyn gazed at her daughter for several minutes, her heart dancing. Then she unfolded the blanket further to look at the miniature fingers, which she kissed one at a time.

"Oh, God, I love you, Patricia. I love you, darling."

Bing Crosby's voice floated across the room from the television set. He was singing "White Christmas." Marilyn brought the baby's face against her own and sobbed with joy.

"Hey, Mom, I'm home!"

Patricia Johnson slammed the front door, checked her appearance in the hall mirror, and then walked with as much confidence as she could muster into the kitchen to find her mother at the breakfast table making out a grocery list. It was a sunny spring Saturday afternoon.

"Hi, honey."

Then Marilyn looked up in shock. Patricia's normally dark blonde hair was bleached almost platinum.

Daughter faced mother resolutely. "How do you like it?"

Her mother gasped. "What have you done?"

"Looks great, don't you think?" The question held a note of false bravado.

Marilyn said, "Oh, honey, it's not you. Why on earth . . . ?"

"It's the latest thing, Mom!" Patricia said defensively. "Robin had it done. Her mother didn't mind. And Nancy is going real blonde, too. Anyway, I really love it. It looks good."

Her mother smiled. She had never refused her daughter anything. Marilyn remembered her own youth and bit her lip. "Well, it's different. I guess I'll get used to it. It *is* pretty. But it makes you look older."

"Tom is crazy about it," Patricia said. "And he's asked me to the prom. Isn't that great? I knew he would."

"He's a sweet boy," Marilyn replied, looking into the happy face of her daughter. Patricia's wide-set eyes, short, straight nose, and full little figure never failed to fill her up with maternal pride. Marilyn attended all the Upper Arlington High School football games, even though she had no interest, to watch Patricia lead cheers. She was a popular, bewitching child with a winning smile that came easily to her soft, generous mouth.

The past seventeen years were the happiest in Marilyn's life. The relationship between mother and daughter had been close, loving, and more emotionally satisfying than any other she had ever known.

"He's not a boy, Mom," Patricia said, interrupting her mother's reverie. "Tom's going to be eighteen in a month."

"That's a dangerous age," Marilyn teased. "You better keep an eye on him."

"Mom!" Patricia remonstrated with feigned indignation. "This is 1980!"

"I know, darling. I was just kidding."

"What about you and Walter?"

Marilyn smiled at her daughter. "What about him?"

"You can't fool me. He's the reason you've been on that crash diet."

Marilyn blanched. She weighed almost one hundred and forty-five pounds, much too heavy for her frame. Her hips had broadened, and her thighs and breasts had grown heavier. There was a small roll around her waist now, too, and she could no longer ignore the existence of two chins. Her brown hair had strands of gray, which she chose not to color.

"What's the matter, Mom?"

"Nothing, why?"

"You look sad."

"Not at all, pumpkin. Just thinking how grown up you are now, graduating next month and all."

"You didn't answer me about Walter."

Walter Bender, at fifty-five, a year older than Marilyn, was a hearty insurance sales manager who Marilyn had been seeing for six years. A widower, Walter had been attentive, sensitive, and gentle with Marilyn, a thoughtful and experienced lover. Sex for Marilyn had at last become natural, unselfish, and joyous. She no longer had to prove she was the sexiest woman on Earth. She was astonished at the beautiful sense of shared passion she felt with Walter when they were in bed.

They met when Marilyn started working as a receptionist and general assistant at his office in downtown Columbus. Their attraction grew slowly, and as Marilyn's proficiency in her job grew, Walter came to rely on the attractive widow as much in business affairs in the office as he did emotionally when they were alone together.

"Walter is coming for dinner, if that's what you mean," Marilyn said.

"You know what I'm talking about, Mom. Are you going to marry him or not?"

"I'm thinking about it, honey. He's barbecuing some steaks for us tonight."

There was a pause, then Patricia said, "Gosh, I won't be here. We've got senior class play rehearsals tonight."

"I wish you'd forget that acting nonsense. Honestly, darling, you should be going to Ohio State with Gina and Ashley."

"God, Mom, let's not go through all that again. Mr. Bains says I have talent, a flair."

Marilyn stood up and drew her daughter into her arms, kissing the side of her face.

"Just be sure you know what you want. I was an actress once myself."

"You're kidding!"

"It's true. Not a very good one. School plays. A little theater. That kind of thing. But it wasn't the sort of life I wanted, not really."

The Boeing 747 landed at Los Angeles International Airport. The platinum blonde with the bright smile walked out of the American Airlines baggage claim area to find a taxi. The driver stowed her suitcases in the trunk.

"Where to?" he inquired, taking in the girl's figure speculatively.

"Take me to the Hollywood Holiday Inn."

"No problem."

"I'm going to like it here," the young woman said.

"Staying long?"

"Yes. I'm an actress. My mother was an actress, too."

"Walter," Marilyn called from the kitchen. "Do you want some cake to go with the ice cream?"

"Hell yes, darlin'. Let's go whole hog."

His wife of six years walked heavily into the living room. She carried a plate in each hand containing scoops of vanilla ice cream and generous slices of chocolate cake. Marilyn gave one to Walter, and as she did, she bent to kiss the top of his balding head.

"We ought to be ashamed of ourselves," she said, giggling. "We both weigh a ton."

"Yeah, why not? The heavier you get the more there is to love."

She found a place beside him on the divan, placing her dessert on the coffee table.

"What's on the tube tonight, honey?"

Walter flicked the remote control to turn on the television set. "I looked at the *TV Guide*. There's an old movie on. *Niagara*."

Marilyn smiled.

"It's a Marilyn Monroe picture. God, I was crazy about her. I almost got to see her once when she came through Columbus on a publicity tour. Jesus, she was gorgeous. A real sex bomb. They don't make 'em like that anymore."

"You're making me jealous, honey."

"Norma, she was never in the same league with you."

"I know," his wife replied.

Norma and Walter Bender held hands and settled back to watch the movie.

ELVIS
PRESLEY

BY MARILYN BECK

*E*lvis hovered at the head of the stairs, pulled the hood of the sweatshirt down low over his forehead, drew a labored breath, and nervously made his descent to the first floor of the mansion.

Heart racing, trying desperately to appear nonchalant, he passed the living room, where the housekeeper was busy with midmorning dusting and the study, where David and Mark were absorbed in a game of pool at the antique Brunswick table.

Then he was out the door, into the battered tan Chevy van, down the driveway, and by the front gates with a half-wave to the guard.

His foot pushing hard on the pedal, he took off down Elvis Presley Boulevard with a roar.

He felt like a figure caught in a surrealist painting.

Nothing seemed real . . . the brightness of the day, the traffic that clogged the street, the racking memories of recent hours. He had no idea where he was going, what he would do. All he knew was he was free—and behind him in Graceland lay a body that might have been his twin.

A nervous laugh escaped his mouth, clenched tight with tension. Would it work? Would they believe it was his lifeless form sprawled on the plush purple carpet of the lavish bathroom? He knew it would. It had to! They would bury the body of the impostor—while Elvis Aron Presley returned to the life of anonymity he had left when he was still a teen, a life free of pressures, demands, stress, and the endless fears that not even drugs nor gluttonous quantities of food could drown.

The events of the last hours washed over him; he was swept back to his bedroom, with Ginger lying beside him.

It had been a night, like countless other nights, when not even repeated doses of Demerol and Valium would bring sleep.

Ginger had stirred into consciousness when he left their bed at 9:00 A.M. "Go back to sleep," he had told her, and she did, while he groped through the darkness of the room with its black-out drapes and into his sanctuary—the combination bathroom-office-study-lounge.

He tried to read, leafed through *The Shroud of Turin*, a book about Jesus and the evolution of Christian theology. But he couldn't concentrate on anything but the dread of the nightclub engagements he was to start in several days.

Some of his recent performances had been disasters. In Baltimore, he had overloaded on pills to mask the pain of a twisted ankle, forgotten the words to a song, and demanded of the audience, "Gimme the lyrics to the damn thing"—and had to be helped as he stumbled offstage twenty minutes later.

One reviewer compared him to Judy Garland in her sad final days. Another started his review by noting Elvis' "eyelids were almost as heavy as his paunch."

Elvis stood before the mirror that covered one wall of the bathroom. Staring back was a bloated form with double chin, fleshy jowls, distended abdomen—even his hands were swollen.

He could hear the shocked intake, the derisive whispers coming from the crowd when he made his next entrance onstage. The press would be lying in wait.

It was nothing new. They had all seemed to be out to get him for years, even Walter Cronkite, a man who represented all things good and patriotic to Elvis. He could recall the shame and humiliation that had stung him two years earlier, on the night of his fortieth birthday, when he turned on *The CBS Evening News* in time to hear Cronkite characterize him as "fat and forty."

Diet pills and fasts, binges and purges, girdles beneath skintight costumes—it had gone on for years—and now he would never be forced to put himself on public exhibition again. "Let someone else do it," he muttered as he sped down the highway. "God knows enough of them are trying."

Certainly, Elvis knew it. If he hadn't, this bizarre, night-marish day would never have happened. And he wouldn't be on the way to a new life.

He remembered that recent night when the boys returned from a cruise of the bars in downtown Memphis and told him of a Presley impersonator they'd seen performing at a seedy club. On a whim, Elvis said, "I want to see him." It'd be a kick, a respite from the boredom that assailed him.

His aides went into action. When Elvis was in the mood to go to the movies, a theater was rented, closed to the public. Now Elvis wanted to go slumming, and so a call was made to the club: "Elvis is coming in, clear out the place."

They traveled in their typical caravan: Elvis with a portion of his entourage in one of his fleet of luxury autos; the rest of the "Memphis Mafia" following in another car.

They sauntered into the club and ordered drinks. Elvis motioned for the show to start, laughed when he heard the first strains of "Hound Dog" being played on the darkened stage—then froze as the spotlight caught the performer in its beam. The likeness was uncanny; so was the similarity in voice. "Hey, boss, you better be careful, someone's going to mistake this guy for you," one of the boys teased. Elvis shushed him, staring trance-like at the stage. Finally, he whispered to Joe, "Get me his name and telephone number."

He had no idea why he wanted the information. But this morning, sitting in his bathroom/sanctuary in Graceland with a mood of gloom settling ever more deeply upon him, he had become convinced his introduction to the impersonator had been preordained. God had brought him into his life to allow Elvis to find a path to peace.

Pulling the drawstring of his indigo-blue pajama bottoms tighter over his mountainous stomach, he rummaged through a pile of papers until he found a slip with the impersonator's telephone number. He dialed, identified himself to the startled listener, and instructed him to drive to Graceland. "I'll call downstairs and tell them I'm expecting a faith healer—they're used to that. Disguise yourself. Don't wear an Elvis get-up, for God's sake. Wear something with a hood. Identify yourself to the gateman as Reverend Good. Then come upstairs. I'll be waiting for you."

It had been amazingly easy. His boys had been used to his meetings with mystics, occultists, and spiritualists. And when he was with them he had privacy.

There had been no need for whispers. The bedroom, where Ginger was sleeping, was only thirty feet away, but the bathroom's heavy wooden door and tiled walls served as an effective buffer against noise.

Elvis wanted to know all about him: why and how he had become a Presley impersonator; the details of his background, his life.

He was a loner, without family or friends. He drifted from city to city, from club to club, and was planning to move on from Memphis that day. He had changed his name from Joel Kinsley to Elvis Preston in homage to his idol—and hoped to cash in on the resemblance. He had undergone cosmetic surgery to heighten that resemblance; there had been reconstruction of his nose, lips, chin, and cheeks.

"Where do you get your money? Little dives like the place I saw you in pay only peanuts."

Silence. Then . . . "I deal . . . a little drugs."

Elvis laughed. "Aw, bullshit! Just a little? Take off your shirt."

His arms looked like a pincushion, and Elvis knew why. For years Elvis had injected prescription drugs—Tuinal, Demerol, Dilaudid—into the muscles of his body. God only knew what Preston shot up, but the results—and the telltale marks—were the same.

"Want somethin' now?" Elvis asked and pulled open a drawer piled high with supplies—pain pills to relieve the muscular aches from performing, opium, uppers, downers, antidepressants. He had taken them for years, several times secretly admitted to private hospitals to "dry out." But lately nothing had helped him overcome an overwhelming sense of depression and apathy.

Elvis grabbed a handful of pills from the drawer and held them out to his guest. Preston studied them a moment, then shrugged. "What the hell," he said and downed them without benefit of water.

Preston got very high. He was excited as Elvis asked, "How'd you like to cover my gig for me in Vegas?" Then, disorientation and dizziness came. He forced himself erect, stumbled toward the sink, and fell, his head crashing against the wall.

Elvis shook him, demanding, "Get up. Hey, snap out of it!" Preston's mouth was agape, his body frozen in a contorted pose.

"My God, he's dead!" Elvis whispered. His hand reached out for the door, then stopped. He moved toward the phone and halted. He had to call someone. The police had to be told. But why? . . . *Wait a second . . . maybe I've found my way out . . . let 'em think it's me who died.*

He'd had it all, and none of it meant anything to him—the women, the cars, the planes, the luxury, the fame. What he wanted was the happiness he had known when he was just a kid playing along the muddy banks of the Tupelo creeks, strumming his guitar to the accompaniment of crickets and frogs and later making a living driving a truck. And never worrying that friends were only friends because of what his money could buy.

"It could work, it will work!" he breathed. Then he froze. "The fingerprints! They'll check the friggin' fingerprints!"

The sudden, crushing thought immobilized him. Then, just as suddenly, a memory tumbled from the storehouse of his mind, of a conversation he'd had with a buddy from the Memphis coroner's office at the time Spencer Tracy died in 1967. "They're such nitpickers out there in Hollywood, they leave nothing to chance. They'll even take Tracy's fingerprints—as if they couldn't recognize him," scoffed the Tennessee pathologist's aide. "Nah, we don't do that here; identification is enough—certainly should be, particularly with a face the whole world knows."

As Elvis completed his replay of the conversation, all doubt left him and a rush of adrenaline washed away the residue of the Demerol within his system, providing a high greater than he had enjoyed in years.

He worked quickly. In what seemed like mere seconds the inert form on the floor was dressed in Elvis' pajama bottoms, and Elvis had put on his visitor's sweatsuit.

He breathed deeply, started for the door, then stopped, glanced in the mirror, and grabbed for a razor.

"The sideburns have to go," he muttered. Cleanshaven, he ducked his head under the faucet and washed his hair free of oily lotion, then stood back and laughed. "Hell, I hardly recognize me."

Now, some four hours later, he laughed again as Preston's van rumbled its way through the countryside outside Memphis—to the accompaniment of radio news bulletins about Elvis Presley's death.

"Good riddance!" he said through a bitter grin. "It's about time you were buried." The boys and Colonel Tom had worried because he had become so reclusive. "Well, no one has to worry anymore. I'm gonna kick up my heels."

He still had no direction, no goal, no idea where he would sleep, how he would live or make a living. But such a thing didn't matter for the moment. In the glove compartment he had found Preston's wallet with three hundred dollar bills— obviously a drug dealing cache.

By late afternoon, news of his death and tributes to him and his music were just about all you could get on the radio and TV.

"The passing of the immortal Elvis Presley has saddened the world," intoned one newscaster.

"Thousands have crowded the gates of Graceland, un-willing to believe their idol is dead," reported another.

The airwaves were flooded with his music and with testimonials from world leaders and the giants of show business.

"I didn't think it would be like this . . . I didn't think there would be this much fuss," he said to himself.

By late afternoon fatigue started to set in, and pulling off the highway, he slowed to a stop beside a weather-wasted auto court with a peeling sign announcing EATS—ROOMS FOR RENT.

He glanced in the rearview mirror, tossed the hood of his sweatshirt over his hair, and strolled into the diner.

A blonde, attractive waitress with a short cotton skirt and breasts that strained against her blouse stood staring at footage of Elvis Presley on a black-and-white TV, tears streaming down her face.

She looked in the direction of the door, and Elvis gifted her with the slow, sensual smile that had elicited excited shrieks from countless females.

Her response was immediate.

"What's the stupid grin for? What the hell you looking at, you fat slob?" she said.

Startled, he sat down at the counter and ordered a burger and fries. When she slapped the plate down in front of him, she announced, "That'll be two-fifty. You pay now."

He looked confused. It had been years since he had paid for a purchase. A member of his entourage was always there to handle such matters. He suddenly felt like a stranger in a strange land.

"Money, I—"

She cut him short. "Hey, buddy, no money, no food."

She started to pull the plate away when he remembered Preston's wallet.

"I'll be back," he said, and moments later returned from the van to hand her a $100 bill.

"You must be kidding . . . you rob a bank? You expect me to change that?"

"Keep it." He shrugged. "Just give me a room to sack out."

He fell into a deep, immediate sleep—for the first time in years without the benefit of barbiturates.

Early-morning sunlight streaming through the torn window shade woke him. He shot up, confused. In recent years he had lived a nocturnal life, up all night, usually closeted in a darkened bedroom during the day. "What the hell, where am I?"

And then he remembered—and lay back against the pillow with a smile. He was at peace with himself and his situation and wondered why he was having no second thoughts about what he had done, or the course he had set for himself.

He allowed his mind to drift back to the very beginning. People would write later that he had been born into a poor, ignorance-ridden Southern household, but the poverty and ignorance hadn't mattered at the time; Elvis could only recall happiness as a child adored and pampered by his mother.

His thoughts then shot forward to the life he had known as a star; the feelings of inferiority that engulfed him when he was thrust into the company of notables; the insecurities, the stress, the depression and paranoia that had made existence joyless. Presidents and movie moguls and renowned beauties had courted him—and only made him more acutely aware of all he lacked in culture, education, and refinement. He had never felt comfortable with any of them.

When he first came to Hollywood to make movies, he tried to become a part of the sophisticated world that beckoned him. He went to parties and hated them. He attended formal Filmland banquets and despaired over using the wrong fork or over the misuse of grammar in conversation with dinner companions.

After a while, he seldom ventured out of his Memphis mansion at night. He was at ease there, with his family of roughneck aides/confidants/bodyguards with whom he shared the same common, Southern roots. They invited girls there, they all ate the foods he loved—heavy, gravy-laden meals washed down with swigs of orange soda pop straight out of the bottle—in the formal dining room. He was in his castle—and he truly felt like a king.

Now, lying on a narrow bed in a cell-like room at an auto court, he was a million miles removed from the kingdom that had been his—from even the small band of people with whom he felt close.

He missed his father; he thought of the pain he was putting him through and wished he could contact Vernon—but he knew he didn't dare. Being away from Ginger was a relief; she was sweet, but her presence had become cloying. Being away from Colonel Parker was an even greater relief; no longer would there be someone pushing, always pushing, for him to perform.

He yearned to be with Lisa Marie, but ties with his daughter had been infrequent, at best, since his divorce from Priscilla. And maybe she'd be better off not having to live in his shadow any longer. The world would forget him soon enough—he was sure of that. "I'm just leavin' a fickle public—before they turn their back on me.

"I'm goin' to make me a new life," he announced to the empty room.

Elvis jumped from the bed. He pulled on his sweats, washed his face, ran wet fingers through his hair, and went out to face the world. He was alone and on his own for the first time in twenty-two years—since Colonel Tom Parker entered his life in 1955.

The sun bore down. "A sweatsuit is nothin' to wear in August; better get me some new clothes," he decided.

He lumbered across the highway to a general store, stopped for a moment in front of a rack with newspaper headlines screaming ELVIS DIES! and suddenly realized he had no coins—no money at all.

He made his way back across the road to the van, retrieving the two remaining one hundred dollar bills from Preston's wallet. Inside the musty store, he asked if they sold blue jeans and shirts.

"Size?" said the store owner.

"Size?" Elvis parroted. He had no idea of his size. His clothes were always custom-made, ordered by others, laid out for him to wear.

"You simple, son?" said the store owner.

"No, it's just . . ."

"Go look around back there. And look for large—extra large."

The pants came to $9.98, the shirt $7.50. Elvis held out a hundred dollar bill and got the same reaction he had received from the waitress the night before.

"Where'd ya get money like that? You expect me to have change—especially first thing in the morning?"

"Keep the change," said Elvis as he grabbed the bag of clothes and marched to the door. He felt frustrated, irritated.

And he didn't know why. He did know he would have to do something to earn some money, though. Even if he didn't waste his last $100, it wasn't going to last long.

He slid behind the wheel of the van and, after an hour's drive, pulled the car into a construction site where a massive-shouldered, middle-aged man was directing a crew of carpenters.

"Need an extra worker?" Elvis asked, and was rewarded with the remark, "You don't look like you've ever worked a day in your life. You look like a marshmallow. What can you do?"

"I can . . . I studied to be an electrician once," Elvis replied.

"Great." The sarcasm was obvious. "Well, it takes no studyin' to lift lumber. You want to do that, I can use a carpenter's helper."

Within an hour, Elvis' arms were in pain, his back felt as if it had been run over by a truck, his legs were stiff and sore. Rivulets of sweat ran down his face, onto his chest—and images of the swimming pool and verdant lawns of Graceland swam before his eyes.

He tried until he could try no longer and an hour later, he quit. "I'm sorry, I can't lift no more," he said to the foreman. He asked for no money; he wanted nothing but to escape the stares of contempt that followed his retreat.

He drove until he was out of sight of the crew, then stopped, laid his head down on the steering wheel, and cried.

For over twenty years, he had been conditioned for nothing more strenuous than completing a performance. Toward the end, even a short walk had become such an effort that during Las Vegas engagements he had been transported by golf cart from his dressing room to the stage.

"And what do I do now?" he murmured through his sobs. Once he had driven a truck. "That don't take no muscles," he said. "I'll find a job as a truck driver."

He found one the next day but lost it by afternoon when he dropped a crate of ceramic figurines he was unloading.

He took a room with a bath—$40 for a month's rent in advance—and spent the following day in bed, listening to the radio accounts of the funeral plans for Elvis Presley, reading newspaper reports about the thousands who had come from all across the U.S. and Europe and as far away as Japan, Germany, and Australia to mourn the once raw redneck from Tupelo, Mississippi.

They called him the biggest name in music, hailed him as a revolutionary force, the king of rock and roll. Walter Cronkite referred to him as a great American folk hero. Commentators recounted the highlights of his life, his triumphs, the glory that had been his. No mention was made of the downslides in his career, of the performances that had been savaged by critics.

"Mama, you'd be so proud," he whispered.

He recalled having read a comment from one of his schoolmates in a *Rolling Stone* magazine article. "All Elvis ever seemed interested in was his guitar; I don't know if he would have been able to survive in any field but music."

That statement haunted him as one day flowed into the next, one month followed another, with nothing to distinguish one from the other but the menial jobs he picked up—and lost within a week or two.

He was on his own for the first time in his life. He had gone from mother to mentor, Tom Parker—never needing to learn to fend for himself. Now he was no one—and was treated that way. He had sought anonymity but found it less and less appealing as he slipped even deeper into its abyss. Money hadn't mattered when he was a teenager. He thought it mattered even less while he was King, with a cortege to see to his every whim. But now he was just a middle-aged, overweight, dirt poor drifter and found no joy in worrying if he had the money to buy a six-pack or a ticket to a movie house.

It was also no fun going to bed alone at night—night after night.

For years he had his choice of the world's most beautiful women—and had had so many, so often, that eventually his sexual drive diminished. Now it had returned full force—and with it frustration and humiliation. Women whose dreams were filled with erotic fantasies of Elvis Presley rejected the advances he made and looked at him with disdain.

He slept alone, often dreaming of the women he had bedded, of the countless beauties selected for his approval by the boys. Frequently, he awoke with his sheets wet and sticky.

One morning in December, he awoke with a sharp, driving need he couldn't, wouldn't analyze: to gaze upon the Memphis mansion that had once been his home.

He donned the sweatsuit he had worn the day he fled from Graceland four months earlier. Two hours later, he was standing across the street from the Graceland gates with their ornamental figure of Elvis Presley playing a guitar.

There was a line of thousands waiting to make the pilgrimage to his grave—matrons, middle-aged men, teenagers, children—all of them seemed to have the same somber, reverential expression.

A sense of sadness and loss washed over him, yet there was also an inexplicable feeling of pride as his eyes took in the peddlers hawking Presley memorabilia along the sidewalk—and the proliferation of Presley souvenir shops lining the street. None had been there when he had been King of Graceland.

The hood of his sweatshirt pulled low over his forehead, dark glasses hiding his eyes, he wandered into a store, saw his likeness grinning back at him from LOVE ME TENDER T-shirts, notebooks, lunch boxes, medallions. There were dollar bills— selling for $8—with his portrait in place of George Washington's. There were Elvis ashtrays, figurines, posters, bath towels, bubble gum, Christmas tree ornaments.

"We got over a hundred different Elvis items, and the stuff keeps sellin'," said the chatty, rotund merchant. "Can't keep the stuff in stock. That Colonel Parker is really somethin'. Before Elvis was even buried, the Colonel was working out all the marketing arrangements with the president of the firm who's putting most of this stuff out. I guess Parker felt he had merchandised Elvis into becoming a star—so he should also merchandise him in death. And he's keepin' a close eye on everything. Everyone tried to cash in on Elvis' death, and a lot of them tried right away. But a week after Elvis died, Colonel Parker had already gotten two hundred legal actions started to get unauthorized stuff off the market."

Elvis' hand reached out to touch a black velvet painting of a young, thin Elvis Presley, and the merchant said, "Looks good, doesn't he? Elvis looks young and slim on everything we sell. That's how people want to remember him. And that's what Colonel Parker wanted; maintaining Elvis' dignity, givin' him class."

He paused a moment, then said, "You know, Elvis was a god to millions of people around the world—and they need something to touch, to hold, that will keep him with them."

Elvis felt a sudden need to walk upon the lawns of Graceland once more—to gaze upon the burial sight countless thousands had visited.

He waited in what seemed an unending line as a uniformed guard allowed them through the metal gates in groups, twenty-five at a time. Finally, he was beyond the heavy stone walls—and home again. The view of the mansion and Graceland's thirteen acres of trees and pasture stretched out before him. Off in the distance, he could see his palomino grazing in a field. He plodded onward with the group of strangers, along the sloping, quarter-mile driveway, merely another face in a sea of faces, to the Meditation Garden. And there the procession halted—and a strained silence fell.

Before them was a Corinthian-style mausoleum, with four stained glass windows and eight white columns bracketing the twin graves of Elvis and his mother, Gladys. A sob could be heard, and then another, then a whispered prayer. A teenage girl, her face a study in sorrow, plucked blades of grass and kissed them gently. A child bent down to lay a bouquet of daisies upon the 800-pound casket of Elvis Aron Presley, buried under a 2,000-pound granite slab to prevent thievery of the body.

A coffin-length bronze plaque bore the message: "He had a God-given talent that he shared with the world. . . . He revolutionized the field of music and received its highest awards."

Also inscribed on the plaque, the final ode of Vernon Presley to his son: "God saw that he needed some rest and called him home to be with Him."

Pain, sorrow, regret flooded over Elvis.

He turned his head and through tear-filled eyes saw the mansion in the background. He turned back and realized it was Dick Grob—who had been his chief of security—on duty at the burial site. Their eyes met and for a moment Elvis felt panic; Grob would surely recognize him. But he didn't. Elvis felt no relief, but inexplicably experienced acute disappointment.

Then he realized why. *"Enough!"* he thought. He wanted the charade to be over. He wanted to return to Lisa Marie, to Graceland—to Elvis Presley.

He pulled back the hood from his head, yanked off the sunglasses, worked his way to Dick Grob's side, and said, "Dick, it's Elvis."

"Yes, it is," said Grob, nodding solemnly at the grave. "It's still hard for any of us to really accept that fact."

"You don't understand," Elvis said. He put his hand out, but Grob turned away, and a guard approached and motioned him to leave.

Elvis allowed himself to be led away, feeling like the central character in a nightmare. The sideburns were gone, his hair was cropped close. But how could Dick Grob not recognize him?

His father . . . he would find his father.

And then he saw him! Vernon was crossing the grounds from the mansion to the trailer quarters where Elvis' cousin Billy Smith lived.

"Dad! Dad!" Elvis broke away from the crowd and bolted across the lawn—the guard chasing after him, Dick Grob close behind. The crowd was stunned as Grob executed a flying tackle of Elvis' legs, then held him spread-eagle on the ground as he ordered, "Get a squad car over here. We've got another nut on our hands."

The next half hour—and the hour after that—were a blur to Elvis. His pleas to contact Vernon Presley went unheeded, his body was grabbed and unceremoniously dumped into the back of a police car. At the police station a weary watch commander told him, "Son, I'm not going to throw you in jail. The city couldn't afford to put up with all the nuts who think they're Elvis. I'm just going to warn you—stay away from Graceland. Leave the family in peace; they've suffered enough. Do you know how many people they've got coming around and saying they're Elvis, and how many people are going around done up like Elvis?"

He would soon find out.

Three months later, in March 1978, *Rolling Stone* magazine reported: "More than a hundred impersonators are keeping the Elvis Presley legend alive throughout the United States, with shows ranging from small nightclub acts to sophisticated Las Vegas productions."

Later, the same publication announced that the nation's army of Elvis imitators had grown to an estimated 600. And that merely counted those who were trying to cash in on Presley's likeness and songs. It didn't take into account the endless scores who tried to look like Elvis, who insisted on dressing like Elvis, with no thought of commercial gain.

As the months passed, Elvis became more and more determined—and desperate—to make his real identity known.

It had been a year since his "death." His system had been cleansed of drugs, his body had lost its bloat. He looked better than he had in years—and less like the man who sneaked out of Graceland on August 16, 1977 than did hundreds of Presley imitators.

"I've got to gain weight, and let my hair and sideburns grow before I can make anyone believe me," he told himself.

He ate all the greasy food he had once loved, and for which he no longer had an appetite. He drank malts, downed ice cream by the gallon. And the weight built up. His stomach once again became a mountain; the double chins and jowls returned—framed anew by ear-length sideburns. He looked like the overblown man he used to be—but no more so than hundreds of other Elvis lookalikes.

He tried to phone his father. The telephone number had been changed.

He called Colonel Parker's office, identifying himself to the secretary. The receiver was slammed into its cradle.

He tried Ginger, the woman he had planned to marry. It was a wrong number.

Certainly Priscilla and Lisa Marie would recognize him. He would go to his ex-wife, to his daughter. The number was unlisted; guards patrolled the house.

His right-hand man, Joe Esposito, his half-brothers, David and Rick, the dozens of people who had been in his employ throughout the years, the scores of acquaintances on whom he had lavished gifts. He tried to approach them all. And failed.

He went to the F.B.I. and announced, "I'm Elvis Presley. Take my fingerprints and I'll prove it."

He was escorted out of the building by a guard who said, "Take care, and if you're looking for me again, just ask for Napoleon Bonaparte."

He confided in his landlady, sought her advice—and was evicted.

He told the story to the grocery store owner where he had been employed for several weeks as a box boy. He was fired.

Soon he was telling everyone he met he was Elvis Presley, asking anyone he knew what he should do. The inevitable response: an embarrassed stare, a shrug, a hasty retreat.

Finally, he stopped trying and became engulfed in an incapacitating depression.

And then one day, sprawled on the pull-out bed in the one-room apartment he rented by the week, his eyes drifted to the back page of the supermarket tabloid he had purchased two days earlier and deposited unread on the floor. A headline caught his attention: CLONE CONVENTION. He reached down, pulled the paper to him, and read of a Las Vegas gathering of Elvis Presley lookalikes at which thousands were expected—and where Colonel Parker was to help select the winner of a Presley singing competition.

Depression, lethargy vanished. He laughed. He raised his arms, made a victory sign. He had a reason to live again, to hope again. He could go home again. He would go to Las Vegas. He would sing for Colonel Parker. And the nightmare would be over.

He needed money. And he needed to have a costume made. He achieved this by working days at a gas station and nights at a donut shop where he also stocked up on left-over product.

A month later, he boarded a late-night bus bound for Las Vegas, but was too excited to sleep as he anticipated his return to the city where he had once been the Superstar of Superstars.

He found a room near the bus depot in downtown Vegas, washed, shaved, and changed into his tailor-made, formfitting leather suit adorned with rhinestones and a massive western belt. He did a quick pirouette and said to his reflection in the mirror, "You gonna try to tell me anyone won't recognize me now?"

The convention was already getting under way; the singing competition would be held that night. He jumped in a taxi—he was going to arrive in style—oblivious to the cab driver's murmured "Another nut!" and asked to be taken to a hotel at the edge of the downtown area, in the seediest section of the seedy area known as Glitter Gulch.

Some ten minutes later, he was strolling into a meeting hall with faded, flocked red wallpaper, worn paisley carpeting—and into a sea of Elvis Presley clones. They were everywhere; they clogged the room, they crowded before tables where vendors hawked Presley albums and memorabilia. It was a scene from a Fellini movie, a walk through a house of mirrors.

It would all be over soon, he assured himself. Elvis would try to locate Colonel Parker; even if he couldn't, he'd be there to hear him sing—and he'd know. Colonel Parker would know.

He approached a man wearing white shoes and a checkered polyester suit adorned with a paper label that bore a hand-scrawled "Host." Elvis asked how he could find Colonel Parker.

"He's not here, never exactly said he would be," Elvis was told. When he pressed, and said he had read a newspaper item that said the Colonel would help judge the singing, the response was a shrugged, "Don't know where anyone got that idea; you know those damn newspapers. They're always wrong."

A sudden nausea washed over Elvis, pain clutched at his innards—and he bolted toward the sign that said MEN.

He raced into a bathroom booth. Vomit erupted with violent force as he clung to the urine-stained latrine. Finally, there was nothing left for Elvis Presley but tears. Sobs racked his body as he kneeled—a man praying at a porcelain altar—and cried out to God to save him.

Some fifteen minutes later, weak and woozy, he made his way like a sleepwalker back to the main room. *There's still a chance,* he told himself as he fought to beat down his depression and approached a desk where applications for the singing competition were being taken.

"Hey, you do look a lot like Elvis," said the woman who took his entry fee and advised him, "It's a couple hours until the show. Why don't you go mingle."

He tried. But if he was in a sea of mirror-images, he was also a fish out of water in a crowd whose only common denominator was discussing the places they'd imitated Elvis, the lengths to which they'd gone to "Preslify" their appearances.

He stood among them but felt a million miles removed, growing more and more morose as he thought of the life he had led the past year. *I can't, I won't return to that life,* he screamed within, and told himself, *You don't have to. Everything will be straightened out as soon as they hear you sing. You don't need to have the Colonel here; someone will tell him. And the newspapers will find out.*

He was the fifty-second contestant to perform. By the time he was called to the stage, the judges seemed bored and exhausted, and Elvis' nerves were stretched to the breaking point.

He asked the orchestra to play "Heartbreak Hotel." He stood before the mike and started to sing the 1956 song that had metamorphosed him into a myth at the age of twenty-one.

He couldn't find the key, couldn't recall the words. He stood frozen for a minute, tried again, but was paralyzed with fear.

"Mister, what's going on? We've got a lot of people out here waiting their turns," called out a voice from the darkness.

Elvis nodded dumbly, stared blindly ahead, then finally motioned to the band, grabbed the mike, drew a deep breath, and began. "Well, since my baby left me, well, I found a new place to dwell. It's down at the end of a lonely street . . . that's the Heartbreak Hotel . . . "

His words came out in an off-key croak. Snickers floated through the room.

"That's it. That's enough, you're off," said the promoter at the rear of the hall, with a glance at the judges for confirmation.

"You don't understand, I am Elvis Presley," Elvis cried out desperately. "Let me try again. I'm nervous, I'm not feeling well. But can't you see I am Elvis Presley!"

They led him off the stage, out of the convention center, and onto the street.

The next day his body was found, wrists slit, in the dingy downtown hotel room where he had registered the afternoon before as Elvis Preston.

No mention was made of his passing—and as far as is known, no fingerprints were taken.

The following fragment, produced verbatim, was found among the presidential papers of the late President John F. Kennedy (1961–65, and 1969–73). He asked that these be sealed until his death. It was obtained under the Freedom of Information Act. Members of his family were unaware of its existence. It is unknown whether it was intended to be published as is, or even published at all. One family member, who asked not to be identified, said he had heard President Kennedy speak of an *outline* of a "personal" autobiography not long before his death on June 10, 1987 at the age of seventy from complications arising from a sailboat racing accident.

—*L.W.*

JOHN F.
KENNEDY

BY LES WHITTEN

The night before, in Fort Worth, I heard on the radio that overcast skies were expected in Dallas, and I turned to Jackie before we went to sleep and told her it might rain.

"Well," she had said, sighing resignedly, "let it come down." I knew the quotation came from somewhere and I asked her, and she tried to remember and then said, yes, it was from *Macbeth*. Banquo, walking with his son at night, had said something like, "It will rain tonight," and one of the murderers sent by Macbeth had murmured, "Let it come down," and had stabbed Banquo.

"Well," I said, turning the conversation away from that sort of thought, "when I think of the pot I am beginning to get from this Texas food, I feel more like Falstaff than Macbeth."

It did not rain in Dallas. The skies cleared. We did without the bubbletop on the limousine so I could wave at the crowds, which would get us better TV coverage. I was not thinking about the crowds as I smiled and waved, but about the fall of Diem, the president we had installed in Saigon, and how much the CIA had or didn't have to do with it. Beside me, I heard Jackie gasp and I stopped thinking about Vietnam for a moment and turned to her.

Her hat had been caught by a small gust of wind, and she raised her hand to hold it to her head. I remember smiling at her efforts, and then I felt this great crashing just above my right shoulder blade.

◈

When I came to, the doctor was staring into my eyes, and groggy as I was, I tried to smile and ask him what the hell was going on, but it came out as a gurgle and I realized I had tubes in my throat and an ache there as well as in my back.

It was two days more, four in all, before I was enough out from under the drugs to learn what happened. Kenny O'Donnell laid it out for me, but in a tense, hesitant way that made me uncomfortable. I had been shot by a crazy ex-marine, a left-winger, which was an irony, since Dallas was the capital of the American Right. "Hoover swears he acted alone," Kenny said.

"Do you believe him?" I asked in a whisper, the best my throat would do.

"Yes," he said. "On this I believe him."

"What does the ex-marine say?"

"Nothing. A striptease joint owner killed him."

I thought he was being sardonic. "That's not funny, Kenny," I said.

"No, it's true." I saw the tears come into his eyes. Kenny was not the crying kind. "Nothing is ever going to be funny again, Jack," he said. "Jackie tried to get in front of you after the first bullet hit you."

"The first bullet . . . ?" I knew what he was going to say and closed my eyes against it so I would not have to see the terrible tears in his eyes, to spare myself at least that.

"The second bullet killed her. Instantly."

I only half heard the rest of it: the theories about why this Oswald had shot me, about why the striptease man had shot Oswald, the evidence Hoover had come up with. I wondered where Bobby and Teddy were. Maybe they heard the silence, because they came in, and Bobby took my hand while Teddy stood there crying.

"You don't mind me asking Kenny to tell you? I knew Teddy and I would have broken down in the middle," Bobby said, never able to get a single millimeter, not one, between what he was saying and what his heart was saying.

"No. Mother? The kids? How are they taking it?"

"Mother thought it was another one, like Joe or Kathleen"—my dead brother and dead sister, who had died in air crashes—"but she's all right now. The kids are holding up."

I thought of Jackie, all the things done and all the things undone, and felt a grief and remorse so heavy in my heart that I wanted to die, to be done with it. Forever and ever.

"I wish it had been me," I rasped.

<hr />

Lyndon was wonderful during those weeks, and later when it went sour I would still be grateful for the way he was. He deferred to the family in every aspect for the national funeral we held for Jackie. She lay in state in the Rotunda—Lyndon and John McCormack, the House Speaker, had taken care of that—and all that day Bobby had Beethoven's Seventh piped in there. She had loved it so. I watched on TV as the crowds filed past the catafalque, but had to turn off the sound when the second movement started because I knew I could not have borne it.

It was a month before I got back into the oval office, and then for only part of the day. Bobby, Kenny, and the rest met with me every morning. Lyndon took a backseat now, but reluctantly, because he knew how very damned well he had done.

We all knew that the only positive thing that could come out of Jackie's death was to build a monument to her from our New Frontier programs. We subtly put it that way to Jim Eastland and Ev Dirksen and other senate southerners and conservatives. Jackie would not have approved, but not because she did not feel deeply for the disadvantaged, because she did, in spite of the bad rap she got from the media. But it was not her style: she had always been more in tune with poetry than politics.

Sometimes I found myself in dialogue with her when I was unable to sleep. "Robert Frost never got a single Negro past a poll-watcher in southern Alabama," I reasoned with her over my using her death to further the civil rights bill.

"And all the U.S. marshals with all the guns in the world never got a man to look at snowy woods in the evening in a new way," she seemed to answer. "Jack, don't use me like this."

But I did, and by February I was sure I was going to get a civil rights bill through, and a war on poverty bill, and maybe medicare, even with the tax cut and a shaved-down budget.

More and more I worried about Vietnam. We had twenty thousand troops there and were lying about it, sometimes saying fifteen thousand, sometimes seventeen, and it was driving Bobby up walls and me, too. The French had gotten beached as a world power ten years before at Dienbienphu, and I didn't want to see us wandering around Vietnam like Snow White in the Haunted Wood. But I didn't want to look mushy on the communists, either.

Eisenhower had put almost a thousand military advisors in Vietnam before I took office, and when I had tried to talk with him about it, he got very stiff and military as if it ill-behooved a former Navy ensign to question the deployments of "le grand general." It was at such times when Ike was out-de Gaulleing de Gaulle that I found him, well, most galling.

But in the end, I wasn't any better. I let the Pentagon have its way, and McNamara, my defense secretary, and Lyndon did nothing to stop me, and bit by bit we sent in training troops, then planes, and all of a sudden we were in a shooting war. Bobby put it to me in a ham-handed way in March, four months before I had been shot.

"I'm tired of us lying, tired of this war, tired of us backing our new bunch of thieves in Saigon. George Aiken"—an ancient senatorial leprechaun from Vermont—"was at supper last night and said, 'Why don't we just march out and declare ourselves the winner,' and the whole table laughed—*with* him and *at* me when I tried to defend us."

I was in my rocker and was acutely aware of its rapid creaking as we tried to figure out how we could withdraw, and with a little more honor than Aiken had in mind.

"The hawks will slash us to bits if I just pull out," I said. "And I need their support on the domestic stuff."

"You've got a hawk in your own nest," Bobby said, meaning Lyndon. I thought about that a while.

"Without him there wouldn't be any nest," I said. I had beaten Nixon by just over a hundred thousand votes. I would never have won, never have carried Texas and so much of the South without Lyndon.

I had known when I took him on the ticket that he was compulsive. I had underestimated *how* compulsive. I had counted on his loyalty not to undercut me. He didn't see it as disloyalty, but as protecting me from Bobby and the other doves. Finally, I agreed to a meeting about Lyndon with my inner circle.

"Cut him off the ticket when you make the announcement that you're going to run again," Kenny counseled. "We can get him to say his heart's bad and find him a little something that'll let him look at himself without weeping when he shaves."

Bobby backed Kenny, and we talked about putting Lyndon on the Supreme Court, or giving him State or Defense, but I couldn't bring myself to dump him. I couldn't forget how classy he had been after I was shot, and besides I felt I could control him. They all left grumbling. And I felt badly torn.

It was about then, three months before the Republican convention, that I began to get dizzy spells. I called in Patrick Mowberry from Massachusetts General to check me out because I knew I could trust him to tell me the truth and then handle the press well if the news was good and shut up if it was bad. I knew the news wasn't good when he told me he couldn't do an accurate assessment unless he could get me someplace with a full lab, X rays, and the new electronic scanners.

"You're saying it may be my brain," I said. He looked uneasy. He had taken care of Dad when he began to fade, and I asked him to be as blunt with me now as he had been with the family then. "I want to know what you *think*," I said.

"I think you should let me give you a full run of tests. If you're okay, you're okay. If the trauma got to your head more than we thought, then you'd better think about not running for a second term."

"With Goldwater"—the senator from Arizona—"a sure pushover?" I asked exasperatedly. "Pat, I could beat him running from the balcony of a Scully Square whorehouse."

He smiled and spoke more about the tests, and finally I agreed to come to Boston sometime soon and take them if we could make it look like I was just dropping in for a routine check-up on the way back from a weekend at Hyannis Port.

As often happens when you want to avoid finding out what is really wrong with you, the symptoms went away, and I put off seeing Mowberry. I declared for the nomination, but said the affairs of the nation, from Vietnam to the economy, would tie me up too much to campaign. Lyndon took the stump for me.

In June, all hell broke loose in Mississippi. Three civil rights workers, two of them white, disappeared after being seized by a mob and I asked Hoover to take a look. He came over with that pious sag-jaw look of his.

"My sources say the Klan killed them," he said. "We are extending every cooperation to the Mississippi authorities."

"The Mississippi authorities, my ass!" I barked at him. "The goddamned Mississippi authorities are who's to blame. I want *us* to break the backs of the scumbags who took these people off. And I want it fast!"

I had never forgiven him for spying on me and a Danish woman during World War II. His gumshoes had followed us from her hotel room to church and back to the hotel room. His pretense had been that she was a spy, which was horse manure, and that it might be used against Dad, who was ambassador to London.

"Fast may be several weeks, Mr. President," Hoover said. I knew he detested me and he knew I detested him.

"In several weeks I may have to find me a new FBI chief if it's not resolved," I said coldly. The old faggot, if that was what he was, knew I was bluffing. The country loved him. And he had once hinted to Kenny that he had evidence I had been less than

Saint Paul-pure with regard to women, which, alas, was true. "I want daily reports on progress," I told him, furious that we both knew he was outside my control.

The hostility of our talk gave me a renewed dizzy spell. I ignored it and concentrated on using the Mississippi horrors to push the civil rights bill through. Again, Lyndon was magnificent, arm-twisting, deal-swapping, and in *Atlanta,* calling for the bill's passage with a speech beginning, "We shall overcome . . . " When the filibustering was done, it cleared the Senate with fifteen votes; the most powerful civil rights measure in history.

The conventions were imminent, and Bobby and Kenny and most of the rest still felt I should push Lyndon out. But I simply could not do it. We had our final meeting at Bobby's place on Hickory Hill, and Ethel brought the drinks in with the kind of junk snacks Bobby loved. I laid it all down.

"Firing him would be no good politically, even though I could beat Goldwater with Kenny"—the least likely politician imaginable—"as a running mate, no good legislatively because if we dump him, no friend of his on Capitol Hill will vote even to pay the White House carpenter, no good strategically because, to quote him, I'd rather have him inside our tent pissing out than outside pissing in . . . and no good morally. He stays."

We argued until past midnight, and they did get me to ask him for a commitment to help get us out of Vietnam and on some other matters where he'd also been a sage-in-bloom Machiavelli behind my back.

That night I lay awake in many-splendored anguish, hating my job, hating the fact of Jackie's death, hating the subterfuge and deception of smuggling in women. I was going to be fifty before the end of my second term, and I was getting too old to play high school, although the Lincoln bedroom was, in fact, a good deal better than the back of a convertible on the vineyard.

The truth was, I could never bring myself to *like* Lyndon, and I felt guilty about it. He had done much more *for* me than he had ever done *to* me. But, dammit, there was something that reminded me of Hoover about him, a kind of hangdog look he got around me. Or maybe it was just that, like Hoover, I knew Lyndon did not really approve of me, as I did not of him.

Next morning, I crossed over to his office in the Executive Office building to let him know I wanted him on the ticket again. "I should have told you sooner," I said.

He looked both exultant and relieved. "I didn't ask. Don't blame yourself," he said. "I know Bobby and some of the rest want me off. I appreciate you doing the right thing." He mixed us both Scotch and water.

"I wouldn't say they wanted you off. They just had some concerns." He let my necessary lie pass, but his eyes got slinty. He knew their "concerns" meant that he was going to be making concessions. I told him what they were: "You'll have to back me on getting out of Vietnam, for one thing."

"Jesus, how could I do more?"

That crafty expression on his sourdough face always made me spiteful. "Dammit, Lyndon, you make all the right sounds on TV and then you and your cronies in the Senate and God knows who at the Pentagon get the leak machine going and make it look like if I don't send another regiment, or a carrier, or the B-

52s over there, then the communists are going to invade the farm and tie Grandma's knickers to the barn and rape her and the cow both."

He smiled. Maybe the only time we ever liked each other was when I talked to him on his level. "I'm sincere about Vietnam," he said. "If we let Russia's gooks beat our gooks, then we'll lose face everywhere in the world. The day we pull out of Indochina is the day Castro and Khrushchev begin to take over Latin America. It's that simple."

Simple to him, maybe. Lyndon thought of himself as the great persuader, and he was, but only when he was persuading from power. Now he wasn't. I heard every argument ever made on Vietnam, and he knew it. And besides, I had what he wanted: a yea or nay on the vice presidency. It gave me a nasty little thrill of pleasure, feeling my supremacy over him.

"It's no use, Lyndon." I waited for his answer.

"I could do what you ask, but it would hurt," he tried to maneuver. "If I agree, could I count on you in sixty-eight?"

"No, that'll be Bobby's year." I was losing patience. "Jesus," I burst out at him, "I've given you more power than any vice president in history ever had . . . " But he was angry, and got reckless as he sometimes did.

"What the hell has Bobby ever done for this country, Jack? A stooge for Joe McCarthy, a nobody, his brother's brother, that's all. Dear Mary, Martha, and Lazarus, I was sweating my butt for Roosevelt before he began pulling his pud. I got a Silver Star in the war, damn near got my ass shot off, like you did. I was on the Hill working the twenty-goddamn-fifth hour every day when Bobby was pissing his didies . . . "

I listened, not so much to the words, but for how much lay beneath. Was he making his agonized polemic so that I would not ask him for more concessions? This was his way. I'd seen it in the Senate, although there, *he* had been Victor McLaglen, and *I* had been Gunga Din.

"Lyndon," I broke in sharply, "let me put it down cold and hard. I want you on the ticket, but you will have to play on my team, not circulate in the stands on behalf of my opponents. That means my team on Vietnam, on oil, on farm subsidies, on defense spending, on everything that has 'New Frontier' branded on it. You're damned right there's plenty of people that want you off. I have pacified my tigers on your behalf, but you have got to throw them some meat."

His face closed up. He had lost. "Meat, hell! You're telling me to throw them what's left of my balls!"

◈

In July, I watched the Republican convention on three TV screens as I worked and before I went to sleep. Most of the time I did not need the sound. I knew what they were saying. Worse, I knew what the extremists among them were thinking: that we should just drop a little old nuclear bomb on Hanoi and end it all. Yeah, well, I had just wrenched a nuclear test ban treaty from the Russians a year ago, and the CIA, if I could believe them, was saying the Chinese would be setting off a nuclear device in the fall. This was no time for thoughts of "nuking 'em."

Goldwater knew better than to indulge himself the way his supporters did, but he was their captive and they were their history's. Bill Scranton, who'd been governor of Pennsylvania and had run against Goldwater as the moderate "conscience of the Republican Party," was a lovely man with a lovely sense of humor. He called me up after he was walloped by Goldwater at their convention in San Francisco and asked me if it was too late to apply for the job of vice president on the Democratic ticket.

We both laughed, but mine was a little hollow. His jest showed how widely known was the disaffection between Lyndon and myself. Nevertheless, we made a big show of togetherness at our convention in Boston later that month. I was renominated unanimously.

I had more dizzy spells in early August. I now admitted to myself that they were brought on by stress. On August 2, despite the fact that we had gotten word to the North Vietnamese through back channels that, after the elections, we would be making a major bid for peace, there was some kind of attack on one of our destroyers in the Gulf of Tonkin. It was unclear, and the stupid Pentagon couldn't honestly seem to find out for sure, whether our destroyer or one of the North Vietnamese patrol boats fired first.

The hawks wanted to blast Hanoi off the map. I managed to keep it down to blowing up a couple dozen of their patrol craft and bombing a few of their cities. But it definitely escalated things. Lyndon, as he had reluctantly promised, kept out of it. But at a cabinet meeting the day after the attack, I got one of those I-told-you-so looks from him.

Then, on August 4, the bodies of the three civil rights workers were found buried near Philadelphia, Mississippi. I called in Hoover again and this time his unwillingness to act fast would have made Saint Francis apoplectic. I had to lay down on the couch for fifteen minutes after he left. I knew the wisest thing would be to see Mowberry, but I put it off again. And the truth is, from August on to September I felt fine.

There had been so much speculation about the efforts to kill me in Dallas that I had named a commission to study it. They had taken evidence, visited the site, held a reenactment. They had heard wild stories about the CIA, the Mafia, pro- and anti-Castro Cubans, the right wing, the South Vietnamese, even Lyndon, being behind it. Kenny's first words to me about Oswald acting alone, however, still seemed to me the most logical, really the only explanation.

On September 27, the commission finally issued its report and I read it through, skimming some, but staying up until four to reach its end. I felt it was a fine job, covering the terrain as well as anybody could.

But I couldn't go back to sleep. All the "what ifs" came back to me. What if Jackie had not thrown herself over me? It appeared that her action jarred me out of the way of the bullet that struck her. What if I had ordered the bubbletop? What if I skipped the motorcade, or skipped Dallas altogether? I had, after all, known it was Hatesville and could just as well have gone straight to Austin. I turned and tossed with guilt and remorse in spite of my weariness, then at last fell asleep.

When I woke an hour or two later, I didn't just have the dizziness, but also a numbness in my right hand. It was almost as if the computer in my head were telling my right hand not to push back the covers, not to reach for the phone. I used my left hand and told the switchboard to get Bobby and Kenny over fast. By the time they got there, I was feeling okay, but was still in the bedroom. Kenny looked at me much as that doctor had when I first came to in Dallas.

"What do you see?" I said, trying to be the tough guy.

"Constricted pupils."

"It's the lack of light," I said.

"They look like pinpoints," Bobby said. "There's something wrong with you. It's time to see Mowberry."

I tried to get up from the bed, but the dizziness hit me fully and I slumped back. "Okay," I said weakly, "okay."

In fact, it was past time, because now if the results were bad, my successor was already in place. It would have to be Lyndon. I went to Massachusetts General for what looked like a routine check-up on the way back from a weekend at Hyannis Port. Mowberry reviewed my medical records that went all the way back to my wartime back injury, which still afflicted me.

At the end of the day, he came to my room and I knew everything I needed to know from the look on his grizzled old face. I had guessed correctly after that impromptu examination he had given me in the White House a half-year before.

"The brain," I said, rather than asked.

"Yep, not irreversibly, but yep."

"I'll have to drop out?"

"Yep."

I began to cry. He stood there waiting patiently for me to stop. Goddamn it, I thought, a hater, an unstable cipher, but one with near perfect aim, kills my wife, messes up my brain, changes the course of history. All my work, all my abilities wasted by his one moment of insanity and luck, this miserable drifter's one reprieve from failure. I had always felt only the vaguest sense of a God, but now lying there, I called on him, not for help, for there wasn't any help he could give, but in outrage at what he had let happen to me. It was a good three minutes before I could talk to Mowberry.

"Not irreversible?" I grasped the straw he had offered.

"*Maybe* not irreversible. I want to do more tests, lots more. I want to think about it. I want to talk with a lot of other people. I could even be wrong."

"What's the chance of being wrong?"

"On the *short* term, none," he said. "The encephalogram and the brain scan show the vertigo is due to brain wave irregularities. They're worse now than when I ran them on the portable machine down there in Washington. Your brain isn't getting reliable messages to your extremities."

All very well, I thought. However, what was really going through my head was not electrical brain waves, but the thought that I would have to give up the presidency. And not to Bobby. I could in theory ask Lyndon to resign the nomination, could try one last wild manipulation. But that would be nuts. The party might not even go along with me. Barring some act as unpredictable as the bullets of Dallas, Lyndon would be sworn in next January.

"What about the rest of this term?" I asked.

"Serve it out. It's just a few months. My guess is that the symptoms will dissipate once you make up your mind that, beginning in January, you're going to focus on getting well."

"Getting well?" I said abruptly. "Pat, most of the time I don't even feel sick! Couldn't you be wrong?" He raised his hands slightly and let them fall against his legs but said nothing. "Okay, I'm sick," I said.

He smiled, and I felt easier. "Admitting that," he said, "is the first step toward getting well."

Mowberry, more to avoid any public questions than from any doubt about his judgment, called in a half-dozen other specialists. They came in late at night, discreet as priests, and by morning all had concurred. I called Bobby so he could tell the family and our crew and then called Lyndon. We notified the networks that I would make an announcement at noon, but the news had leaked by ten-thirty—from Lyndon's people, I would bet, wanting to make sure I didn't change my mind.

In my broadcast, I told the country what Mowberry had told me. I said I would serve out my term as president, and would be making campaign speeches for Lyndon and whomever the party decided should be his running mate. Bobby had already said he didn't want it. Lyndon would never have stood still for him anyway. I was already sure it would be Hubert Humphrey, the senator from Minnesota. Thank God he was on hand.

Goldwater self-destructed even before November. And on Election Day he got less than forty percent of the popular vote.

Between then and Lyndon's inauguration in January, the symptoms didn't return and I worked hard to accomplish everything I possibly could. The sympathy of the country and the Congress helped.

I sent staff people to Thailand to talk with the North Vietnamese and Vietcong. As a good faith gesture, I pulled back the carriers, stopped bombing, and withdrew two thousand troops. For their part, they did not expand their territory. Why should they? One day, they were going to get the whole shebang anyway.

On December 4, Hoover finally arrested twenty-one men for killing the civil rights workers. Bobby got a grand jury going and eighteen of them were indicted on January 15, five days before Lyndon was sworn in.

The prime rate edged up a quarter point in January, at, of all places, a Boston bank, and I made personal calls and got it knocked back to $4\frac{1}{2}$ percent. I parceled out $83 billion in anti-poverty funds. I got a disarmament feeler out to the Soviets, with Lyndon's promises to keep it going.

I also got him to go along with the phasing out of the Army Reserve, merging the viable units with the National Guard. Japanese Premier Soto visited me early in January, and he and Lyndon hit it off and we even talked about how, if we could get out of Vietnam, we could begin some kind of dialogue with the Chinese. In those last months I had never felt more vigorous, more—as the newsmen said—"presidential."

The day before I stepped down, I had a telephone call from Khrushchev, who had been kicked out of office in October, replaced by two sourpusses named Brezhnev and Kosygin. Despite our scary moments over the Cuban missiles, I had always felt a grudging respect for Khrushchev's toughness, and he had commiserated at length with me after Dallas.

"Dizzy spells, my Ukrainian ass," he said through his translator. "The eagles have pushed you out, Mr. President, the eagles, led by our Texas friend, Mr. Lyndon Johnson."

"You don't mean eagles, you mean hawks." I laughed.

I heard him arguing with his translator. "Eagles, hawks, the large predatory birds," the intimidated and somewhat confused translator said. "Those people who oppose you in Vietnam."

"Hawks," I said. "No, Mr. Premier, that lunatic in Dallas pushed me out. Come visit me in retirement and I'll show you the medical reports."

"Ah, doctors, who can trust them," he said, "and it is now Mr. Former Premier."

"What will happen to you?"

"Nothing if I keep low, which I intend. These two are no Stalins, you know. No worse than your Nixon. In fact, they are interchangeable with Nixon." The man was irrepressible. We were talking by open telephone, with every intelligence agency in the world, no doubt, listening in, including the KGB. I heard him pause, then continue volubly. "You could put either one of them in charge over there and put your Nixon here, and there would be no difference. It would only mean that Nixon would have to drink vodka martinis instead of the gin ones."

"And Premier Kosygin and Party Chairman Brezhnev would have to throw out the first pitch in baseball."

Khrushchev guffawed. "Why not? We invented baseball."

On January 20, Lyndon was sworn in. I administered the oath, a departure from tradition, and Lady Bird held the family bible. This time there was bulletproof glass all around the speaker's stand and at the reviewing stand where we would watch the parade down Pennsylvania Avenue. The times they were a-changing.

During Lyndon's speech, my heart tumbled. I thought of that bright day four years ago, the snow fresh-cleared at the Capitol and Jackie looking more beautiful and younger than ever, and Robert Frost having a hard time reading the poem, and the hopes, the hopes, the hopes, now all gone.

Lyndon retained most of my cabinet: Rusk at State, McNamara at Defense, Dillon at Treasury, and several others. Why should he fire them? We had picked the best. He kept Bobby on as attorney general, too, although that was not going to last.

I did what Mowberry said, loafing at the compound in Hyannis Port, spending the winter in Palm Beach. I read, flirted halfheartedly, played with the children, got exercise, suffered a return of the dizzy spells, although none as serious as before. In May, part of my life took a change for the better in a way I wouldn't have guessed in a million years.

The genesis was in 1954 during my first term as a senator when, at a speech to students at Northwestern, I met a bright, brash kid interested in journalism. She was probably as pretty a blonde as I had ever seen, and a Phi Beta Kappa to boot. I was newly married and the girl—her name was Ann Marie Wayes— was only twenty-two, so I put her out of my mind.

In the late fifties, she came to Washington and was soon covering Capitol Hill and I, in the biblical sense of the word, was soon covering her, in an infrequent and, to me, at least, casual manner. After I was elected president, I managed to see her a few times when I was on junkets. Sexually, she had been everything one could ask for, but where could it have led?

In late 1962, she was conducting an investigation of racketeering influences on some midwestern congressmen, and a goon threw acid in her face. The acid had not badly damaged her looks, but she was substantially blinded and would never be able to see any more than forms. I visited her at the hospital and was impressed as hell by her pluck. She felt she was finished as a reporter, but was determined to become a lawyer. She went to law school, Harvard no less.

The spring after I left office, I got a nice note at Hyannis Port asking me if I ever had drinks with "fellow disableds." We met at the Harvard Club in town for supper. I thought she was as pretty as ever and made a pass at her which, somewhat to my surprise, she turned aside.

"I'm not looking for one-nighters, or even ten-nighters," she said. "Every professor I meet seems to think he's the right man to do a favor for the poor little match girl."

"Dammit, Ann Marie," I cajoled her, "I'm not a professor. I can understand you turning down the former president of the United States, but a former lover . . . "

"Emphasis twice on *former*," she bantered back. "If I can turn down a professor who helps determine whether or not I make law journal, I can certainly say no to a brain-damaged ex-pol."

The next week I invited her out to Hyannis Port, and we walked on the beach, and then I met her in town again, and pretty soon she was no longer saying no to the brain-damaged ex-pol and we were no longer former lovers. She was fifteen years younger than I was, but then Jackie was twelve years younger, and Ann Marie loved political talk, the whole political scene, my pol friends, and soon, me. By fall, I asked her if she would marry me when she got out of Harvard Law.

The fact that she was a Methodist did not sit well with the family, but the fact that we obviously loved each other did. She put off the marriage until she had a job in a good Boston firm that paid her enough to support herself. She also wanted a baby and was determined to keep practicing law right up to delivery. I was as happy the day I married her as I had ever been.

She got on well with the kids, but her blindness made her more companion than mother. Holding her hand, they would rush down the beach, and if she tumbled over, cursing in frustration, they hoisted her up and went more slowly. I knew it was going to be all right when I saw them giving her shells to feel as they identified them.

My dizzy spells had still not stopped, but Mowberry ran tests every three months, and at least I wasn't getting any worse. On his advice, I tried to avoid stress, but things were happening that made it hard for me to sit still.

By then, Lyndon and McNamara had decided they could win in Vietnam. Lyndon announced we were moving in a total of 125,000 troops, beginning with the First Cavalry. Bobby had quit the cabinet in August of 1965, and, without directly attacking Lyndon, declared for the Senate from Massachusetts as a peace candidate in 1966. I made one visit to Lyndon about Vietnam, and he was cordial but patronizing, as if he were again majority leader and I were a junior senator whose vote on a bill he needed but could scrape through without.

I campaigned for Bobby, and like everyone else in the country was drawn into the Vietnam controversy. I found more and more that our positions ran counter to Lyndon, and the press put me up against the wall: "Aren't you saying that your views are diametrically opposed to the man you picked as vice president?"

I weaseled as best I could with such statements as, "Both the President and I are eager to end the war . . . " But when push came to shove, I felt now as Bobby did: The only way to end the war was to withdraw our troops, making whatever allowances we could for those Vietnamese whose cause we had upheld and who, therefore, were likely to be eradicated by the Communists.

Other things about Lyndon's administration also irritated me. He sent the Marines to the Dominican Republic to block a left-of-center government from taking over, falsely promulgating lists of "Communist leaders"—one turned out to be a twelve-year-old boy. Meanwhile, his misunderstandings with France led her to pull out of NATO.

Bobby's campaign for the Senate was against a black Republican, Edward Brooke. Bobby won handily, making him the junior senator from Massachusetts to our kid brother, Teddy, surely one for the dynastic book of records.

Next May, I set my own record. I turned fifty. Mother had a party at the compound. I looked around at them: gallant mother; Ann Marie, chin up, tinted glasses covering the filmed eyes which had become for me sort of the way eyes were supposed to look; everybody's kids; my brothers and sisters; Kenny; Pierre with his stogie, getting plump; Larry; Dave . . . all of them. We had been, were, a close optimistic clan, the friends now as much family as the family. I thanked God for letting me be here. But for Him—or luck—I would have died when the Japs blew up PT-109, or when the nut in Dallas shot me.

Even as I smiled to myself over my change in outlook since cursing God two and a half years ago for forcing me out of the presidency, I felt that stab of anguish that would never fully go away. Jackie had flung herself over me and because of that I was here and she was in Arlington. I trembled and felt Ann Marie's strong hand gripping mine tightly, and went on with the party.

As the year continued, I began to get a sense of things sliding out of control in Washington. Thirty-five thousand anti-war demonstrators swarmed up Capitol Hill, and some marched on the Pentagon. Six hundred were arrested. Bloody race riots broke out in Newark and in Detroit.

By December, Bobby had made up his mind to run against Lyndon for the presidency. Gene McCarthy, like Hubert, a Minnesota senator but with a strong peace record, had already begun to campaign. I talked long and hard with Bobby, saying he needed four more years in the Senate. But he was hard-headed.

Despite my misgivings, I agreed to campaign as hard as I could for him. For his Vietnam plank, we drafted a plan for getting the hell out and taking with us the hundred thousand or so people most closely identified with us. Even if we used a hundred thousand dollars each to resettle them in the U.S. or France or whatever, it would be cheaper than the war. And it would end the hemorrhaging—of our soldier's blood, of our civility, of our influence abroad, of our national pride. We would then bulwark Thailand, Malaysia, and the other neighbors, which we would have to do anyway. We'd try to get something going with China to keep Vietnam *and* China off balance.

I spent a lot of time talking to Bobby about his becoming more flexible and willing to compromise on little issues so he could win the big ones. One night, in a West Virginia motel after he had pacified the state's senior senator, promising not to burn the coal companies too fiercely, I nudged him and said, "God knows, I've done everything I could to groom you as my successor." The idea had tickled him and we had chortled. We were brothers and pals and we both felt very good about each other.

In January, after Lyndon declared solemnly that the war had turned a corner and a long road to peace was in view, the Vietcong staged its "Tet Offensive" against thirty provincial capitals, took Hue temporarily, and actually held our embassy in Saigon for six hours. I was now sure that Bobby or McCarthy would beat him for the nomination. The war had become a debacle.

In early March, Lyndon called and asked me to supper with him and Lady Bird. From his voice, I knew he was on the edge. We four ate upstairs in what in my time had been a sitting room. It felt odd to be there without Jackie but with a new wife, now pregnant. There was candlelight and choice food that I was sure Lady Bird had selected, and California chardonnay and cabernet that I was sure Lyndon had left to the staff to pick. Indeed, he was hitting the Scotch with some diligence.

I saw how exhausted he was and how worried Lady Bird was about him and I thought, *I am glad not to have your job right now, although I thought almost as fast that I would never have let it get to where it was destroying me this way.*

We made small talk about babies, my health and his, the way the Senate had changed, almost anything but the war and

Bobby's race for the presidency. I was sure that it was the latter and not the former that had prompted the invitation. I found out it was both. After the custard pie, which I knew he shouldn't be eating with his heart problem, he hit his spoon on a glass, an oddly formal gesture, both gauche and touching.

"Jack, I'm not going to try for another term," he said. "The war . . ." he began, then looked at Lady Bird and put his head in his hands for a moment, and said to us, "I'm a dog eating his own guts and trying to tell himself it's sirloin. I'm lied out and cried out and I can't do it anymore."

In face of this new honesty, my own evaporated. "You did everything a man could," I dissembled, but he was far beyond the point of being consoled. He said almost hysterically:

"I got my ass kicked by a bunch of gooks. They did to me what we did to George the Third, and for the same reason. I bankrupted my country fighting pygmies. And the worst of it is, they won't even get what we got out of England: freedom."

"Lyndon," his wife said gently but firmly.

He got a hold of himself and said he planned to go on television March 31 to make his announcement. I was still reeling from the thunderclap when he sounded another one.

"Jack, I want you to back Hubert for the presidency."

It was then that I saw how distanced he had let himself get from reality. I loved Hubert Humphrey. Everybody did. But he was too stained with Lyndon's policies, too weakened by playing Lyndon's lackey to unify the country. It would take a Bobby to do it, I thought more loyally than accurately—or a me.

"I asked you because Hubert asked me to," Lyndon said.

"You know I can't do that," I said as kindly as I could.

"Bobby will wreck us worse than I did," Lyndon said. "Look into his heart, Jack, and yours, the only way you can. Bobby can't compromise. Oh, he's fine when you sic him on a Hoffa, or a George Wallace, or the Mafia. But I'm talking about someone who has the sweetness to make the lions lie down with the lambs, the hawks with the doves. Like Hubert . . . "

"Lyndon, I can't . . . "

" . . . or you."

He let those two words sit there before us—the purpose for this supper—and I realized he was not distanced from reality at all. What I had taken for his mania was in fact his artfulness. He was telling me that he wanted me to succeed him, to serve again after a hiatus of four years like Grover Cleveland had done, and that he wanted loyal Hubert as my running mate. Thoughts crashed through my mind so wildly that I was sure they would lead to a dizzy spell.

Vaingloriously, I thought of Satan offering Jesus the dominions of the earth. I thought of Bobby, and of a poem I read about him after he had campaigned in Harlem for me in 1960: "In the fumy, twilight slum, beats the beat of Bobby's drum . . . " it began. I looked at Lyndon's droopy, tortured face.

I knew enough never to underestimate his insights, the more so because I saw what he meant about Bobby. No one matched Bobby in the intensity of a campaign speech on a fumy night, binding his listeners—particularly if they were the disinherited—to him with passion. But when it came to keeping hostile elements from each other's throat, Bobby simply did not function. He joined with one of the hostile elements and fought bloodthirstily against the others.

"I'm not saying this because I hate Bobby," Lyndon said, pleading with me now, "although I do. I'm thinking that the country is coming apart: the war, the race riots, the economy. Jack, Bobby will just tear it further. Christ, he'll be lucky if some crazy bastard doesn't do to him what Oswald tried to do to you.

"Ann Marie, you've got a good picture of us all as a fine, young, objective newswoman," Lyndon begged. "Talk to Jack. Search out his heart." The man was shameless. He could never keep pathos from falling away to bathos, never stop short of overkill.

"Listen," I said to all three of them, "I am not going to run for president with a brain that may not work when I need it most. Much less against my own brother." But he had planted a seed in my vitals that began to root the instant Ann Marie and I left the White House.

"You had your last check-up four months ago," Ann Marie said to me when we were in the White House car on the way to Andrews Air Force Base. Lyndon had a small jet waiting there to take us home. I nodded at the driver's back and then gave a mock look around the car. Lyndon would not only have the driver report anything we said back to him that same night, but probably had the car bugged as well.

"I'm past due to see Mowberry," I conceded.

Not until we were home in bed did we dare talk about it in detail. "I love Bobby," she said. "You know I do. More than any of them, he smoothed out the religious thing for us. But . . . "

" . . . Lyndon may be right," I said for her.

"In four years the Senate will take some of that out of him, some of that . . . " she began.

" . . . rigidity. He's already doing better," I said. We had been married long enough so that we tended to finish each other's sentences.

" . . . but he needs a little more compassion . . . " she said.

" . . . for the strong. He has it for the weak, God knows."

The next morning, I drove to Boston with Ann Marie. Mowberry could make my mind up for me if he said I was unfit, which is not to say that I hoped my scans had taken a turn for the worse. When he got me off the machines, he studied the charts and smiled.

"Steady as a clam at neap tide," he said. "Whatever Ann Marie's doing," he said, nodding at her, "don't stop." He had kept me on Dilantin, more as a precaution than because he feared a seizure, and now he suggested I stop taking them. "I want you back in three months. I might just have some good news for you."

"You're saying it's . . . healing?"

"Well, more that it may be rearranging. Back to before you were shot. Maybe reversing itself, like we hoped."

"So that even under stress . . . ?"

" . . . *if* there's no change in three months, stress would be manageable. You'd be as you were before November 1963."

Three months would make it just over two months before the convention. With Lyndon out, it was going to be a horse race between Hubert and Bobby, with Gene McCarthy holding the balance. There were giant imponderables. Hubert and

McCarthy were both Minnesotans, had been close until Vietnam had separated them.

But Hubert would now put space between himself and Lyndon. McCarthy might back him—except that Bobby and McCarthy had been much alike on Vietnam all along. "If I did run," I said to Ann Marie, "my candidacy would simplify things, position us better than anybody else against Nixon."

". . . except that Bobby won't drop out."

"That's not certain. He knows I have another four years coming. He knows he'd be my natural successor. If I took on Hubert as my V.P., I could get him to promise to let Bobby run for president in seventy-two. Maybe."

"And maybe not. Look, Jack, I've always wanted to make love with a president *in* the White House, but there are too many ganglia flapping around on this thing. Maybe some of them inside your head, too. You're not sure whether you're cured yet."

I turned to her and took her dear face in my hands. "If the stress of thinking at one and the same time of running for president and of making love to you doesn't give me a dizzy spell, then, sweetheart, I am impervious."

Lyndon made his announcement, and there was a momentary national sigh of relief. But five days later, Dr. King was killed in Memphis. Riots broke out all over the country. A sizable chunk of downtown Washington was looted and burned. Anti-war students shut down Columbia University for two weeks, and there were acts of violence, and sit-ins, and bombings all through May.

Bobby seemed to be picking up more and more strength, reaping the whirlwind. He was very up. I knew the feeling from

1960. You begin to practice after-dinner speeches in the East Room and wonder whether your next guest of honor should be Casals or Pope Paul. I didn't have the heart to tell him what had been festering in my mind ever since my talk with Mowberry.

On the first of June, Mowberry ran the tests and came out grinning, taking my arm in his hand. He told me that the graphs were stable and that the sensors showed restoration of all my motor functions. I knew I was cured and that before me was the most difficult choice of my life.

I asked him whether he would run the results past the same panel who had told me to leave office four years ago.

"You're not considering . . . " he started and then stopped with a surprised look at me. I knew he was thinking about Bobby, about Kennedys in general and how they did things and did not do things based on family loyalty.

"I want to be sure . . . in case of anything," I said, feeling ashamed that he had looked into my voracious heart. He queried the panel and the next day they came back with the same answer Mowberry had given me. That night, Ann Marie and I joined Bobby on the campaign trail. He was full of South Dakota and California and all the other states where he had won or was expected to win in the primaries. I felt almost as if we were barging in on his time when we got the campaign staff, most of them old friends of mine, too, out of his room.

"Mowberry says I'm well," I said.

His first reaction was a glowing chipmunk smile, and he jumped from his chair and hugged me. Then he realized that was something I could just as well have told him by phone and the fact that we had flown across the country meant there was more to come, probably a lot more. Before he sat down, he surmised what it was.

"You're wondering what to do," he said, and when I nodded, wanting to leave him with the serve, he said, "What *do* you want to do?"

"You've already guessed that. The question is—what *should* I do? What do *you* want me to do? What does the family want me to do? What would Big Joe"—our name for our father—"want us to do?" Bobby smiled, with humor but not much warmth.

"What do you want him to do?" he asked Ann Marie.

"I want him to do what's right and I want him to be president again and I don't know if both are possible," she said.

"Your serve," he said to me, instinctively hitting on the same tennis metaphor that I had.

"It would be easier for me if we were sure whether you could beat Hubert and Gene."

"I'll get the nomination," he said.

"And the election?"

"Probably that, too," he said.

Well, he might and he might not. I had run against Nixon in 1960 and he was a lot fitter, a lot smarter now. I could beat him. I wasn't sure Bobby or Hubert could. I knew Gene couldn't. In any case, Bobby's assurance left me no room to work around him. I had to take his chance away from him or give up mine.

"You'd be in for eight years, assuming you don't screw up." What I was saying was that if he ran, I was finished. "How much would it hurt you if I took it?" I asked him.

"Lots. I want it now. Bad."

I knew that feeling, too. "You could leave the Senate," I said, "spend the four years in the cabinet or the Supreme Court. Warren is stepping down. I would give you anything you wanted."

"Jack, don't Lyndon me." He thought a while, looking at no one, then rose and went to the window and thought some more. It was even possible he was praying, something he was more likely to do at such times than I was. Finally, he came back, his eyes angry and his face tight. "If you want it, I'll drop out. But you know goddamn well it ruins me for seventy-two. There's enough dynasty talk already. Besides, there'll be Teddy. How the hell do you think he'll feel about waiting even longer?"

"Not good," I said, buying time, shaken myself now that he had said, however reluctantly, that he would drop out. And yet I knew that while he might be furious with me now, he would break his ass to drop out with grace, turn over his delegates and campaign for me. So, once again it was my serve. He had deferred to me, but in a way that let me know he would never in his heart forgive me if I took him up on it.

The two of us sat there voiceless, lost in calculations about our feelings for each other, for ourselves, for the family, the country. It was not one of us but Ann Marie who spoke. "You can't do it," she said softly to me. "Ever since your family has been in politics, since your grandfather was mayor of Boston, you've all been looked on as opportunists. And why not? You took the Senate away from Lodge, a perfectly fine senator in fifty-two, tried to take the vice-presidential nomination away from Estes Kefauver in fifty-six, and took the presidency away from Hubert, who God knows deserved it, in sixty.

"And, Bobby, you've never tried a real case and yet you took over as attorney general and then bumped Ed Brooke, who would have been the first Negro senator, a good senator, and now you're trying to take the shot at the presidency from Hubert again. And here Jack is, trying to take that from you. Sure, you're idealists, wanting to help the weak against the strong, but there is something insatiable about it, like sharks.

"Is Teddy going to be in your hotel room in seventy-two?" she asked, turning to Bobby, then to me, "or yours, telling one of you that it's his turn, as if you were divvying up an order of french fries? Do you Kennedys think you have some divine right to the White House, like kings of France?"

She was saying what neither Bobby nor I could say, and we both listened to her, fascinated, knowing she loved us and—as both lawyer and journalist—saw us perhaps as clearly as anyone ever had, and as uncompromisingly.

"What I am saying, Jack, because you are my concern, really, not Bobby, except in an ancillary way, is that the devouring has gone far enough. Somebody has to call a halt. And you are the one who should do it. Let Bobby have it. Back him. Help him every way you can. Your head is cured and what an asset you will be for him against Nixon! If he wants you in the cabinet or on the court, take it and serve him. Moderate him, as he did with you during the talks on the missile crisis. But, dear Jesus, let this greed come to an end!"

When she stopped, she was out of breath and I was heartsick. She was right. It had to stop somewhere. Bobby had given the nomination to me, and now I must give it back. And while I could do it without anger at him, since I, not he, had been the grasper, I could not give it back to him without pain.

I rose from my chair and he from his simultaneously. We needed no words. We hugged each other, Kennedys who had fought everyone and had won and had almost fought each other. The tears came to my eyes, the tears of a child who had been forced to give up a toy he loved beyond love. But slowly as we held each other, in my heart, in my mind, I began to feel a great catharsis.

I'm giving up the toy, I have become the man. Sure, if by some unknowable stroke of fate, Bobby dropped out before the convention, I would jump in and carry out his work, our work. But he wasn't going to and I was going to help him as he had so ably helped me. We broke and looked for something to say.

"What's next?" was all I could think of.

"Big victory celebration on June 5 after I win in California."

"In San Francisco?" It was a city that loved Kennedys.

"No, Los Angeles."

I thought of Orange County and Los Angeles and all the dangerous nuttiness that was abroad in that city, the far right wing and the smoldering coals of Watts and the student riots and maniacs from every violence-prone political and nationalist movement in the country.

"Hold it in San Francisco," I said, suddenly and senselessly afraid, my voice a plea.

"I've got San Francisco sewn up. I need Los Angeles."

I thought of Dallas and how I could have gone to Austin that day, but that I already had Austin and needed Dallas, needed the motorcade, needed the TV coverage with the plastic bubbletop off. I thought of the forecast of rain and what Jackie had said about letting it come down. And then I thought of what had come down instead of rain.

"I have a bad feeling about Los Angeles, Bobby," I said again. "The brain business has made a seer of me." I tried to make a somber joke of it. Yet my tone and intent were serious.

But Bobby's mind was already back on the campaign trail, his hand, his ambition stretching out for the merry-go-round's gold ring. "If anything should happen in Los Angeles, or *anywhere*," he said, triumphant, fraternal, believing in this moment of joy that nothing ever could, but remembering my words to him all those months ago, "I'll know I've done everything I could to groom my successor." He laughed aloud. When I saw him so happy, I loved him the way only a brother who has already lost one brother can love. And that was the way he loved me back.

KURT
COBAIN

BY ORLANDO RAMIREZ

THE FINAL DAYS

*D*on't get pissed off if I get up and walk out in the middle of this," said a surprisingly clear-eyed Kurt Cobain as he settled into the plush cushions of an oversized wing chair in the penthouse suite of the Oriental Beverly Hills.

At one time this kind of too-fancy-by-half hotel would have been anathema to the seldom seen god of grunge rock, but its luxury spoke of the big bucks behind the Lolla-palooza XX tour, which Cobain was set to headline.

With or without his former Nirvana bandmates was still unknown. But Cobain seemed to have another agenda as he sat down for his first interview—other than a few random appearances on the Net—in more than thirteen years. At the time, possibly only he knew it would be one of his last.

"Do I look like a 'total vegetable' to you?" pleaded Cobain, toying with the frayed sleeve of the pajama top he wore over a pair of torn jeans. His appearance wasn't much different than when he burst upon the rock scene in 1991. His blue eyes still had the penetrating power that glared from a million T-shirts since his absence from the music scene. But there were wisps of gray in his rapidly thinning hair and his creased forehead and mangled ear still bore the scars of his botched 1994 suicide attempt.

"That was just Courtney's favorite fantasy," he said, referring to the *60 Minutes* report of more than ten years before when Courtney Love, the former Mrs. Cobain, told Tabitha Soren that Cobain's suicide attempt had left him "drooling, incoherent, a total vegetable."

At that time, the two were locked in a bitter custody dispute over their daughter, Frances Bean. The custody hearing, which was broadcast live on the old MTV network, was capped by a dramatic courtroom appearance by Cobain in which he pleaded to care for his daughter. But Cobain was no match for Love's lawyer, the combative Marcia Clark. It was assumed that the judge's denial of visitation rights caused Cobain to retreat farther into his remote Northern California compound and a heroin habit.

"It hit me so hard," he said of the lost years after the ruling. "I felt abandoned, and there's no point in not being blunt. I wanted to die. I wanted to die every day. I had no choice but to medicate myself. After the trial, the whole world thought I was a drugged-out schizophrenic. I figured it was easier to live up to their expectations.

"The whole outside world seemed like a strange planet to me. And if you have enough money, heroin is the perfect drug. You get people to care for you and you can stay in your pajamas all day."

He paused for a minute and retrieved a pack of his trademark Winston Lights from the ripped pocket of his pajama top. He took a puff and a thin watery cough seemed to erupt like a hairball from his muscular throat. An aide then rushed to his side with a glass of water. He tugged the sleeves of his pajama tops. His veins were not for display.

"Look at Keith Richards," he said, settling into the plush contour of the chair. "He was always going to be the next rock fatality. But he showed them. Burying Woody, Charlie, then Mick. I was considering asking him to tour with me. Wouldn't that be a trip! We could call ourselves the Old Barbarians!"

The boast didn't seem so funny given Richards' recent appearance on *The Late Show with David Letterman*, where the aging rocker seemed disoriented and insisted on calling Letterman "Jay," a reference to the now-disgraced former "other" talk show host.

"I don't know who to have back me up," he said, finally addressing the question that was on everybody's mind. "I was thinking of asking Michael, but he doesn't need this. He's got his movies. His Academy Awards. He doesn't need this—now that he's got his hairpiece."

The sudden splash of vitriol seemed out of place given Stipe's long and faithful friendship with Cobain. Stipe is credited with helping Cobain detox after the 1994 suicide attempt, then recording the classic *Shift the Blame* album, where Cobain and the former singer of REM teamed with Larry Mullen and Adam Clayton of U2 to form the first alternative supergroup.

Cobain then paused to reconsider. "You know, Michael was the only one to keep in touch all those years. He'd call and I wouldn't come to the phone. Even after I had the phone disconnected, he'd fly out and there he'd be all of a sudden, sitting on the porch eating an apple. That was when he was still wearing all those silly hats. Back when we'd compare hairlines."

When asked if he missed his compound, Cobain shrugged. "It's just another part of the same prison. It doesn't much matter where you go. The confusion is still as deep."

Confusion?

"I made a fucking foolish mistake," he said, sipping at the water. "I thought that as you got older that it wouldn't hurt as much, that you could escape this prison, but all I found is that the prison walls got higher. The people would still climb the walls trying to get at this thing called Kurt Cobain.

"All I wanted was to be forgotten. I was tired of bitching about celebrity. Everybody was tired of hearing me bitch about celebrity. I thought if I just stopped playing one that it would all eventually end, that people would forget and that the prison would just like, you know, melt away. It just doesn't make sense that I became more popular after I disappeared."

That fact was what was fueling the big money—some sources quote a figure of $100 million—behind Cobain's return. In the many years of his absence, his following had grown with succeeding generations finding some sort of spiritual reckoning in songs like "Smells Like Teen Spirit," "Lithium," and "Rape Me."

"I wrote most of the lyrics on the dashboard of the car on the way to the studio," admitted Cobain. "It's not like a tremendous amount of thought went into those songs. And then the stuff from *Shift the Blame*—that was mostly Michael. I was just the guitar player in that group."

Cobain was being somewhat disingenuous about the album that stands as the apogee of punk/alternative rock. It sold fifteen million copies and led to a tour that fell apart after a few weeks. Some reports said that the pressure led Cobain back into heroin use, making him miss shows. But Stipe's recent autobiographical CD-ROM of the period hints at a failed relationship between him and Cobain.

Several long seconds passed before Cobain responded to the question about the nature of his relationship with Stipe. He moved to stub out his cigarette, but the Oriental had complied with the recent federal regulation banning the manufacture and distribution of smoking paraphernalia, so he let the butt fall into the water glass, sputter, then die. An aide whisked away the glass.

"I love Michael," he said finally. "We never talked about what happened on that tour. For me to say this happened or that happened is bullshit. Take from it what you want. The reason I quit the tour is that I was puking my guts out before every show. I was puking air, and quite literally, my gut told me to get out.

"It was stupid of me to think it wouldn't have become some big fucking scam. At first it was going to be some small halls. Then before we knew it, it was these stadiums with tickets being sold by MTV. I'd walk out onto the stage and could feel the floor shake with the applause of those people and I kept thinking, 'You stupid fucks, this isn't music, it's merchandise.'

"I'm glad that tour lost so much money," he said, reaching into his pocket for another cigarette. "Michael was way too far up the ass of those MTV mobsters. If there's anything I'm glad about, it's that that evil Viacom empire saw its first defeat because of the bile I spewed in the catering rooms on the way to the stages of the precious few stadiums we played."

A malicious glint came to Cobain's eye. He was energized suddenly. Yes, he helped bring down MTV and was proud of it. But wasn't the first video channel the reason for his success?

"I hated doing fucking videos," he says. "Besides, you couldn't find anything by Nirvana on MTV after I bailed on that tour, and kids still got into the music. We became like an underground band again. And it just showed how stupid and pitiful MTV was."

If so, then why did Cobain refuse to respond to the subpoena issued by the Congressional committee investigating the music video scandal?

"It was just more television. It was McCarthyism for the '90s. Newt Gingrich and all his 'counterculture' crap. They wanted me to go play the drugged-out rock star and shit on all the kids in their bedrooms playing our CDs. No way was I going to march in that ignorant parade.

"That was an amazing time," he said, running a frail hand through his thinning mane. "You had Stone (Gossard of Pearl Jam) and Mariah Carey sitting next to each other before that committee, mouthing the same lines. Then Tabitha turns state's witness and what's his name, that Congress guy who used to play for the Seahawks (former vice president Steve Largent), had the nerve to say he'd listened to all the Nirvana records.

"Jocks," he sneered. "I always hated fucking jocks."

The interview ended there. Cobain glanced about the room, frowned, lifted himself from the chair, and disappeared into another room. A loud conversation could be heard taking place behind closed doors. Moments later, an aide, a willowy brunette, returned to say that the publicist would call to set another date.

Weeks passed. Rumors mounted. Cobain was back on heroin. The tour was canceled. Nirvana was getting back together. Then a group called The Kurt Cobain Project was announced as the lead act on Lollapalooza XX. Then—silence.

Just as suddenly there was a call. Be ready to board a red-eye flight to the West Coast. Cobain wanted to talk. He was rehearsing the band at his compound. Certain issues had to be set straight.

At the small rural airport, a Cobain aide was waiting. The Cobain compound was set high in the hills, hidden among old-growth redwoods. The only clue that you were approaching the hideaway of the reclusive rock star was the graffiti that began almost a mile away.

WELCOME TO NIRVANA read one message sprayed on the side of a gas station. Farther down, HERE WE ARE NOW,

ENTERTAIN US was scrawled on a deserted van. And just before rounding the bend to the compound was the more professionally lettered KURT COBAIN IS A FALSE IDOL, which had been crossed out and covered with various epithets.

Despite this buildup, it was still a shock to confront the gates of the Cobain compound as they loomed suddenly out of the rainy fog that hugged the mountain slope. On that day about twenty men and women, boys and girls, some as old as fifty, others as young as nine or ten, stood vigil. Most affected the long, stringy hair and cardigan sweaters of their idol. They stood around campfires warming themselves, some strumming guitars and singing the songs that had become even more popular in the absence of their writer. Some had taken up semi-permanent residence at the gates of the compound and were often compared to the camp followers of the Grateful Dead before that band perished in a suspicious aircraft disaster.

Others, from as far away as Turkey and Australia, were there only for a few hours as part of the Cobain Pilgrimage, which began in Cobain's hometown of Aberdeen, Washington, passed through Seattle, stopped at the site of his botched 1994 suicide attempt, then visited the compound before moving to Los Angeles and a stop at the home Cobain had shared with Courtney Love before their split.

The walls of the compound were painted pink. It might be called a shocking pink, but the faithful referred to it as Pepto-Bismol pink in reference to Cobain's celebrated stomach distress. A row of blinking Christmas lights was strung along the upper perimeter of the wall, but the festive lights only served to subvert the eye from the jagged row of razor wire along the top of the ten-foot-high walls. A closer inspection also revealed a sophisticated series of surveillance cameras and motion detectors.

The gates themselves, massive steel and wood and remote-controlled, had been painted with a mural of Cobain, angel wings sprouting from his back, with his torso cut away and his interior organs on display much like the anatomical dolls he once collected—an obvious take-off on the cover of the *In Utero* album. Candles burned in notches carved in the wood by fans. The accumulated wax from years of the practice had given the gates a dull sheen.

To enter, the aide called ahead and gave a password, and the car barely slowed as the faithful dodged out of the way as the gates swung open. Two burly guards hurled the brazen few who tried to enter just before the gates slammed shut.

The compound itself was a vision of serenity. There was a large main house made of redwood. Beyond that, in a grove of redwood trees, was a trailer, vintage 1965, that was also painted Pepto-Bismol pink and decorated with strings of Christmas lights. This was Cobain's residence. The big house was for the guards and other aides and that day for the various technicians who hovered around the rehearsal room set up in the ballroom.

A quick glance around the rehearsal space revealed a simple drum set, a bass amp, a single guitar amp. Everybody was waiting. The roadies talked among themselves about the recent Counting Crows reunion tour and how Adam Duritz didn't speak to the other members until they reached the steps of the stage.

Then Krist Novoselic entered from outdoors. The six-foot-seven bass player appeared tanned and healthy, a bottle of beer in hand. His wife/manager Shelli trailed a few steps behind.

He sat down on a stool and picked up his bass. There was a slight buzz to his amplifier, then he asked, "Anybody seen Dave?"

When there was no reply, he returned to his instrument and called to his technician to complain about the condition of the equipment.

"That's how Kurt wants it," said the technician with a shrug.

"That's stupid, considering how technology has progressed in fifteen years," replied Novoselic.

Shelli took a seat next to the reporter and began running down Novoselic's activities since Nirvana disbanded after Cobain's 1994 suicide attempt. There was the year they spent in Croatia helping relief efforts. Then the tour with the Melvins, followed by the failed attempt at a solo album.

"Krist was ready to give up then," said Shelli, "but then he got on the cable access and found his true calling. None of us ever expected he'd end up being a talk show host."

The show, *Calling All Cows,* which drew on Novoselic's underground contacts, was a surprise success because it eschewed the regular formula. Many episodes were taped as Novoselic drove from bar to bar with that week's guest.

Shelli was quick to point out that it was Novoselic who contacted Cobain when he heard about the Lollapalooza XX tour. After all, it couldn't be Nirvana without Novoselic, who had been Cobain's partner since their days in Aberdeen. And despite the occasional slur Novoselic let slip about Cobain on his talk show, the two were able to resolve their differences.

When asked if Novoselic was receiving a percentage, she bristled. "This tour is not as lucrative as it may seem."

Just then, drummer Dave Grohl entered and settled behind his set. Since the breakup of Nirvana he'd been the drummer in demand. Tom Petty, Pearl Jam, the Clash reunion album and tour, the ill-fated Peter Buck Band, and the Bono solo tour were among the various high-profile projects in which he'd held down the beat. Then there were his solo albums, self-produced affairs that displayed an unexpected flair as a songwriter.

Grohl seemed almost diffident as he waited for Cobain to appear or not appear. He was not the first Nirvana drummer, and the Cobain-Novoselic nexus had always been the force that held the group together. Later, in an unguarded moment, he let it be known that the Nirvana reunion held no special sentiment for him. "Playing for the Clash was much more exciting than this."

Like Novoselic, the sticking point for Grohl seemed to be money. There was no three-way split. No democracy among equals. They were on salary. It was definitely the Kurt Cobain Project.

The center of all this attention soon appeared—followed by his retinue of handlers—and took up his left-handed guitar without so much as a glance at his bandmates. Cobain wore jeans, a T-shirt, and sunglasses with wide white frames. His head hung low as he began to strum the opening chords to "All Apologies." Novoselic and Grohl fell in behind him. Cobain began singing in a low mumble, but by the time the chorus kicked in, he was screaming—on key as always.

"It was always about the music," shouted Shelli Novoselic as the band reached a crescendo.

But after the auspicious start, the music became hard work. "Sliver" faltered before it started. "Pennyroyal Tea" dissolved when Cobain forgot the chorus. An hour was spent on aimless jamming. Cobain wandered off. Novoselic and Grohl exchanged looks, then abandoned their instruments. Novoselic headed back to the hotel. Grohl was overheard telling his manager that they'd need to hire a second guitarist to cover for Cobain "if he insists on playing all smacked-up."

The crew and hangers-on moved to the far end of the ballroom where the caterers had set up a late breakfast. The talk was dispirited. After the first rehearsal, it looked like the Nirvana reunion was headed toward disaster. Cobain was obviously under the influence of something.

The representative of the Lollapalooza organization was unperturbed.

"This is just the start," he said. "They haven't played together in fifteen years. If we need to bring in other musicians, no problem. We did that with the Chili Peppers."

That tour, Lollapalooza XVII, set the format for the revitalized concert series. A dinosaur of alternative rock was signed to headline as a draw for the older crowd, then a modern alternative act like Little Whore Tribe or Prog was second-billed to placate the younger demographics. The lower levels of the bill sometimes supported upcoming acts, but in the last couple of years those slots had been filled with aging punkers like the re-formed Replacements, Liz Phair, and the now ironically named Sonic Youth.

The Lollapalooza representative defended the practice.

"We do extensive polling," he said. "These are the names that get the highest numbers."

What bands received the highest numbers?

"Nirvana was No. 1. KISS was a close second."

The original KISS or KISS: The Next Generation, the band of new cast members put together by Paul Stanley?

"Both, actually," responded the Lollapalooza representative. "Perry (Farrell) thought that the two together would be best. But far and away, we wanted Nirvana. They were supposed to headline back in 1994, but you know what happened."

When asked if there were any concerns about Cobain's mental state on the part of the money people, the Lollapalooza representative replied, "We're insured."

An uneasy calm settled over the camp. Grohl could be heard upstairs jamming with some friends. The lights were on in Cobain's trailer.

Then the aide appeared. "Kurt is ready to talk," she said and led the way to the trailer.

"Maybe four or five people have been in here," she said on the walk over. "This is so rare."

She knocked on the door and it swung open. Once inside, the cramped surroundings revealed themselves to be covered with objects of every sort. There were numerous dolls from various parts of the world, a collection of antique Gameboys, a mannequin dressed in pajamas, its face smeared with makeup, sat in a corner. Next to it rested a shotgun. On the arm of the drab sofa was what looked like a Colt .45 pistol. A large, flat screen hung from the wall, the monitor divided into six channels. One broadcasted the news from Tokyo, another carried the MoonSat live feed, Classic MTV was on another, a London billiards show filled another segment, one monitored the ballroom of the main house, and the last screen monitored the front gate.

"You'd be amazed at what I see going on there," said Cobain, entering from the back bedroom of the double-wide. He was wearing reading glasses that he slipped off and let dangle from a chain around his neck.

"At first I hated these people," he said, clearing the other channels off the screen to gaze at the thirty or so diehards waiting outside the gates. "Now it's like they're ants and I'm the picnic. I tape the most outrageous things. Last year there was this kid, maybe no more than four. He had his own tiny guitar and amp and sang all of 'Nevermind' in order from beginning to end. I was thinking today of finding him and sending him out on tour in my place."

He returned to the MoonSat feed, the EC satellite survey of the lunar landscape forming the perfect setting for this otherworldly mood. Then he put on an old Howlin' Wolf record. Vinyl.

"I like it best when the record skips," he said, pulling the ubiquitous pack of Winston Lights from between the cushions of the sofa. He picked up the pistol and pulled the trigger. A flame shot out of the barrel. He calmly lit the cigarette.

"I was just talking to Courtney," he said matter-of-factly. "She said she heard the rehearsal was for shit." His hand drew a circle in the air as if to describe the tangle of satellites and transmissions buzzing above his head that link his trailer to his ex-wife's London townhouse.

"I figure Shelli called her. Those two have been such good friends since the hearing." It was obvious that Cobain still harbored some bitterness against Novoselic's wife for testifying against him at Frances Bean's custody hearing.

Just how did he manage to speak to Courtney?

"The Bean called while I was at the rehearsal," he said, referring to his daughter. "Courtney happened to pick up, although it was Bean's private phone."

Cobain revealed for the first time that he was in regular contact with his daughter. "We speak almost every day," he said. "We fax each other drawings and collages all the time. She started calling me on her own about four years ago. She gets awfully bored and lonely cooped up in those European hotels with the countess or duchess or whatever she is."

Love had recently married Baron Phillipe Beringer de Rothschild, an heir of the banking fortune. It was her fourth marriage. After Cobain, she had briefly married actor Brad Pitt, then had a long-term marriage to ex-Smashing Pumpkin Billy Corgan, who died after an unsuccessful liver transplant.

"She's like any fifteen-year-old," Cobain said of his daughter. "She hates her stepfather. Hates her stepbrother. Her mother is too preoccupied with her shopping and Net chat. It's just too ironic to be funny."

Cobain, of course, was referring to his own childhood. His parents, an auto mechanic and a secretary, divorced when he was eight. He then bounced from parent to parent to relatives before he finally struck out on his own, often sleeping below the bridges in Aberdeen.

"It's just funny to see how the genes play out," he said. "It's not funny for Bean, that's for sure. But in the war between me and her mother, it's amazing to see how much she ended up resembling me, even though her mother wouldn't let me near her for about ten years."

When asked if Frances had inherited any of his musical talent, Cobain laughed. "She's got a bad stomach, if that's what you mean." He was referring to his legendary digestive problems, which many cite as the impetus for much of his tortured writing.

"She can sing and she plays drums, but I hope she avoids the Sean Lennon or Jade Jagger route," he said of two rock royalty offspring who had had recent hits recycling their fathers' hits.

"Bean has more sense than to record 'Lithium' with a Bulgarian choir." The younger Lennon had recently done similar with his father's song "Mother."

Cobain squirmed in his chair for a moment. "It's her life," he said, waving his cigarette in the air. "She can fuck it up anyway she wants."

His restlessness forced the issue. He seemed ready to end the interview at any moment, but the big questions still had to be asked: Why the tour? Why now? Money or art?

"I think about something Neil Young once said—'It's not me, it's the music.' You see, I am as disturbed and amazed and all the fuck else that there are still people outside the gates of my house, that tons of money roll in although I don't do a fucking thing. What's going on? Why these songs? It was all supposed to end when we crossed the millennium, but it's just as fucked up and crazy.

"Although I don't do anything to encourage it, the dialogue is still taking place. It's time for me to step in and add my two cents. There's nothing else for me to do."

But why this tour?

"Because I can't sit down and answer every question that ends up in my file on the Net. Sometimes I open up that file and read through the stuff they're talking about and I gotta comment. I've tried, but they no longer believe it's me. There are so many frauds out there."

His eyes flashed darkly.

"Did you see that video of that convention in Laughlin? They had Japanese Kurt Cobains. Iranian Cobains. African girls dressed like Courtney." He laughed at the idea of the host of Kurt Cobain impersonators that had sprung up in his absence.

"No matter what I say, it comes off like I'm bellyaching." He laughed at his own joke.

Lollapalooza XX seemed such an odd choice given Cobain's complaint that his last tour, the one with Stipe, had been too big.

"There's no in between anymore," he replied. "The demand is that I either play the enormodomes or nothing. And nothing is looking better by the second."

Did that mean he was having second thoughts? Were Krist and Dave still part of the plan?

"I don't know. It's weird," he said. "I don't know what to expect from either of them. When I walked into the rehearsal this afternoon, I could feel all this pent-up hostility on their part—and mine."

When asked if he would form another backing group if the reunion continued on its rocky path, Cobain shrugged. "Maybe I'll get a band of lookalikes, and challenge the audience to guess which one is the real whatever."

The mood suddenly shifted. Cobain picked up the lighter in the shape of a revolver.

"Courtney was right. It would have been better if I hadn't fucked up in 1994. A living legend is just dead weight."

What did happen in 1994? Did he really intend to commit suicide?

"I blew a golden opportunity. I obviously meant to do it," he said, lifting the hair on the side of his head to show his mangled ear. "Do you think I'd just blow off my ear for attention?"

When asked if he regretted the attempt, he replied, "Next time I'll have better aim."

Two weeks later Kurt Cobain was dead. Earlier in the day he had arrived from Los Angeles after rehearsals with the Kurt Cobain Project, but shortly after 3:10 A.M. authorities say the forty-two-year-old singer/songwriter set fire to his trailer.

According to investigators, an accelerant similar to kerosene was spread through every room of the double-wide trailer and that once the match was struck—those closest to him believe it was his pistol-shaped lighter—it exploded into flames so intense they set fire to nearby trees. Fans holding vigil outside the gate were the first to call 911, having been awakened by the blast and the trees burning like Roman candles in the otherwise dark compound.

There was immediate speculation that this was a hoax. Many maintain that Cobain had faked his death to escape the celebrity that had become such a burden that he rarely ventured outside his compound walls. They also add that the pressure of his first tour in more than eleven years may have caused him to seek a way out.

However, Cobain had been exhibiting bizarre behavior in the preceding week, and it was confirmed by a close aide that Cobain had increased his heroin use as his stomach problems had recurred.

As further evidence, authorities released the records that showed Cobain had made a phone call to his daughter, Frances Bean Cobain, earlier in the day.

"He said, 'No matter what happens, remember I love you,'" Frances Bean told a London tabloid. "I said, 'What kind of bullshit is that?' He never told me he loved me. I should have known."

Further, those closest cite the master tapes of a new album that Cobain had dispatched to Dreamworks, his longtime label. Titled *I Hate Myself and I Want to Die,* it was a collection of thirteen songs recorded in the last three years.

"It sounds like he recorded it in his bedroom on a four-track," said a source at Dreamworks. "It's just him and his guitar. A drum machine in places. A few overdubbed harmonies and samples off old blues records."

Most of the songs, said the source, were Cobain originals, but two were covers of songs by Leadbelly and Joni Mitchell.

"He was apparently deep into the blues," said the source. "If anything, it sounds like one of those old field recordings done by the Smithsonian of backwoods musicians singing on their front porch."

Officially, Dreamworks had no plans to release the album. Legally, it may have been unable to do so. Cobain's recording contract with Dreamworks had lapsed, having been signed more than ten years ago. A press statement from CEO Jeffrey Katzenberg said that given the tragic events it would be "inappropriate" to issue the recording.

Pirate copies had been offered on the Net beginning at $5,000, but inquiries had provided no more than a few fragments gleaned by hackers off the Dreamworks in-house system.

"He seemed to be in good spirits," said Freddy Mercury Martinez, the twenty-four-year-old drummer Cobain had recruited after the attempted reunion with Nirvana bandmates Krist Novoselic and Dave Grohl had failed. Novoselic was known to be bitter, while Grohl merely moved on to his next project, a tour with Layne Staley.

"He was really getting into the music again. He was pretty rusty. He couldn't remember all the chords all the time. But I figured that after a couple of weeks we'd be rocking," said Martinez.

Older associates painted a bleaker picture. As the rehearsals moved to Los Angeles, Cobain's mood seemed to darken. He was uncommunicative and in turns harsh and apologetic.

"In other words, the same old Kurt," said one close source.

Another source, who wished to remain anonymous, told of a night spent with Cobain in the back of a hired limousine cruising the Sunset Strip in search of drugs. This source said that Cobain ordered the driver to stop at the site of the old Viper Room, now an annex of the Tower Media shopping center.

"He kept telling the driver, 'Take me to the spot where River Phoenix died.' Except the driver had no idea who River Phoenix was or what the Viper Room was. It was eerie, kind of like that movie with Tom Cruise and Glenn Close—*Sunset Boulevard–The Musical.*"

Once they located the spot, Cobain got out of the limousine, kneeled by the side door, and began rocking back and forth.

"Then these kids recognized him," said the source. "And he just got real mad when they asked if it was really him. He started cursing at them and then got back in the car, and told the driver to cruise this one street off Hollywood Boulevard until he saw some guys.

"They were obviously dealing and Kurt called them over and they started talking and Kurt asked if they knew where he could cop some heroin."

According to the source, Cobain let the two dealers into the limousine and conveyed their directions to the driver. After stopping at an ATM where Cobain withdrew $1,500, they drove to a park in the Hollywood Hills, where the two went off to score heroin.

"We sat in the back in the dark, waiting, and I was scared," said the source. "I kept begging him, 'Kurt, don't be so stupid.' But he just suddenly turned really vicious and mean, calling me all kinds of names. He'd been halfway sweet up to that point.

"They came back and were going to do it all up there, but I kept complaining, so as soon as the car reached Sunset, Kurt had the driver stop and told me to get out."

According to the limousine driver, he drove to a house on Highland Avenue where Cobain exited with the two men. Cobain told the driver to return when paged, but the page never came and the driver handed off the responsibility to the manager of the limousine service. According to their records, Cobain never paged.

Cobain was missing for two days. Authorities tried to reconstruct what occurred over that period. He withdrew several more thousand dollars from his ATM, but according to the LAPD sources, videotapes of the transactions showed a young woman with long stringy hair and a tall man with short hair making the withdrawals.

The two dealers who got into the limousine had neither come forward nor been found. Cobain was said to have been spotted at a private club in West Hollywood where a number of Cobain impersonators were putting on a show, but that was generally discounted as rumor.

"The best guess is that he was wasted in some cheap motel," said a member of the Lollapalooza production team. "He missed two rehearsals and a photo shoot. When he showed up, his eyes were glazed and his clothes were filthy."

"Kurt had been doing heroin for years," said a source who worked in the Cobain compound. "Except he managed it so he was able to function. He said he used it just to keep his stomach problems under control."

"For a while, before the tour, he switched to methadone because he wasn't sure he could get a steady supply (of heroin) while he was out on the road. But then he got to L.A. and it was like old times. He was scoring out on the street, doing it up in strange places, and trying to hide it from those closest to him."

It is known that director/producer Michael Stipe, the former lead singer for REM, had visited with Cobain several times during the rehearsals. When contacted, Stipe refused to comment other than to say he was "deeply saddened" by the death.

According to the source at Dreamworks, it was Stipe who encouraged Cobain to release *I Hate Myself and I Want to Die.*

"Stipe had acted as intermediary for (Dreamworks chairman David) Geffen," said the source. "He convinced him to release it although both Geffen and Cobain were reluctant. But Stipe's influence is such that anything he says goes."

To sweeten the deal, Stipe offered to come out of retirement and make a few "surprise" appearances during the tour, where he and Cobain would perform several songs from *Shift the Blame.*

However, a crew from Sweden shooting background footage for a documentary captured an apparent argument taking place between Cobain and Stipe. The argument began, according to sources, when Stipe confronted Cobain about his disappearance.

The two could be seen standing in the anteroom of the rehearsal hall. They were out of range of the team's microphones, but at one point Cobain staggered toward Stipe in an aggressive manner. Stipe, however, stepped away and Cobain fell to the floor. When Stipe offered his hand to help Cobain up, it was batted away and Stipe walked away in exasperation.

"Michael did his best," said an anonymous source in Stipe's production company. "But Kurt was blowin' it. After it all fell apart, Cobain kept calling Michael, promising to stop using junk, pleading with him to help get the band together. It was clear Cobain was scared. But after the first couple of messages weren't returned, he just turned mean and said some really spiteful things."

The tape also captured a rehearsal that was far from polished. Cobain, drummer Martinez, and bass player Yuri Cowles (formerly of Yoyo) played a leaden version of "Rape Me," then fell into an aimless blues jam.

"The Lollapalooza people were scared," said the Dreamworks source. "By that point, just a couple of weeks before the tour, the band should have been more together. Perry (Lollapalooza founder Farrell) insisted they get a second guitarist to cover and Kurt just went off on him."

A spokeswoman for Farrell's office confirmed that they had auditioned guitarists, but only at Cobain's request. She also denied that Lollapalooza had a "handshake deal" with the re-formed Stone Temple Pilots to substitute for Cobain.

However, a member of STP's management said that Farrell had contacted the band and inquired after their availability following the incident with Stipe.

"It was all done very informally," said the source. "But it was clear to STP that Lollapalooza was looking for a way out after it was evident that Stipe wasn't going to be involved."

Many speculated that Farrell had hoped Stipe would step in and bring some order to the chaotic Cobain rehearsals. Others felt that Farrell had only used Cobain as bait to get Stipe on the tour. Whatever the motive, it seemed that Cobain thought he had been kicked off the tour at the time of his death.

In fact, only three days after Cobain's death, STP was named as the lead act for Lollapalooza XX.

Cobain's return to Northern California was a scheduled break in the rehearsals. He flew in a private jet from Los Angeles with only one aide accompanying him. From the airport, he took a helicopter to his compound. Members of his staff say that he seemed to be in good spirits and that he spent his first day back transferring the tracks for *I Hate Myself and I Want to Die* onto a CD-ROM disc from a series of tapes.

That evening he was said to be in a good mood but was somewhat lethargic. He skipped dinner, retired to his trailer early, and was apparently watching TV when one of the security guards made his rounds at 2:00 A.M.

According to phone company logs, Cobain placed two calls, one to London to his daughter, Frances Bean, and the other to Los Angeles. That number was not disclosed, but inside sources say the call was to Stipe.

Authorities speculate that sometime during the night Cobain left the trailer and entered the garage where the accelerant, used to power an emergency generator, was kept.

When firetrucks arrived seventeen minutes after the first 911 call, members of the compound staff were trying to fight the blaze with garden hoses. The firefighters extinguished the blaze in two minutes.

The flames were so intense that the trailer's aluminum siding had caught fire. Inside the rubble were the remains of a single individual. Of the few intact sections of the skeleton, the skull "exhibited striations consistent with Mr. Cobain's wounds from an earlier suicide attempt."

The news and accompanying amateur video of the blaze was soon on the Net and broadcast around the world. In the days following, there was much fingerprinting of those close to Cobain.

"But nobody was really close to him," said a member of his staff. "He had people around him to do what he wanted them to do. But there was no one you could really call a friend. His fame was so monstrous that it just shut him off. It's a miracle he lived as long as he did."

In the days that followed, an outpouring of grief reached a worldwide crescendo. Copycat suicides were reported from locations as diverse as Edinburgh, Scotland; Raleigh, North Carolina; and the Czech Republic.

Mass gatherings were held in major cities, with a candlelight parade down the Champs-Élysées to the Tuileries Gardens in Paris the most spectacular. Even in the smallest towns across the world, faithful fans of Nirvana and Kurt Cobain congregated to hold their own vigils.

There was also such an increase of traffic on the Net that the premier computer mail subscriber service had to temporarily halt operation for the first time due to fear of a system overload.

Commentators from every end of the spectrum offered their opinions. President Andrew Cuomo said Cobain's passing was the "end of an era."

Satchel Farrow Allen spoke for the younger generation when he said, "Cobain's death is a perfect example of the older generation's self-absorption and media-dependency."

"Forty-two is still young," said one fan outside the gates of the Cobain compound, where thousands of mourners gathered. "He didn't have to give up so soon."

Many believe that Cobain did not die, that the fire was an elaborate ruse for him to escape the prison created by his fame. In the days after, a number of Cobain sightings had been reported from Maui to Los Angeles to Bangkok.

But the final word belonged to ex-wife Courtney Love Cobain Pitt Corgan Rothschild: "This ain't no *Eddie and the Cruisers*. Kurt's dead. Let him stay dead. That's all he ever wanted, anyway."

ANNE
FRANK

BY ARMAND DEUTSCH
& SUSAN GRANGER

*A*nne Frank's father, Otto, was born in Berlin in 1895, the son of loving middle-class parents. By 1932, he was a highly respected executive at Kolen & Co., a firm that supplied products to the homemaker. He had a close-knit, happy family. It never occurred to Otto that he and his wife, Edith, would not grow old together, enjoying their friends, their home, their holidays, and, most of all, guiding the development of their beloved daughters. Margot, the elder, was the serious one. Annelies Marie, three years younger, and called Anne, was an outgoing, inquisitive little chatterbox with countless friends. They would mature, marry, and bring grandchildren to the family. If Otto had realized what his future would be as the head of a Jewish family, of the untapped qualities he would have to call upon, he surely would have been overwhelmed.

Adolf Hitler became chancellor of the Third Reich in 1933. As edict after edict blasted from Nazi headquarters, as violence reared its ugly head, Otto was among the first to understand that life for German Jews would very quickly become intolerable, and he carefully weighed his options. He could beat an orderly retreat now, run the risk of fleeing later, or subject his family to a third unthinkable alternative. He did not hesitate.

Finding an escape route was not difficult. His colleagues agreed that Otto would become managing director of their Amsterdam affiliate. He journeyed to Amsterdam, where he acquired a pleasant apartment, not unlike the one they were forced to leave.

Only then did he inform Edith of their need to relocate. She was shocked but admitted that this situation was deplorable. Who would have thought, only a short time ago, that Jews would be increasingly segregated, with ration cards, separate schools, arm bands, and ever-increasing taunts from the troopers roaming the streets? "Surely, the worst must be over. Is it necessary to completely disrupt our lives?" she asked. "Yes," Otto replied, "if we are to save them." Shock quickly gave way to a feeling of gratitude at her husband's foresight. Determined that the emigration not be traumatic for the girls, they simply told them Papa had been transferred.

The family enjoyed Amsterdam from the start. The Dutch despised the Nazis and went out of their way to be welcoming. Herman and Petronella Van Daan, business acquaintances, became good friends. Closest, however, despite the age difference, was an office employee, Miep Santrouschitz, and her fiancé, Henk Gies. The day the family attended the wedding of Miep and Henk was a joyous one.

Regrettably, having no crystal ball, Otto Frank could not have foreseen the speed with which the Nazi legions would roll over Europe. By 1941, Holland was occupied, and it was quickly apparent that the Nazis planned to waste no time dealing with Holland's "Jewish problem."

Dutch Christians flaunted their disgust. Many sewed the yellow "JOOD" on their own clothing, lifted their hats to Jews on the street, and allocated extra produce to Jewish ration cards. The Germans struck back harshly. Any Christian showing sympathy to a Jew would be deported or executed.

Despair gripped Otto. He had already lived through this once, but this time the noose around his neck was tighter, the borders were sealed, and flight was not an option. The life of a Jew caught in this net, he reflected bitterly, was of little value. He was many times on the verge of yielding to the inevitable. The New Order could extend after the natural lifespan of Margot and Anne. It was always the thought of his daughters that made him realize that he had no right to give up. He could no longer repress the sickening reality that had been building below the surface of his mind.

One day at the office, he asked Miep to stay after the others had left. Calmly, he said to her, "Miep, Edith and I have decided that, with the children, we are going into hiding." He paused to let his words sink in. "Up the stairway above this office are some unused rooms. No one ever goes there. They are completely forgotten. That is where we will hide." Looking her directly in the eye, he inquired quietly, "Miep, are you and Henk willing to take on the responsibility of taking care of us? You will be our lifeline. Without you, we will not survive. It is much to ask, you must think carefully. Give me your answer after you have talked it over with Henk." Miep replied instantly, "I do not need to ask Henk. We will not be the first Dutch to hide friends. This is our fight, too. Of course we will do it." Otto sat silent for a moment, then said, "I have no words to thank you."

He showed Miep how a bookcase placed in front of the stairs swung open on a hinge, serving as a door. Miep followed him up the staircase to the landing and was stunned by the mustiness, peeling wallpaper, and wretched quarters. Calmly, Otto showed her the living arrangements. The moderately sized room in which they were standing would serve as Edith and Otto's bedroom. Margot and Anne would share a long hallway-like room. There was a spartan bathroom to serve them all. Each room had a window already covered with thick homemade curtains.

Everywhere there were boxes, sacks, and furnishings. "As you see," Otto gestured, "I have been preparing for this for some time." He led Miep up another flight of stairs to an attic room with a stove, sink, cabinets, and an adjoining closet-sized garret. "We hope," Otto said, "to make an orderly transition."

It was not to be. A week later, Margot received a card ordering her to appear for deportation to Berlin. Desperately, the Franks, along with Miep and Henk, moved additional supplies every night. On a Saturday night early in July, under cover of a pouring rain, the Frank family went into hiding.

The full impact of their imprisonment did not hit them immediately. All were totally occupied in making order out of chaos, and gradually, the airless quarters became habitable. Each morning, the family went up to the second landing, where they remained for the day. Any noise could be fatal. Edith never adjusted but never complained, always doing her part. Margot, naturally shy, retreated into a shell but never shirked any duties. Anne, alone, retained her irrepressible nature. Day and night, she dreamed of freedom, peeping through the heavy curtain at the sky. She scribbled for hours in her cloth-bound diary, her most precious possession, and hid it carefully, eliciting promises from everyone never to look at it. Otto's quiet leadership was heroic.

Each evening, Miep signaled when the last worker left the building. Activity then filled the hiding place. Shoes could be worn, the toilet flushed, and conversation could flow in a normal voice: all things they took for granted before and now so appreciated.

Miep and Henk's largest problem was providing food for four extra mouths. They used forged ration cards, but constantly worried because if they ever became ill, the lifeline would be severed. Early every morning, Miep carried the daily treasure trove up the steps.

Otto realized that idleness was their worst enemy. He became a virtual drill sergeant, commanding them to always remain busy cooking, writing, cleaning, or sewing clothes. For Anne and Margot, school under Otto meant longer hours and more homework than they had ever known.

Miep and Henk paid daily visits, and these meant almost as much to the Franks as did their daily food supply. Everyone peppered them with questions about the outside world. Anne constantly begged them to spend the night, offering to move in with her parents. Finally, on a quiet Saturday night, Miep and Henk stayed upstairs at Prinsengracht 263. Edith miraculously turned their rationed food into a tasty meal. They left in the morning, shaken to the core. It was only then that they realized the horror of living in hiding, and they never forgot the experience.

Fearing daily for their lives, Herman and Petronella Van Daan and their sixteen-year-old son, Peter, were forced to be in hiding as well, followed soon after by Miep's dentist, Albert Dussel. Now there were eight hungry mouths to feed. Fortunately, Herman had cultivated the friendship of a butcher who so hated the Nazis that he became their major supplier. Margot moved in with her parents; Anne shared her narrow room with Dr. Dussel. The Van Daans slept in a bed on the attic floor that had to be rolled against the wall before the others made their daily trip up the stairs. Peter, a dark, handsome boy, slept in the garret. Anne was attracted to him, but privacy was so impossible that they were only able to manage an occasional furtive kiss.

Each night, Otto descended the stairs to hear the news on Radio Free Europe. The speed of allied advances was quickening. Liberation did not seem too far off. For morale purposes, he only passed on the good news, but he had no illusions, because as long as Dutch guilders were rewarded for every Jew reported, the odds on eventual capture far outweighed freedom for the secret inhabitants of Prinsengracht 263.

Otto was right. On August 4, 1944, twenty-five months after going into hiding, Nazi boots marched up the stairs. The eight Jews were pulled into the street, pushed into a van, and herded like cattle to Nazi police headquarters. They were then loaded onto a train bound for Westerbork Detention Camp. At the camp, German soldiers, with shouts and rifle butts, pushed them onto the station platform.

Family units were instantly separated; adults marched off to internment barracks and children to the prophetically named Orphanage. It was by the merest chance that Margot and Anne were able to remain together.

The descent into dehumanization proceeded with mechanical efficiency, taking only a day. Along the way, girls who fell behind or lost their place were shot. Arms were tattooed and heads shaved. They were made to undress, dip their feet in violet water to be disinfected, then stand under sprays of icy showers. There were no towels. Naked and dripping, they were led to basins containing a sharp greenish anti-lice lotion to apply all over their shivering bodies. Evil-smelling prison clothes were distributed. Anne received a long skirt which fell to her heels and a blouse with a number and a large yellow Star of David on the sleeve. There were no underclothes. Finally, they were hurried into the Orphanage, a windowless hall filled with hard, blanketless cots. Talking was prohibited.

Margot and Anne tumbled numbly onto their bunks, irrevocably changed from the two girls who only a few days before were hiding in the Annex. In the blur of the day's events, Anne's mind clearly recalled the sight of her parents being marched away. Her eyes closed.

Each day at roll call, the girls stood in neat rows as the S.S. officials checked their numbers. If any were unaccounted for, they all had to kneel and hold their hands above their heads as punishment while a search was made for the missing. Although their prison garb and tattoos made escape through the guarded barbed wire unthinkable, their captors seemed obsessed that they would run away. The guards also had a far more valid fear of the infections and disease permeating the camp.

Early one morning, Anne awakened to find Margot with her body curled up and wracked by fever. She was quickly taken away. Anne later heard it was typhus, but she never saw her sister again. Totally bereaved, Anne yearned for her completely forgotten diary.

Some weeks later—Anne had lost all sense of time—she was herded in the usual brutal manner along with the other girls to the station, where they boarded a tightly packed cattle car. Minutes later, the train lurched forward to an unknown destination. Anne had learned instinctively that survival meant acceptance of events without feeling, and that the line between life and death was a shadowy matter of indifference. She had no idea how long she was aboard the stifling train when it suddenly stopped. The sign on the platform read BERGEN-BELSEN. Rubbing her eyes against the daylight, Anne saw a line of German soldiers, each with a large dog held on a tight leash. The snarling dogs made her whole body shudder with fear.

The girls, already "processed" in Westerbork, were quickly marched across large green fields surrounded by barbed wire to a tented area. An S.S. officer counted the prisoners. A thin, watery gruel was handed out. As she drank it, Anne watched with envy the birds that could fly so freely. In spite of herself, she remembered the hours she'd spent watching the flight of birds from the Annex.

The new arrivals were shown how to break large batteries into parts and separate them into baskets. It was dirty, hard work. It wasn't long before Anne developed a wracking cough and fell behind in her daily quota. A few days later, she fainted. The guards had difficulty bringing her around; her emaciated body was covered with sores and scabs. She was taken to the hospital, realizing a dream shared by all the girls. There she was allowed to wash and was given salve to protect her skin from lice and fleas. Her rations were increased. She found a blanket underneath her bunk and wrapped herself in it tightly. She prayed day and night that she would not recover sufficiently to be returned to the labor force.

One morning, she felt a warm hand on her forehead. Unused to any kindness, she looked up, startled. Standing over her was an emaciated but beautiful green-eyed girl a few years older than herself. "My name is Leah, little one," she whispered. "I will try to help you." She walked away, leaving Anne wondering and puzzled. Hours later, she came back. "I'm a prisoner, too," she explained. "There is not enough staff, so a few of us have been ordered to help. Don't give up hope." Suddenly, she popped a tiny square of chocolate into Anne's mouth. "I steal well," she said and vanished.

As Leah made her daily rounds, she ignored Anne completely. Her late-night bedside chats were short and infrequent, but each encounter was a lifeline for Anne, who had lost her family, her childhood, her adolescence, and her dignity. Now she did not feel entirely alone. Leah had renewed her desire to live.

One night, Leah said to her softly, "I hear the Nazis when they're secretly listening to forbidden radio transmissions. The allies are close at hand. We will be freed soon, little one." She put a bit of salve on Anne's cracked lips and slipped away.

Three nights later, prisoners throughout the camp were awakened by violent noises. Air raid alarms, sirens, and shouting filled the air. Each captive, shivering in the darkness, felt death close at hand. Just as suddenly, an eerie silence fell over Bergen-Belsen. The Nazis were gone, vanished, and British liberators quickly spread through the camp. For most prisoners, it was too much to absorb, but not so for Anne. From the moment Leah told her freedom was coming, she knew it would.

Medical corpsmen entered the infirmary with horrified disbelief. They immediately began treating the human wreckage they encountered, establishing a professional field hospital. Sheets and pillows appeared. Floors were scrubbed down. Thick, nourishing soup was provided. All was done with sympathetic clucking sounds of encouragement in a language the prisoners did not comprehend but understood perfectly. For some, it was too late; their bodies were taken away. Most, however, survived and grew stronger.

The magic phrase "You are free. You may go." was repeated daily throughout the camp by the British. Gradually, more and more prisoners streamed out of the gates. But Leah was far too smart. "The sad thing," she told Anne, "is that, while they are free to go, most will wander with no destination." Anne told Leah of her time in hiding, of her father's courage, and of her final capture. Painfully, she spoke of her family's fate. It was a release to share her anguish with her protector.

Anne's frail body grew stronger, but she lived in mortal fear that Leah would disappear. "I won't be leaving you, little one," Leah comforted her. "The British have asked me to stay on and help." Anne's eyes welled with tears. Leah leaned over and kissed her forehead. At that moment, Anne summoned the courage to ask the question that was never far from her mind: "Leah, why did you pick me out? Why was it me you saved?"

To Anne's surprise, Leah began to weep. For a long time, Anne sat silently. Finally, Leah spoke: "Everyone is vulnerable but you were the most, little one. I needed to help someone. You see, I, too, am alone. I have lost the one person who was my whole life."

It was Anne's turn to hold Leah's hand as she spoke of her early life. She was born in Vienna. Her father, a good provider, died when Leah was ten. Her mother struggled to support and educate her. At the University of Vienna, she met Leonard, a fellow student. They fell madly in love, and knowing Hitler would enter Austria at any moment, they quickly married. With Leah's mother, they fled to Hungary, where they had relatives, but their respite was short-lived. Hungary was captured early in 1944, and the Gestapo picked them up within days. During their time in a bleak holding area, Leah's mother, like so many thousands, took ill and died.

When a guard told Leah she was being shipped off to Bergen-Belsen, Leonard overheard and whispered, "I will find you." Leah finished, "This is why we must stay here as long as they will let us. Leonard will come for me if he is alive." Anne said softly, "Leah, do not give up hope. You are an angel. Wonderful things happen to angels."

As time passed, Leah's spirits sagged. Anne, however, turned out to be an excellent prophet. One day, Leonard appeared at Bergen-Belsen. "I told you I'd find you," he whispered quietly to Leah, enveloping her tightly in his arms, tears streaming down both their faces. As Anne watched the thin, handsome man embracing her savior, she, too, was moved to tears of joy.

Leonard told them he had survived Auschwitz and a death march before he was liberated. Like thousands, he headed for the American zone, thinking his problems would be solved. Disillusionment came quickly, however. Everywhere he found sympathetic American officials, overburdened with escapees, unable to cope with more.

"Then," said Leonard, "I met Nathan Schapelski, a refugee himself. He found two key people: a caring American officer and a Burgemeister who hated the Nazis. He was determined to create a refugee community dedicated to rebuilding as many lives as possible. Munchberg is a monument to Nathan's energy and ability.

"He helped me get travel papers so I could come and find you. I thank God you survived. I'm taking you back to Munchberg." Without a word from Leah, he patted Anne's trembling hand, adding, "You are coming with us."

The nourishing food, decent living conditions, and clear mountain air of what was called by everyone "Nathan's Miracle" helped restore Anne's health. Everyone worked, with Anne and Leah assigned to help settle new arrivals.

When the High Holy Days arrived, the community observed them for the first time in years. The Yahrzeit memorial candles were lit, followed by the release of uncontrollable sobs. All wept for murdered loved ones and for the virtual obliteration of entire generations. Anne wept for her family, the cruelty of the world, and her inability to grasp why she had been spared. For everyone, it was a much-needed spiritual catharsis.

It was a basic rule that Munchberg was not a place to settle, but a way station to regain health and then move on so others could follow. Nathan had established an office to assist people to realize their choices of destination. Israel was the dream of many. Leah and Leonard yearned to go there to build a new life. In May of 1948, the British mandate on Palestine was terminated.

On June 12, Anne's eighteenth birthday, Leah and Leonard hosted a celebration. They were brimming with excitement and jubilant as they told her: "We have done what we can here; our future is in Israel. Come with us." They were the only family she had left in the world—at least that she knew about. "I would love to . . . " she began, looking at them lovingly, "but I can't. I must go home to Amsterdam to see if there's anyone . . . " she choked, "anyone I know left." With understanding, Leah put her arms around Anne's shoulders. "Yes, it's time," she agreed. "You must make peace within yourself." Leah then gave Anne the tiny gold Star of David she wore on a chain around her neck, saying, "Wear this to keep me with you until we meet again."

There were only a few Dutch refugees, but arrangements were made for them to go to their destination by truck. Anne deeply doubted her decision. Leah and Leonard meant security; now she was again heading for the unknown. At the border, an official welcomed them warmly. Armed with her new papers, Anne set out for Miep and Henk's home with a pounding heart. It would be so wonderful to see them! She knocked on the door, but there was no answer. The door was firmly bolted. The flat was empty.

Stunned, she wandered down the street. She was in the country she loved but totally alone. Suddenly, she was startled to hear a man's voice call out, "Anne!" Anne stared at him without recognition. He was of medium height, stocky, blue-eyed, and pleasant looking.

"Anne, don't you remember me?" he asked. "Willem Ledermann." "Willem?" she gasped. For three years, he had sat behind her in class at the Sixth Public Montessori School. He told Anne that he and his father, a diamond cutter, had escaped to Switzerland. When he heard Anne's story, he said, "Come and stay with us. Let me help you through this graveyard of memories."

Anne accepted gratefully. In the small, neat apartment she met Willem's father. "You are very welcome here," he said, with his hand on her shoulder. There was only one bedroom, but father and son made up the couch in the living room as a bed. Willem said, "Regard this as a fine hotel room. We wish we had a palace for you." Together they laughed. Before she went to bed, Willem said, "Tomorrow we will go to the Jewish Committee office. They work wonders in locating people. I feel it will be a lucky day." His confident voice soothed her. She slept soundly.

The next morning, after a brief wait at the bustling Committee office, Anne told the lady at the desk her name and that she had been a prisoner at Bergen-Belsen. The woman looked at her searchingly and asked her to wait. A half hour later, another woman came and escorted her with Willem to a small private office. "I have happy news for you, Anne," she said. "Our records show that your father was here a few months ago asking about you. We could find nothing, but he left his telephone number. We reached him." She held Anne's hand and went on. "He will be here for you very soon."

Anne would have fainted, but Willem's strong arms held her. "Hold fast," he said, "so you can enjoy this reunion." Anne sat quietly, clutching Leah's talisman. The office door flew open, and her father burst into the room. Wordlessly, he lifted her up and hugged her tightly, squeezing the air from her lungs. Then this controlled, disciplined man sat and wept. "Stay here a bit," Willem advised as he left. "This is a happy moment, but it must be very hard to bear."

Finally, they made their way to Otto's new small, neat apartment, and spent the rest of the day and far into the night exchanging stories. Otto told Anne he had learned that her mother had died shortly after the two were separated. Anne sadly told her father about Margot. She learned that her father had survived Auschwitz. After the liberation, he made his way to Odessa, where a large transport ship took survivors to Marseilles, then to Belgium, and finally to Holland. He went directly to Miep's flat, where he stayed until he located a place for himself. Once again, he took over the reins of his business. He lived very quietly. Except for regular visits with Miep and

Henk, he saw few people. This reunion was one he no longer even dreamed about.

Before going to bed, Anne telephoned Miep and listened to her shouts of unrestrained joy. It was agreed that they would come over to Otto's for morning coffee.

They appeared bright and early. Anne and Miep fell into each other's arms, weeping. Henk and Otto blew their noses loudly. Coffee was poured. Anne said, "I thought about the two of you all night. How in the world did you do it? Every day for two years: work, feed all of us, and find time to sleep. Everyone in the Annex would have died of starvation without you." Henk answered, "We talk of it often. Frankly, we don't know how we did it, but we are very proud. It is by far the most important thing we will ever do. It was our way of fighting the Nazis."

A moment of silence followed before Otto replied, "There is nothing my daughter and I can say except . . ." He smiled. "More coffee?" The Gies declined, saying they had to go to work, and parted with heartfelt embraces. Anne and her father sat quietly for a long time.

For several weeks, Anne was unable to adjust to the fact that she was actually at home and her father had survived. A lassitude descended upon her; she wanted only to absorb the feeling of safety and reunion. Her father doted on her. She saw Miep and Henk often. Willem called her or saw her every day. They had coffee, took walks, went to films. Imperceptibly, she felt herself responding to the love he so obviously felt for her. He held a rather menial job in the office of a construction company, but his hopes and ambitions were far higher than that.

One evening after supper, her father said, "Anne, I have something that belongs to you and the moment has come to return it." To her total amazement, he handed her the tattered diary. "I thought it was lost," she said, flabbergasted. "Miep found it in the Annex. She saved it and gave it to me," he explained. Anne looked at her diary blankly. "This book is from another world, one I want to forget." Gravely, her father said, "I don't think that will be possible, Anne. I asked Miep and Henk not to mention anything about this since your return, but there is something you must know."

He told her that one Sunday over coffee he read a section of the diary to some friends. Without exception, they were extremely moved by it. One man asked if he could show several passages to a publisher friend. "At first I resisted, but they all urged me to do it. Finally, I agreed. In record time, I received word that the publisher wanted the excerpt and would pay for it." Anne's jaw dropped, but she said nothing. Her father continued, "That excerpt immediately attracted comment and attention, and other offers came in increasing numbers. I even had to seek the help of a lawyer. The original publisher printed the entire diary."

"Papa, how could you?" Anne blurted. "My quarrels with Margot, my stolen kisses, all my private thoughts are being shared by everybody." Otto handed her a large packet of clippings. "Anne, read these. Your diary has already been published in three countries. Whether you like it or not, you are well on your way to being regarded as an important writer. Be proud of it. Enjoy it. Yesterday I visited the lawyer and arranged that all of the money from the diary go to you."

That evening, Anne shared all of this with Willem. He responded, "I know nothing of these matters. The thing I wanted to talk to you about is that I intend to ask your father's permission to marry you. I love you. Will you be my wife?" Anne gave him a mischievous smile, her dark eyes twinkling. She kissed him passionately, murmuring, "I wondered why you didn't ask sooner." Otto was not surprised. He had formed a high opinion of Willem and felt strongly that he would be a steadfast and loving husband. Anne and Willem were married with only their fathers, Miep, and Henk present.

They had little time to settle into a domestic routine. Letters poured in praising the diary, with the correspondents sharing their own wartime experiences. Handling the mail began to take a considerable amount of her father's and Willem's time. Calls from her lawyer increased, too. Offers to print the diary and requests to speak multiplied. Anne's fame as the child who bore witness to the Holocaust grew in Holland and neighboring countries.

Royalty checks began coming in. Gradually, her earnings exceeded Willem's salary. Anne found these developments incomprehensible. Certainly nothing prepared her for the call from her attorney advising that an excellent offer had been received from the McCracken Publishing Company to publish the diary in the United States. The contract called for Anne to come to the United States at the publisher's expense if the book was well received. She would be needed for interviews and public appearances.

For the first time, Anne felt a surge of excitement. She told Willem she was eager to sign the contract but could not possibly do it unless he would be at her side, and he readily agreed. She began to accept speaking engagements, limiting her appearances to universities and Jewish groups. Most important, they started taking English lessons in the event, as Anne put it, "America likes my diary." Eventually, a long letter arrived for Anne from Peter McCracken, the owner of the publishing company. The first edition of *The Diary of Anne Frank* was selling beyond expectations. When could she and Willem sail for New York? As soon as her lawyer advised him, tickets would be delivered. He would meet them at the dock and looked forward to it eagerly.

From then on, events moved swiftly. In short order, Anne and Willem, hearts pounding, were waving farewell to Otto, Miep, and Henk and sailing off like explorers. They were amazed by the huge ship, but for the most part kept to themselves. Anne pronounced it their belated honeymoon. One week later, they were gazing in awe at New York's skyline as the ship gradually eased to the dock.

When the ship docked, Anne and Willem were stunned to see reporters and photographers jamming the pier. Almost immediately, there was a knock on their stateroom door and a pleasant-looking, tweedy, pipe-smoking man entered. He greeted them warmly. "I'm Peter McCracken, your publisher, here as promised. Welcome to America. Anne, you will be treated like a reigning movie queen. Your diary has taken this country by storm. People are shocked and moved. We'll talk about it on the way to your hotel. I'll get you through the swarm of news people outside. Trust me." Trust him she did, and thus began a friendship that would always have meaning in her life.

Peter led them down the gangway. They posed briefly for photographers, and the reporters reluctantly accepted Peter's repeated announcement, "No questions now." Once ensconced in a chauffeured limousine, Peter went on, "When we get to the hotel, you will meet Jenny Johnson of our publicity department. I'm certain you will like her. She'll be with you every step of the way. Her only purpose is to make life easier for you. The lecture bureau we hired has arranged a superb tour. It will be a bit tiring at times, but they have worked hard to keep it within bounds. Don't be frightened, Anne." Anne smiled at him. "Peter," she said, "after what I have lived through, I'm not frightened. I admit I am a bit apprehensive. This is quite a change in my life." Willem added, "No one has had more changes in life than Anne. We're looking forward to this as an adventure." "And," added Peter, "something that will make you a great deal of money."

In their luxurious hotel suite, Peter introduced Anne and Willem to Jenny, an attractive, articulate woman just a few years older than Anne. "I'm so glad that Peter chose me to do this," she said with a sincere smile. "When you are ready, we'll talk a bit about some of the details of the tour." Peter said his good-byes, kissing Anne warmly on the cheek, murmuring, "I will see you tomorrow, my new friend."

Jenny waited while they unpacked and freshened up. Over tea, she told them that Anne would speak to amazingly diverse audiences in New York, Philadelphia, Chicago, St. Louis, Los Angeles, and San Francisco. As they traced the route on a map, Jenny reassured them, "You will settle into a routine of speaking, signing books, giving autographs, and moving on.

There is no time for anything more, I'm afraid." Then she turned full face to Anne, asking seriously, "Do you want to tell me something about your subject? Maybe we could go over it together." "No, Jenny, I don't," Anne replied. "I've thought about little else this past week, and I think I'm ready." Jenny laughed. "You won't have to wait long. Your first speech is tomorrow at noon. It is sponsored by the New York Overseas Club and tickets are totally sold out. I will pick you up at 11:00 A.M."

Anne and Willem enjoyed a quiet dinner in their room, gazing in wonderment at the twinkling lights of the city Willem called "New Amsterdam." They slept soundly, eager for the tour to begin.

At noon the next day, Anne stood backstage calmly listening to an effusive introduction and walked out to an audience on their feet, applauding wildly. Small, serious, and steadfast, she stood silently until the chairman finally achieved silence. Peter waved to her from the third row. Anne thanked them for being there and then spoke in a pleasant, conversational voice. "My English is far from perfect, so forgive me. I do not want to make a formal speech. Let us spend the next hour talking together. You seem to know so much about me that it should not be hard. Certainly my life has been very different. Much of it has been lived in hiding or in concentration camps. It is your interest in my diary that brings us together today. Some of you kept diaries as children, and I'm sure it never occurred to you that anyone would ever read them. Nor did it ever occur to me. That my diary survived surprised me. That anyone found it interesting seemed odd to me, and that its appeal has brought me to this moment in my life is something I cannot comprehend. Please ask me any questions you want, and I will do my best to answer them." A dozen hands shot up and Anne pointed to one.

Q: How were you able to keep your spirits up living over two years in hiding?

A: Outwardly, we had no choice. Self-pity would have been contagious and brought us all down. How did I feel inside? My diary will tell you: "I simply can't imagine that the world will ever be normal for us again. I do talk about 'after the war,' but then it is only a castle in the air—something that will never happen. If I think back to our old house, my girlfriends, the fun at school, it is past, as if another person lived it all, not me." That is how I really felt.

Q: In the Annex, did you realize that, whatever happened, your adolescent years were lost?

A: I certainly knew it and I mourned them. Let me read you what I wrote: "Cycling, dancing, whistling, feeling young, to know that I am free—that is what I long for. I sometimes ask myself, would anyone, Jew or non-Jew, understand this about me? That I am simply a young girl badly in need of some rollicking fun. I know I could never talk to anyone about it because then I should cry. Crying can bring such relief."

Q: How did your treatment at the hands of the Nazis make you feel about the human race?

A: *If I thought all humanity was that way, I would not want to live. Certainly the Dutch are unbelievably kind and good. I am proud to be a Netherlands citizen. America's revulsion speaks volumes. The Nazis and their government were not human.*

Q: Do the awful concentration camp memories ever leave you?

A: I think of them less often as time passes, but the dreams remain. I have a recurring nightmare of attack dogs leaping at my throat, and I know I will always be afraid of dogs.

Q: Do you and your husband want to have children?

A: No. I am not ready for those responsibilities. I don't think I ever will be. Willem understands. My diary touches on that subject: "Is it true that grown-ups have a more difficult time in hiding than we do? No, I don't think it is. It's twice as hard for us young ones to hold our ground and maintain our opinions at a time when all ideals are being shattered and destroyed, when people are showing their worst side."

Q: Did you have any idea how wonderful a writer you were?

A: Immodestly, I must have known that I had some talent. I wrote in my diary: "I am the best and sharpest critic of my work. I know myself what is and what is not well written. I can't imagine that I can lead the same sort of life as my mother and all the other women who do their work and are then forgotten. I want to go on living even after my death and therefore I am grateful to God for giving me this gift, this possibility of developing myself and writing, of experiencing all that is in me."

Q: Do you plan to write in the future?

A: That has been my plan since I saw my first typewriter at age four, but it is difficult when you know you have done your finest work as a child. I hope I will. My publisher wants me to.

Q: Have you returned to the Annex?

A: Not yet. There are too many ghosts. Perhaps one day I shall.

The hour flew by. Dozens of hands were always raised. When the chairman closed the questioning, Anne pulled up her sleeve. "Here," she said calmly, "is my tattoo to carry the rest of my days. Every survivor has one, but there are few survivors. The government that wanted to kill an entire segment of humanity did a very efficient job. I witnessed it and I believe it could happen again. We must always be vigilant. Any group could be the victim. Thank you very much. I have enjoyed my visit with you." Anne bowed a bit awkwardly and left the platform.

The audience sat silently for a moment, followed by an overwhelming ovation. People stood, shouted, applauded. Many wept. Anne returned, smiled warmly, bowed again, and left.

Anne's tour was launched. Jenny called it, "Anne Frank's conquering of America." For Anne and Willem, one city melded into another. The questions remained in the same vein. The enthusiastic response never varied. There was always a press conference, followed by superb coverage. Willem and Jenny intercepted endless requests which could not be accommodated.

Anne had no time to digest her triumph, which ended three weeks later in San Francisco. Bone-weary, she read the clippings Jenny had saved for her and kept repeating, "I just can't believe it." She slept soundly on the flight back to New York.

The next day Peter paid a visit to their hotel. He said, "Anne, no one could have predicted that your tour would be such a unique success. Your story touched every heart. Your diary is a huge best seller. As your publisher, I am thrilled, but I am also an Anne Frank fan." He paused. "Permit me to suggest that it is time for you two to think about your future. Your choices are wide. Financially, you will never want for anything."

Anne responded, "Thank you, Peter. We have talked about it. Of course we will live in Amsterdam. I won't deny that I love being a celebrity, but we want to buy a home and live quietly. I have never had a chance to do that. Above all, I want to write."

Peter rose, kissed her cheek, and shook hands with Willem. "You have made the right decision: the one that will bring you contentment. I hope," he added, "that you will consider McCracken Publishing." Willem said, "Peter, are there any other publishers?" They laughed. Peter went on, "Willem, it is my belief that Anne will not be able to write if you do not make it your job to manage her life. You will have much to do. Requests for interviews, lectures, articles, all manner of things will pour in and must be evaluated. Fame has its price." Willem answered, "I intend to do just that. I love her and I'm an Anne Frank fan, too."

Peter took an envelope from his pocket. "I have a present for you, Anne," he said. "Jenny told me about Leah and what she means in your life. A reunion is indicated. These are your tickets to Israel. They are expecting you. It will be a private visit with one exception. Prime Minister Ben-Gurion has asked that you speak to the Parliament. Then it will be home to Amsterdam."

Anne replied simply, "Peter, I love you." "Thank you, Anne. Publishers don't hear much of that from authors. This is far from good-bye. We will be telephoning, writing, and seeing each other again. As we say in this country, 'So long.'" Peter paused at the door and said, "Remember, I am your man in America."

Anne, well rested after a few quiet days in New York, was exuberant en route to Israel. "They wanted so much to go to Palestine," she explained, affectionately stroking Willem's hand. "I can't wait to see them."

At the Jerusalem airport, she immediately spotted Leah's smiling, sun-drenched face. The two women hugged, looked at each other in silence, laughing and crying simultaneously. Anne introduced Willem to "her saviors" and they were off to the King David Hotel. "Our apartment is just too small," Leah apologized, "but it will be our headquarters."

As people learned that Anne was at the hotel, crowds formed outside the lobby. Her diary was one of the first contemporary books translated into modern Hebrew. It epitomized the grim reason at the core of Israel's existence. People wanted to see her, touch her, get a photograph taken with her, and give her small gifts. Dates, figs, pomegranates, and flowers filled their room.

Leah and Leonard had taken time off from their jobs. Their apartment, indeed, turned out to be their quiet enclave. They exchanged stories endlessly. Leah and Leonard both loved their new country passionately and were making fine places for themselves. They seldom talked of Bergen-Belsen, but one day Leah said wonderingly, "Who would have dreamed that in a concentration camp I would find a younger sister?" Anne replied quietly, "Or that I, having lost an older sister, would gain one?"

Each day they went sightseeing in Leonard's little car. On the first day, Leah told Anne, "Be prepared for a grand surprise." They stopped, looked up, and she saw they were on ANNE FRANK STREET. "They are springing up all over Israel," Leonard told them. Anne could only shake her head in wonderment. Each day, they were astounded by the energy and spirit of the Israelis. The newspapers had headlined her presence in the city, together with photographs. Everywhere they stopped people appeared as though by magic. They never crowded her, but their smiling, loving faces left no doubt as to their feelings. "They are looking at you, Anne," said Leah, "but they are seeing the young girl hiding from the Nazis writing in her diary."

At night, Leah cooked dinner. "It is hard to eat in a restaurant when the table is surrounded by people," Willem remarked wryly. Their hosts pleaded that they move to Israel, but were always met with the same answer, "We love you, but we are Dutch."

The atmosphere was electric when she addressed the Israeli Parliament. Prime Minister Ben-Gurion's introduction was a welcoming tribute. Anne began, "For me, it is not next year in Jerusalem, it is today . . . " and concluded by saying that Israel was the spiritual home of her diary. The prime minister declared her an honorary citizen. Applause rained down upon her. She always regarded this as her most moving public appearance.

As the trip ended, Anne told Leah and Leonard, "I want to be part of your great adventure. I am making more money than I ever dreamed of. I am going to send a contribution to you to donate to the project of your choice." It turned out to be the first of many gifts. Leah, in turn, reported minutely on how the money was used, resulting in a steady, happy correspondence.

Anne had left Amsterdam a well-known citizen. She returned a full-fledged celebrity. The city, however, was low-key and its citizens respected the privacy of their most famous adopted daughter. Anne and Willem searched eagerly for a new home, eventually renovating a fine seventeenth-century canal house. "A grand house, a palace," Anne described it in a letter to Leah. It was indeed more luxurious than they ever dreamed, with a spacious bedroom, a guest room, a study for Anne, and an office for Willem. When they settled in, Anne, for the first time in her life, felt an inner peace she never knew existed.

Willem's office was a busy hub. Mail poured in, including many requests for autographs. Sitting in her book-lined study, Anne answered each one. There were daily requests for magazine articles and lectures. Universities vied for the chance to honor her as a commencement speaker. Jenny advised her that there were enough requests to warrant a second U.S. tour.

Anne firmly declined them all. She luxuriated in her new home, developing a companionship with Willem that was the rudder of her life. Their social life was with Otto, Miep, and Henk, although they occasionally enjoyed visits from people at the university.

Peter sent Anne a large advance, "for anything you choose to write." She returned the check with a loving letter. "I want no advance from you, my dear friend. Anything I write is yours if you want it. At present, I am thwarted by the inevitable comparisons that will be made to my writing as a child. But who knows? In the meantime, we send you our devoted love—and please kiss Jenny for me."

The tranquility of their lives was interrupted by Otto's decision to move to Switzerland. One night at dinner, he explained to them how, having retired from his firm and without his beloved Edith, he found his life in Amsterdam meaningless and sad. He gloried in Anne's success and was forever grateful that she and Willem had found one another. However, the years in hiding and in the concentration camp had taken their toll. In short, he needed a change of scene. His mother, who lived in Basel, was old and infirm. She needed him and he was ready "to put all of this behind me." He would, he promised, return often. Anne expressed her undying love and gratitude; she and Willem understood perfectly and made him comfortable with his choice.

Several months later, Anne said to her husband, "I can no longer keep this from you. I rarely feel completely well. No matter how long I sleep, I lack the energy I have always had." Willem immediately made an appointment with Dr. Jan Van der Hoag, a highly respected physician, who, after examining Anne said, "Your heartbeat is not as vigorous and regular as I would like. It is tired, and no wonder. It's nothing dangerous at the moment. I am going to give you medicine that should help, and recommend that you rest as much as possible until I see you again in three months."

Anne replied, "Doctor, I was quite certain that would be your diagnosis. We lead a quiet life which we enjoy and will continue it." They decided to tell no one. The medicine did help and the calm routine of their daily lives suited them both. Their regular visits to the doctor showed no change.

One morning, the usually phlegmatic Willem burst into Anne's study in high excitement. "Anne," he said, "I've just had a long conversation with Peter in New York. A famous producer has just read a wonderful script that he wants to present on Broadway. The title is—surprise, surprise—*The Diary of Anne Frank*. Peter has just read it and he's bursting with enthusiasm. He has found a top Broadway agent to represent you and mailed papers for your signature. He urges you to sign so they can move forward." Anne, wide-eyed, responded, "My diary on Broadway! I thought nothing would surprise me anymore, but this . . . "

After the papers were signed, Anne wrote to Jenny, "I wish I could be a fly on the wall and watch this all unfold. Could you possibly find time to keep me posted on the highlights?" Jenny quickly responded with a cable: "I will be your eyes and ears. I will make you feel as if you were here."

As promised, Jenny's long, descriptive letters arrived each week, satisfying her curiosity so completely that Anne joked with Willem, "Bless Jenny. She is writing *The Diary of Producing the Diary of Anne Frank*."

A director was selected and casting began. A fine young actress, Susan Strasberg, was chosen to play Anne. Rehearsals commenced. Peter got permission for Jenny to attend from time to time to report the play's progress to Anne. Emotions ran high, Jenny wrote, from the time the cast first sat around a table reading the script to the moment when they, for the first time, actually moved onto the stage. The director patiently, skillfully coached them until he was satisfied that it was beginning "to look like a play." They would open out of town for six weeks prior to the Broadway opening. Anne pleaded with Willem, "I want so terribly much to be there that night. Can we go?" To which Willem responded, "The doctor has to make that decision, not me."

When Dr. Van der Hoag heard of the proposed trip, he thought long and hard before saying, "Anne, you are doing quite well. Going to New York for the occasion will make you more the center of attention than ever before. Everyone will want to see you, meet you, interview you, photograph you. It would be draining for anyone, but it could lead to serious consequences for you. This is the hardest thing I have ever had to do, but I am forced by my conscience to strongly recommend that you forego it." Anne was surprisingly docile. "I expected it," she told the doctor. "I so wanted to be there, but I find myself taking more short naps every day. They'll just have to struggle through the opening without me."

Peter was so eager to have them attend the opening that they telephoned him and, after pledging him to secrecy, explained why they could not be there. They made light of Anne's condition and Peter, always sensitive, took their cue, but his shock and surprise were palpable. He suggested that Anne write to the producer, explaining that she felt the night belonged to the theater company and her presence would prove a distraction.

It was Willem, of course, who had the splendid idea that softened the blow. "Let's have Leah and Leonard represent you on opening night. Peter can make all the arrangements, and then they can fly here the next morning and tell us absolutely everything."

Six weeks later, on the evening of October 5, 1955, Leah and Leonard sat with Peter at the Cort Theater for the first performance of *The Diary of Anne Frank*. The next morning, a cable arrived from Peter, "However well you hoped it would go, just know that it went a hundred times better. Leah and Leonard are en route. Love, Peter, your man in America."

The New York plane arrived on schedule and, soon afterward, Leah and Leonard burst into the canal house. Both of them masked their shock at seeing Anne looking frail and older. Exuberantly, Leah poured forth the details of the opening. "Anne, Peter was so nice to us. He cried at the play and told us we could tell you. You could feel the excitement going into the theater. The play is so beautiful and the actors were all wonderful! They seem just like the characters you wrote. The set is so grim and real. The play became a mystery thriller. Even though the audience knew how it would come out, everyone was praying that you would not be captured. At the end, with the stage dark, we heard the Nazi boots going up the steps, and as the curtain came down, we heard loud knocking on the door. Everybody gasped."

"Peter took us backstage to meet Susan Strasberg, who plays you," Leonard interjected. "When she came out to take her bows, there was complete silence. At first she thought the audience didn't like the play; then she realized they were returning to reality. 'The applause broke over us in waves,' was the way she described it, adding, 'I have never seen anything like it.' She sends you her love and can't wait to meet you."

Peter corroborated their first impressions with excerpts from the reviews and reported a long line at the box office. "I think the play will run forever," he said on the telephone. "Because of you, Leah and Leonard, we feel we were there and we thank you," they told him.

The canal house was inundated with telegrams and phone calls. Realizing Leah's concern for her health, the two women retreated to Anne's study. She downplayed her condition as "nothing serious" and deftly changed the subject to finances. "I will never understand any of this," she confided to Leah, "but Peter told Willem that royalties from the play will start coming in very soon, in addition to the book royalties. It will mean bigger checks for your projects in Israel. Tell me about them." Leah eagerly related the progress of each until Willem knocked on the door, announcing the midday meal.

The excitement of that night was justified. The play not only had a very long run, but it won every award the theater offered, and, finally, the Pulitzer Prize. The producers quickly assembled touring companies. Not too many months later, it opened simultaneously in seven German cities. *The Diary of Anne Frank* released waves of emotion and guilt from German audiences for what had happened only a few short years before.

When the play opened in Amsterdam on November 27, 1956, Anne and Willem attended with Queen Juliana. The *New*

York Times correspondent reported, "There were audible sobs and one strangled cry at the conclusion as the Germans hammered at the door of the hideout. When the curtain went down, the audience sat in silence for several minutes and rose as the royal party left. There was no applause."

Within a few weeks, Anne's health deteriorated. She was short of breath, and the slightest exertion fatigued her. Dr. Van der Hoag visited the canal house to examine her, but before he had a chance to say anything, Anne spoke. "You don't need to make a report, Doctor. I understand and I have no fear. There were many times in my life when I felt I would not live for an hour. I consider myself the luckiest of women."

She turned to Willem. "I have one piece of unfinished business. The time has come for me to visit the Annex." Startled, Willem cautioned that the steep steps made it impossible. Anne was determined. "Nothing can harm me. I will leave the arrangements to you and the doctor."

A few evenings later, she was driven to Prinsengracht 263 and carried up the narrow stairs. The smallness of the rooms startled her to the core of her being. Memories flooded over her. She walked slowly to the window she had longingly looked out of so many times, then to the desk where she had written her diary, and pronounced herself ready to go home. En route, she said quietly, "Perhaps our ordeal had a purpose." She did not mention the visit again. A few nights later, Anne died quietly in her sleep. She had not yet reached her thirtieth birthday.

Willem's announcement of her passing made headlines around the world. A private service was conducted at her synagogue. The Netherlands Parliament declared that one week following her death there be an official day of mourning with flags flown at half staff. A memorial service was held at the Hague. Queen Juliana attended, and Otto came from Basel. Miep and Henk were there. Leah and Leonard came from Israel. Peter and Jenny flew in from America. The tribute spoken that day was echoed in thousands of services in thousands of cities!

"Her voice, no louder than a child's whisper, speaks for the millions who did not survive. It soars over the shouts of murderers and condemns for all time the degradation of the human spirit."

Shortly after her death, the Annex was officially designated the Anne Frank Museum. "I want to go on living after my death," she had written in her diary. The museum stands today as a mecca for visitors and a testament against man's inhumanity to man.

JAMES
DEAN

BY BOB THOMAS

LATER IN LIFE

*N*obody thought Jimmy Dean could
survive the highway crash. After all,
his silver Porsche Spyder was
crushed like an egg when it
slammed into Donald Turnupseed's
Ford sedan on Route 466. Oddly,
Jimmy might have been less injured
if he hadn't worn a seat belt. His
mechanic, Rolf Wütherich, was
thrown from the Porsche by the
impact. Jimmy hadn't installed a seat
belt on the passenger side, because
he expected to be driving alone in
the Salinas race. Wütherich's injuries

amounted to some cuts and bruises, a broken leg, and a crushed jaw. Jimmy was trapped in a jumble of steel and broken glass.

"That guy's gotta stop!" Jimmy had yelled when he saw the sedan turn in front of him. But young Turnupseed didn't see the low, silvery Porsche zooming toward him at 75 miles per hour.

Sandy Roth and Bill Hickman arrived at the crash scene a few minutes afterward. Sandy was a magazine photographer who was going to shoot Jimmy in the Salinas race. Bill had been dialogue coach on *Giant*. They were aghast at what they saw.

Rolf was lying facedown in a field, a few feet from the Porsche. And Jimmy—what a horrible sight. He lay still in the wreckage, his face obliterated, his blonde hair streaked with red, his arms and legs at crazy angles.

A highway patrolman was taking notes from the dazed Turnupseed, who only had a bruised face. "I couldn't see him," said the college student, "honest to God, I couldn't see him."

The wail of a siren was heard down the highway, and the flashing red lights of the ambulance could be seen in the early evening light. The attendants first laid Rolf on a stretcher and slid him into the upper rack of the ambulance. Then they approached the crumpled Porsche. With gentle hands, they eased Jimmy's limp body out of the driver's window and placed him on the second stretcher, and with siren screaming, the ambulance began the race against death, speeding toward Paso Robles and the War Memorial Hospital.

Within hours, the AP and UPI had spread the news around the world. James Dean had appeared in only one film that the public had seen, *East of Eden*. But his impact on moviegoers, especially teenagers, had been phenomenal. No new star in recent years, not even Marlon Brando, had created such a sensation.

"EDEN" STAR NEAR DEATH IN CRASH screamed the New York *Daily News*. The London tabloids gave the story precedence over the latest cabinet shakeup. The *New York Times* published a three-paragraph wire story on page 36.

Reporters and photographers descended on the sleepy mid-California town of Paso Robles. After six hours, the hospital released the first official bulletin: "Mr. Dean is in a coma. He has suffered fractures of the legs, pelvis, and ribs, as well as multiple lacerations and contusions. He is in very critical condition."

The press maintained an around-the-clock vigil at the hospital. Every bulletin was immediately flashed to the waiting world. The events of Dean's brief life were replayed in newspapers and magazines. Editorialists cited him as a symbol of the times, paralleling his portrayal of the confused farm boy Cal Trask in *East of Eden* with the gifted, erratic actor with a penchant for fast cars.

Schoolgirls held candlelight vigils for Jimmy Dean in Tacoma, Wichita, Natchez, and Concord, New Hampshire. Elizabeth Taylor was driven from Hollywood to Paso Robles in a limousine, her arrival giving the press their first real photo opportunity. The actress' violet eyes were rimmed with red as she stepped before the television microphones, speaking in a soft, halting voice.

"I love Jimmy Dean," Miss Taylor murmured. "It would be a great tragedy if his fine talent were lost just as he is proving himself. I am praying for his recovery."

Life magazine was granted an exclusive shot of Elizabeth Taylor sitting mournfully beside the unconscious Dean. Natalie Wood arrived for a visit three days later, but by then press coverage had diminished, since there had been no new developments in the story. Dean remained in a coma, with no signs of improvement, and doctors were pessimistic about his chances for recovery.

On October 3, 1955, three days after the crash, *Rebel Without a Cause* opened in theaters across the nation. The fascination for James Dean now became a mania. He transformed from the yearning, confused Cal Trask to the angry, confused Jim Stark, doing things and saying things to his parents that millions of American teenagers wished they could do and say.

On Friday and Saturday nights, at movie theaters everywhere, crowds of young people lined up around the block. One fifteen-year-old girl in Boise, Idaho, saw *Rebel Without a Cause* twenty-four times during a six-day period. "He can't die, I love him," she sobbed.

The James Dean story, which had been relegated to brief bulletins ("Mr. Dean's condition is unchanged") during the week following the accident, exploded again. Candlelight vigils were held in every major city. Scores of teenagers all over the country ran away from home to join the youthful throng that knelt silently before the Paso Robles hospital until far into the night. A resourceful entrepreneur managed a brisk business by selling T-shirts with the words: PRAY FOR JIMMY DEAN.

America hadn't seen anything like it since Rudolph Valentino died in 1926. But here was a star who was alive—although just barely—and the suspense over whether or not he would survive was maddening, not only to the country's youth, but to vast numbers of adults who felt kinship with his screen persona.

Serious commentators took note of the phenomenon. One effusive columnist likened the happening to the Children's Crusade. Another highbrow observed that Dean epitomized the postwar generation—confused, lost, purposeless, and rebellious.

The parade of Hollywood figures continued the pilgrimage to Paso Robles. They included fellow actors from his three films: Julie Harris, Dennis Hopper, Sal Mineo, Rock Hudson, Chill Wills, Jane Withers, and Jim Backus. Some of them paused to talk with the swarm of fan magazine writers desperately seeking new angles to a story that had none.

One of the visitors who arrived at the War Memorial Hospital was the distinguished director of *Giant,* George Stevens. A friendly, homespun man, he stopped briefly with reporters outside the hospital to comment that "Jimmy Dean is one of the most extraordinary young actors in America today. His loss would be a great blow to American film. Along with everyone else, I am praying for his recovery."

It was a fateful day, the twenty-seventh of Dean's coma. Doctors led Stevens into the hospital room, where the young man lay motionless, an array of tubes maintaining his tenuous hold on life.

"Jimmy, this is George Stevens," the director said in his flat Midwest tones.

The slender young body, wrapped in casts on his arms and legs, didn't move. Stevens held back tears as he studied the once-handsome face, now marked by savage cuts and massive bruises.

"Jim, I know you can make it," said Stevens. "You're a tough Midwesterner, just like me."

The body lay still.

"I finished the picture, Jimmy," Stevens continued. "Your performance is remarkable. I've never seen anything like it. We just had to dub a few lines in the banquet scene. Don't worry. I got Nick Adams to do it."

The two doctors had witnessed this soliloquy many times before from other visitors, and they listened halfheartedly. But then . . . Dean's big right toe twitched. The doctors stood in disbelief as the patient's mouth began to move. He made sounds.

Stevens himself was astounded. "What did you say, Jimmy?" he asked.

"I said, 'Fuck Nick Adams, I'll do the lines myself.' "

It was a miracle. Radio and television programs were interrupted to announce James Dean's amazing return from near-death (his first words were not disclosed to the press, however). Among the nation's youth, the news spread like a brushfire. Girls gathered in the street to hug one another and weep tears of joy. Boys were equally moved, though less demonstrative; they admired and emulated Jimmy Dean's "cool." A sociologist commented: "It is the greatest period of euphoria for the country's young since V-J Day at the end of World War II."

J. L. Warner and his underlings at Warner Bros. shared the young people's joy. When Dean was first injured, Warner complained, "How the hell are we gonna sell pictures with a dead actor?" Now, he realized, that with Dean's miraculous recovery, Warner Bros. could look forward to a rosy future. Not only was *Rebel Without a Cause* holding strongly at the box office, but in 1956 the company would release what promised to be a super-hit, *Giant*. "That is," said Warner ruefully, "if George Stevens ever finishes cutting the damn thing."

Dean's recovery was slow. So many bones had been shattered that almost his whole body had to be reconstructed. J. L. Warner paid for him to be flown by helicopter to Los Angeles and then brought in a leading orthopedic surgeon from Boston General Hospital to perform the repair work. Warner also flew in a famous plastic surgeon from Geneva to piece together Dean's face.

Fan magazine photographers staked out St. John's Hospital in Santa Monica, on the alert for celebrities visiting Dean. They came in great numbers, and the more polite ones stopped after leaving the hospital to comment on what good spirits Jimmy was in despite the constant pain. There were reports that Marlon Brando had sneaked in a side entrance, but that could not be confirmed.

The media had a field day. *Life* magazine devoted twenty pages of photographs to Dean. He was on the cover of every movie magazine. Television replayed kinescopes of his performances on *Philco TV Playhouse* and *Danger,* as well as his General Electric Theatre dramas, including *The Dark, Dark Hours,* in which he portrayed a killer subdued by a kindly country doctor, played by Ronald Reagan. An alert theater manager in Berkeley offered a retrospective of Dean's two released films, playing *East of Eden* and *Rebel Without a Cause* on alternate nights.

The result was a sellout, and other theaters across the country followed suit.

Hunting desperately for new twists to a well-covered story, fan magazine writers found one when Dean was visited by Pier Angeli. PIER WEEPS OVER JIMMY'S LOST LOVE screamed one magazine cover. The hospital visit allowed writers to rehash stories of how Dean was devastated when the Italian actress jilted him and married Vic Damone and how Dean revved his motorcycle across the street from the wedding.

Ursula Andress also paid a visit to the hospital, and that provided an excuse for stories about her tempestuous affair with Jimmy Dean. Writers reprinted a columnist's crack: "Jimmy Dean is studying German so he can fight in two languages with Ursula Andress."

Another visitor was Vampira, the ghoulish hostess of horror movie programs on television. She arrived in full regalia, knee-length raven hair, milk-white makeup, and funereal black gown. She claimed to have dated Jimmy even though he told Hedda Hopper: "I don't go out with witches." She was denied admittance to his hospital room.

Dean was still in the hospital when the twenty-eighth annual Academy Award nominations were announced on February 23, 1956. In his first important role, *East of Eden,* Dean was nominated for Best Actor. His release from the hospital was well planned by the Warner Bros. publicity department—five days before the deadline for Academy voting.

The scene could have been staged by George Stevens for *Giant*. Three dozen television, newsreel, and still photographers clustered at the steps of St. John's Hospital, accompanied by an equal number of reporters. At high noon, the front doors opened, and out stepped James Dean, flanked by Elizabeth Taylor and Rock Hudson.

Dean blinked and ducked his head in the bright sunlight. His blonde hair was more tousled than usual and he seemed painfully thin, and his face was unsmiling as light bulbs created lightning flashes. After several minutes of posing this way and that, the three stars advanced toward the banks of microphones. Elizabeth Taylor spoke first.

"I'm sure that all of America shares my joy in seeing Jimmy back on his feet and well on his way to recovery," she said.

Rock Hudson leaned down and said, "I feel the same way."

"Now, we don't want to tire Jimmy," said Elizabeth, "but I know he wants to say a few words." She and Hudson helped him toward the microphones.

"I, uh, well, I wanna thank, um um . . . " He continued in the same vein while one reporter asked another, "Wuzzat he's saying?" "Beats me," was the reply. Fortunately, a Warner Bros. publicist handed out copies of Dean's remarks afterward.

When Dean was finally alone in the ambulance with the attendants, he asked, "For God's sake, has anybody here got a drink?" One of them obliged.

While continuing his recovery at his rented house in Studio City, Dean's agents were busy. They had already made two deals for him before the accident, but in view of his worldwide fame, the contracts were obviously inadequate.

NBC Television had signed Dean to play the poor Welsh boy, Morgan Evans, in a new version of *The Corn Is Green*. The network had agreed to pay him $20,000, a large sum for a television appearance. "Now Jimmy's worth fifty thousand," his agents insisted, and NBC reluctantly acquiesced.

MGM had made a deal for Dean to play Rocky Graziano, the champion prizefighter, in *Somebody Up There Likes Me* for $100,000. "Not enough," said the agents, who asked for $200,000. MGM demurred, saying a deal is a deal. Dean said he was not well enough for a boxing movie, and Paul Newman played the role.

The press provided ample coverage when Dean returned to acting almost a year after the accident. Reporters were invited to the first day of rehearsals of *The Corn Is Green* at NBC Studios in Burbank, and they observed that the actor appeared only slightly scarred. He proved his agility driving his motorcycle to work.

Dean's co-star in *The Corn Is Green* was Bette Davis, repeating her film role as the schoolteacher and mentor to the ambitious young man. For American audiences, the locale of the play was changed to Appalachia. Miss Davis approached the sensational young actor warily and was once heard to exclaim in rehearsals, "Speak up, young man, I can't hear a word you're saying."

On September 23, 1956, *The Corn Is Green* achieved a 45 Nielsen rating and a 65.7 share, making it the highest rated drama special in television history.

To capitalize on his proven ability to attract a large audience, Dean's agents were eager to conclude more contracts. "No, wait until *Giant*," he cautioned. "Then we'll go in for the kill."

On October 10, 1956, *Giant* had its world premiere at the Roxy Theater in New York City. With the three major stars in attendance, the premiere attracted more press coverage than any within memory. Interest was heightened not only by anticipation for the movie, but persistent rumors pointed to a simmering feud between the two stars. Columnists insisted there had been a definite chill between Hudson and Dean on location in Marfa, Texas, each claiming that George Stevens was favoring the other.

The premiere did nothing to dispel the rumors. Dean and Hudson didn't speak to each other and declined to be photographed together. Hudson arrived first with his wife, Phyllis Gates, and received a huge ovation. The clamor was so great that the Hudsons couldn't make their way through the crowd and had to enter the theater through a side entrance.

Curtain time arrived and no James Dean. Even Elizabeth Taylor made her appearance on time. Warner Bros. executives sweated profusely as they gazed up Broadway. Then they heard a roar coming from a side street. The noise grew closer—the sound of a motor, accompanied by the growing cheers of the crowd.

Suddenly, Jimmy Dean appeared in front of the Roxy astride a big black Harley Davidson. "Take care of this for me, will you?" he said to the uniformed doorman, and he walked into the theater before a deafening din.

Dean's arrival was front-page news, and *Giant* was hailed by many critics as a modern masterpiece, although a few found Dean's performance too mannered. Warner Bros. predicted *Giant* would prove the biggest grosser in the history of the company.

A week later, the Hollywood premiere of *Giant* was held at Grauman's Chinese Theater. This time, Rock Hudson was determined to upstage Dean, and he and his wife arrived ten minutes after the scheduled curtain. Hudson discovered that Dean, accompanied by Natalie Wood, had been the first celebrity to arrive, and everything afterward had been an anticlimax.

The rivalry was exacerbated the following February when both Dean and Hudson were nominated for Academy Awards as best actor for their roles in *Giant,* prompting more press reports about the so-called feud.

Item in Army Archerd's column in *Daily Variety*: "WB'ites are looking for fireworks in February when Rock Hudson and James Dean report to do a March of Dimes blurb with Elizabeth Taylor. No doubt Liz will stand between 'em at all times."

The fireworks failed to ignite. Eyewitnesses reported that the actors were polite as they made the pitch for the charity drive and that Miss Taylor kept things jocular during the brief filming.

Afterward, Hudson invited Dean into his dressing room, and Dean hesitantly agreed. Hudson closed the door behind them.

"Jimmy, I've been waiting a long time to apologize to you," Rock said as he began to remove the *Giant* costume he had been wearing.

"What for?" Dean asked in surprise.

"For thinking such bad things when you were hurt."

"You can't be blamed for what you're thinking."

"No, this was bad. I actually . . . " Rock hesitated. "I actually hoped you would die."

"Oh?"

"Yes, and I've hated myself for it ever since. I was so goddamn jealous of you and how easy acting comes to you when I have to work like a son of a bitch." He removed his shirt, exposing his broad, muscular chest.

"Hey, Rock, you're a good actor. We just have different styles."

"Yeah, but I'll never achieve what you will. You deserve that Oscar. I'm not in the same league. And I want you to know that I apologize for what I was thinking. I'm glad you're well."

Jimmy blushed and stammered, "Jeez, Rock, it's okay, it's okay."

By now Rock was standing in his jockey shorts, and he leaned down and kissed Jimmy on the mouth.

"Holy shit!" Jimmy exclaimed. He stared unbelievingly at Rock's smiling face. Jimmy could do nothing but sputter while Rock nodded slowly.

"But . . . but what about Phyllis?" Jimmy asked.

"What about her?"

"Well, can you play both sides of the street?"

"Why not?"

Jimmy shook his head. "I . . . I just can't believe it."

"Hey, aren't you the guy that told his draft board, 'You can't draft me, I'm a homosexual'?"

"Yeah, but I'd say anything to stay out of the army."

"C'mon, you can't tell me you haven't . . . "

"Sure I have. I'll try anything. But it screws up my mind if I don't do it the . . . uh, normal way."

Rock shrugged and reached for a shirt. "I gotta go," Jimmy mumbled, rising to leave. As he went out the door, Rock said, "If you ever change your mind . . . "

Neither Rock nor Jimmy won the Oscar. Yul Brynner did.

◆

Before the accident, James Dean's agents had negotiated a new contract with Warner Bros., calling for nine pictures over a six-year period for a salary of $1,000,000. After his recovery, Dean told his agents: "Double it."

Jack L. Warner was apoplectic when he received the ultimatum.

"Why, that ungrateful little son of a bitch," Warner ranted. "I hire the best sawbones in the country to patch him up and get that high-priced quack from Switzerland to put his face back together, and he holds me up for ransom. Fuck him! I'll sue the little bastard and no other studio will be able to hire him. I'll keep him in court so long he'll be playing character parts when he gets out."

A week later, Warners announced a new six-year contract with James Dean, entailing nine pictures at $2,000,000.

The first film under the new contract was a sequel to *East of Eden* called *Eden Revisited*. John Steinbeck wrote a screen treatment continuing the lives of the characters in his novel, Paul Osborn did the screenplay, and Elia Kazan agreed to direct. Principal members of the original cast were reassembled, and filming began in Salinas on April 5, 1957. An alert publicist posed Dean at the corner of Route 466 and Route 33, where he almost lost his life. The AP photograph appeared in newspapers throughout the country.

After six weeks of filming *Eden Revisited,* Elia Kazan resigned as director. "Artistic differences" was cited in the Warner Bros. publicity release. Two days later, the studio announced that James Dean would direct the remainder of the film.

Eden Revisited completed filming six weeks over schedule and $500,000 over budget. Dean then submerged himself in the editing room, poring over one million feet of film. After four months, Jack Warner asked him, "How long is it going to take you to cut that goddamned picture?" Dean replied: "One week longer than George Stevens takes."

Eden Revisited was finally released on February 28, 1958, to a chorus of critical catcalls. Even those who had praised Dean in his first three movies used such phrases as "self-indulgent drivel" and "a pretentious bore." Bosley Crowther wrote in the *New York Times*: "If Dean's verbal stumbling and mumbling grows any worse, the releasing company would be well advised to supply subtitles of his dialogue."

Dean's young fans remained loyal, however, and they flocked to *Eden Revisited* in large numbers. The girls wept loudly at the climactic scene in which Dean was killed by a wheat combine. Despite its huge cost, the film showed a small profit.

Jack Warner remained incensed by Dean's behavior. "Get rid of the little bastard!" he ordered, and a contract settlement was negotiated.

"Hah! That's just what I wanted," exulted Jimmy Dean. "Now I can go for the big bucks."

A newfound avarice was only one of the disturbing changes his friends noticed in James Dean following his recovery from the accident. It was a surprising development, since he had not expressed any concern for money before. During his early acting days in New York and in Hollywood, he had always lived simply, even primitively, dressing with little care for fashion, eating hamburgers and french fries, flopping in friends' spare bedrooms or on living room couches. He had never read his contracts, caring only whether his role was challenging and different.

Now he read the contracts first and the scripts afterward. He was intent on exacting every dollar and concession he could from the studios. "Whatever Brando got, I want fifty thousand more," he told his agents. Brando had become an obsession with him. He still smarted over the time when Brando told him at a party: "You're sick. You need help."

"I'm going to make the world forget Marlon Brando," Dean proclaimed. "Montgomery Clift, too."

Dean's sex life had undergone changes, as well. Women he had idolized and mooned over, like Pier Angeli, no longer interested him. He was intrigued by exotic women, Latin and Asian temptresses who could lead him into areas of sexual adventure. He explored each one for all her secrets, then discarded her for another.

In the aftermath of the accident, Dean seemed to increase the indulgences he had been subject to before. He smoked cigarettes almost constantly, and often drank to excess. One night at Ciro's he was asked to leave because he repeatedly talked back to Danny Thomas as the comedian was performing.

Although speed had almost killed him, Dean refused to abandon the racing life. "It's like falling off a horse," he told an interviewer. "You damn well better get back up and ride that son of a bitch or you'll be scared for the rest of your life."

Defiantly, James Dean bought another Porsche Spyder and raced it at tracks in Sacramento and Riverside. To his chagrin, he never finished better than third.

Following the disaster of *Eden Revisited*, Dean restored his reputation as the screen's most promising young actor. His fifth film was *Payment Deferred*, based on a one-act Tennessee Williams play, directed by George Cukor at MGM. Cukor allowed no misbehavior, and he curbed much of Dean's method-actor excesses. The result was a well-balanced performance that proved Dean's box-office power and brought him another Academy nomination. His salary was $350,000, and thereafter he demanded a flat half-million. Studio heads squawked that such demands would ruin the industry, but most of them submitted scripts to Dean.

As his power in the industry grew, Dean became more aloof from the press. He still maintained contact with a few columnists who had befriended him early in his career, notably Hedda Hopper. She had originally dismissed him as one of the new breed of actor slobs whose lack of discipline and manners she abhorred, but her attitude changed after she recognized the brilliance of his performance in *East of Eden*. She invited him to her home, and he appeared, neat and courteous and carrying a St. Genesius medal Elizabeth Taylor had given him. He proceeded to charm the birds right out of Hedda's hat, and she was his champion all through his long recovery and return to acting. Inevitably, Louella Parsons remained a foe of Dean, using her column to chide him for his salary demands and for the way he used and discarded women.

Aside from Hedda Hopper, Joe Hyams, and a few others, Dean rarely gave interviews and tried to keep his private life private. The fan magazines complained bitterly about his inaccessibility, but that didn't prevent them from splashing their fantasies about his life and loves over their covers.

James Dean's career maintained a steady pace during the next ten years. He continued to be one of the most in-demand stars, and wisely chose a variety of roles. He played Billy the Kid in an all-star western and Iago in a modernized version of *Othello*. He appeared in a biblical epic directed by Henry Hathaway, with whom he had fierce arguments. His only failure was a sex comedy of the kind made popular by Doris Day and Rock Hudson. Critics were almost unanimous in deciding that James Dean should not attempt comedy.

By 1968, James Dean was thirty-seven and had appeared in eighteen films during his fifteen years in the movie industry. He had been in the limelight during all that time and, during the period of his accident and recovery, had tried to avoid publicity, except when necessary to exploit his films. But Dean, like Marlon Brando, Marilyn Monroe, Elvis Presley, and a few other stars, could not escape notoriety.

JAMES DEAN'S SECRET LOVE AFFAIR WITH RITA HAYWORTH
WHY BRANDO HATES DEAN
"I'LL NEVER LOVE ANYONE BUT PIER"—JIMMY DEAN
DEAN RACES FAST CARS TO WIN—OR TO DIE?
WHY JIMMY LOVES 'EM AND LEAVES 'EM.

These were a few of the banner lines that fan magazines carried during the Dean heyday. In the late 1960s, the stories began to dwindle. The reason was simple. In the popularity polls taken by the fan magazines, the name James Dean had dropped far down the list. A new generation of movie fans was choosing its own favorites, names like Jon Voight, Dustin Hoffman, Robert Redford, Steve McQueen.

Critics, too, had grown disenchanted with Dean. They complained about the sameness of his performances: "Dean once again digs into his well-worn bag of tricks and brings forth the same tired mannerisms: the shy smile, the hung head, the mumbled dialogue." The fault was not entirely his. When producers were casting a "James Dean" role, they often did the obvious and hired James Dean.

But Dean no longer looked the young, innocent victim of society. He was in his late thirties and looked it. The years of heavy boozing and constant womanizing were beginning to show in his face. His once-slender body was beginning to bloat. The reports and rumors of his riotous living had eroded his image. The young man who had galvanized the nation with his portrayal of a rebellious new breed had become something of a bore.

The film offers diminished. The major studios no longer placed him high on their lists of casting possibilities. He was sought only for secondary roles or for scripts that popular stars rejected. A few independent producers used his still-familiar name as a means of securing financing for their projects. The scripts were shopworn and only contributed to Dean's image as a fading star.

At the same time, Jimmy Dean discovered a social conscience.

"How can I go on making movies while American citizens are being attacked by police dogs and water guns?" he asked in a famous public statement. He declared that he would abandon his film career and devote himself full-time to the civil rights movement. This was not merely a public gesture. He also announced he was donating a half-million dollars to the Southern Christian Leadership Conference and other organizations in the forefront of the struggle for equal rights.

Dean appeared arm-in-arm with Martin Luther King, Jr. and other leaders in the march at Selma, Alabama, and also took part in lunch counter demonstrations. Southern theater owners declined to book Dean's movies, which further damaged his appeal to Hollywood producers.

Jimmy Dean was an active participant during the 1968 demonstrations at the Democratic convention in Chicago. He became a supporter of Abbie Hoffman, Tom Hayden, and other activists, prompting attacks from Republicans and conservative Democrats. A photograph of Dean with other arrested demonstrators in a Chicago jail appeared on front pages throughout the nation.

Dean's venture into radicalism inevitably led him into the subculture of drugs. He had been drinking alcohol since his late teens and frequently used marijuana. At the Chicago convention, he was introduced to mind-bending drugs and believed that an entirely new world had opened up to him.

"How long has this been going on?" he exclaimed in an interview with *Rolling Stone*. "Where have I been that I missed out on it? My God, this is the best thing that has happened to me since I joined the Actors Studio. It has increased my level of consciousness two or three times. I'm seeing things more clearly now: my life, my work, the world around me. These [drugs] should make me much more valuable as an actor."

Hollywood producers didn't think so. The fact that an actor would openly admit his use of illegal substances made him a bad risk, both from a public relations standpoint and out of fear that he would be unreliable on a movie set.

Movie offers stopped. "That's okay," Dean said boldly. "Maybe Hollywood doesn't want me, but the people do. I'll go back to the theater."

In April of 1971, David Merrick announced he would present a new production of *The Doctor's Dilemma* starring Geraldine Page and James Dean.

"This is both an important and a sentimental event," Merrick told the *New York Times*. "Seventeen years ago, James Dean made his last Broadway appearance in *The Immoralist*—appearing with Geraldine Page."

What Merrick failed to remember was that Dean had posted his notice on the opening night of the play, angering the producers, authors, and his fellow actors. He had received warm notices for *The Immoralist,* in which he played a supporting role to Miss Page and Louis Jourdan, and his resignation harmed the play's chances. The reason he left: Elia Kazan offered him the lead in *East of Eden.*

The Doctor's Dilemma was troubled from the start. Dean appeared for the first rehearsals looking as if he slept in his clothes. He was unshaven and mumbled his lines so consistently that the director said repeatedly, "Please, Mr. Dean, can you speak up?" Dean would deliver several of his lines coherently, then lapse once again into his familiar manner.

After three rehearsals, the director complained to Merrick: "The man is impossible! He has utterly no understanding of Shaw. You can't understand him. He must be replaced."

"No, no!" Geraldine Page insisted. "Jimmy was just the same in *The Immoralist*—rotten in rehearsals, brilliant on opening night. You must give him a chance."

Merrick replaced the director instead. The producer believed correctly that Dean was perfectly cast as Louis Dubedat, the gifted artist and charming scoundrel who is doomed to a tubercular death. A new director was able to deal with the actor's eccentricities, and the play seemed ready to open out of town.

The dress rehearsal in Wilmington went badly. The scenery wouldn't work, and Dean seemed distracted. He walked through his role, and the entire company felt the cold hand of disaster.

"Fifteen minutes, Mr. Dean." The stage manager knocked on the dressing room door but received no response. "Fifteen minutes, Mr. Dean!" Nothing. The stage manager opened the door and his heart stopped. Jimmy Dean was lying on the floor, unconscious.

"My God, it's opening night, and the star is stoned!" the stage manager exclaimed.

"Did you say something?" Jimmy muttered, blinking his eyes.

"I . . . I said, 'Fifteen minutes, Mr. Dean.'"

"Okay." Dean climbed to his feet and sat before the dressing mirror, daubing his face with makeup. The stage manager shook his head and continued his rounds.

Geraldine Page was right: James Dean was brilliant on opening night. His deathbed scene, in which he transformed from the bigamist rake to a tender and loving husband, caused even the stagehands to weep. The audience demanded ten curtain calls, and the critics were exuberant.

The opening in Washington, D.C. drew the same response. On the fifth night of the engagement, the stage manager again found Dean unconscious on the floor. This time he didn't revive. The performance was canceled. Merrick recognized that Dean's addiction was out of control, and he announced that Dean was leaving the cast "for health reasons." He was replaced by Rip Torn.

In 1972, James Dean turned up in Hanoi with Jane Fonda. Both were besieged by international reporters as they left their plane, and Miss Fonda spoke movingly about the need to discover the real truth about "the tragedy we call the Vietnam War." Dean commented: "I am pleased to join Jane in this vital endeavor. Americans have been sold a bill of goods by their leaders, and as a result, a lot of people are dying needlessly down there." He was applauded by the journalists.

Facing a crucial meeting with North Vietnamese leaders, Jane was waiting for Dean in the lobby of their hotel. "We *can't* be late!" she muttered, and she climbed the stairs to Dean's room.

"C'mon in," said a slurred voice.

Jane entered the room and found Jimmy slumped in a chair. A Vietnamese girl was sleeping in the bed.

"For God's sake, Jimmy, we've got to meet these people in fifteen minutes," Jane cried. "Pull yourself together."

"They'll wait," said Jimmy, his eyes half open. "Sit down and try some of this hashish. It's pure, the real thing. Best I ever . . ."

"You are disgusting!"

"Oh, c'mon, Janie, have a little fun. That's the trouble with you—you don't know how to have fun."

"Dammit, do you realize what harm you can do to our case? Can't you see the fun the papers back home would have? 'James Dean Goes to Hanoi for Dope and Dolls!' For Crissake, Jimmy!"

Dean started to cry. "Oh, I'm sorry, Jane, I'm sorry. Don't worry. I'll get myself together and go with you."

"No, you won't! You stay here and don't go near a reporter. And you'd better be sober by the time the plane goes or I'll leave you here."

Dean's behavior in Hanoi remained out of the reporters' view, but reports drifted back to Hollywood. Now he was totally unemployable, not only because of his unreliability but because of his anti-war views. His name was among the most prominent on the Enemies List compiled by the Nixon White House. It mattered little to Jimmy Dean. Soon after the Hanoi trip, he entered his Taos period.

James Dean disappeared. He sold his ranch in Mandeville Canyon, discharged his agents, and dropped out of sight. At first there was little curiosity about his absence. Dean's habits had grown so erratic that nothing he did was surprising anymore. The usual talk at Hollywood cocktail parties was: "Where's Jimmy Dean?" "Who cares?"

People magazine located him. He was living on a mountaintop near Taos, New Mexico, sharing an old adobe ranch with a lovely Indian woman. Dean had refused to speak to the *People* reporter, but several of his friends and neighbors gave insight into how he was living.

Before he started acting in high school, Jimmy Dean had ambitions of becoming an artist. All through his acting career he had calculated that when the career ended—as he expected it to someday—he would turn to art. Now he devoted himself full-time to painting. Descriptions of his works indicated that they were bold, dark, often gloomy landscapes in the Vlaminck manner. He refused all offers to sell his paintings, storing them instead in a barn on his ranch property.

By nosing around Taos, the *People* reporter was able to piece together a description of how James Dean was spending his life. His drug phase had apparently ended, except for the occasional use of peyote with his Indian friends. He had immersed himself in the Indian culture, spending much time on reservations. He taught youngsters how to draw and worked with the elderly, trying to encourage the storytelling tradition.

"Isn't that just like Jimmy Dean to latch on to the Indians?" remarked a Hollywood cynic. "He always did try to out-Brando Brando."

Dean was far removed from such barbs. He had cut all his ties to Hollywood, never saw movies, refused to have a television set in his home. He had dropped out, totally. Photographs taken surreptitiously while he shopped for paint supplies in Taos showed him much changed from the boy in *East of Eden*. His hair was shoulder-length, and a full beard, slightly graying, almost hid his face. Only the eyes disclosed the Jimmy Dean of twenty years before. They still smoldered with fierce intensity, hinting of the passion within.

◆

It was in October of 1978 when the young man walked up the trail that led to the Dean house. He found Jimmy Dean himself sitting on the front porch, a shotgun resting on his lap.

"I think you'd better turn around, boy, and head down that trail—now," Dean said firmly.

"You don't scare me, Mr. Dean," the young man said. "I know all your tricks. That one's out of *The Return of Billy the Kid*."

"State your business."

"I'm here to stop you from pissing away your God-given talent."

Dean laughed mirthlessly. "Talk about tired lines. Can't you do better than that, boy?"

"Don't give me that 'boy' shit. I've already directed two feature pictures."

"My God! The infants are running the nursery."

"Can I talk to you?"

"I'll give you twenty minutes."

His name was Lance Bigelow, and his smooth face and tall slender figure made him seem younger than his age, which was twenty-five. He had the confidence of a twenty-year veteran of the film industry, and when he talked, Dean listened, at first bemused.

"I know this sounds like bullshit to you, Mr. Dean, but it's the God's honest truth—you changed my life," he began. "I was just a snot-nosed kid until I saw *Rebel Without a Cause.*"

"C'mon, I made that picture when you were a baby."

"I know, but when I saw it in UCLA film school, I was knocked out by it. Before that, I was just killing time in college, trying to stay out of Vietnam. Seeing you as Jim Stark made me realize what a powerful thing movies are."

"Okay, okay, get to the pitch. You got eighteen minutes left."

"I wrote a script entirely for you. It's called *Rebel with a Cause.*"

Dean's eyes shot skyward, and he held his head as if in pain.

"Yeah, I know it sounds corny, but hear me out," Bigelow insisted. He outlined the story: a famous movie actor leading a wastrel life finds his career on the skids. Out of boredom he starts dabbling in radical causes and becomes alienated from the film industry and his onetime audience. Still on booze and drugs, he becomes more militant, taking part in bombings. He decides to visit Vietnam so he can see the war firsthand. While there, he finds himself in a battlefield situation such as the ones he once played in films. The life-and-death experience causes a spiritual reawakening, and his soul is free once more.

"I suppose you have the script with you," Dean said.

"That's right," said Bigelow.

"Okay, you can leave it. But I don't promise anything."

"No, you can read it now. I'll wait."

"You're a cocky kid."

"That's right. Just like you."

When Dean finished turning the pages, tears were in his eyes. He laid the script down and said nothing for several moments. "Even if I did agree to do it, there's no way you could finance it with James Dean's name," he said.

"That's my problem. Will you do it?"

Dean pondered. "Yes," he said.

"I knew you would. Now, here are the conditions: SAG minimum against twenty-five percent of the producer's gross. No limos, no Winnebagos. If you're ever on dope or late twice, I'll get Bruce Dern. Agreed?"

"Agreed," said Dean, laughing loudly. "You got more chutzpah than Tony Curtis."

"And for God's sake, shave off that fucking beard."

◈

Rebel with a Cause was filmed in the spring of 1979 on locations in Chicago, Atlanta, and Los Angeles, plus three weeks of battle scenes in the Philippines. With a non-union crew, the budget was held to $1.2 million. No publicity was issued during production. When the film was released in November of 1979, it had the impact of a thunderclap. Lance Bigelow was hailed as the next Francis Coppola, and critics who had once reviled James Dean restored him to their bosoms.

"The greatest comeback since Marlon Brando and *The Godfather*," declared *Time* magazine.

"Here I go again, following Marlon." James Dean sighed.

Rebel with a Cause won eleven nominations for the 1979 Academy Awards, including those for best picture, for Bigelow's script and direction, and for James Dean's performance. The press speculated whether the iconoclastic Dean would reject his Oscar, like Marlon Brando. He remained incommunicado at his Taos ranch.

On the night of the Academy Awards, James Dean was not present in the audience at the Los Angeles Music Center. Tension was growing as the ceremonies proceeded amid speculation over what Dean might do if he won as best actor.

Finally, the moment arrived. Jon Voight tore open the envelope and broke into a wide smile. "Oh, this is wonderful!" he exclaimed. "The winner is—James Dean for *Rebel with a Cause*."

The orchestra played the theme music as Voight peered into the audience. No one advanced down the aisle, and the orchestra repeated the theme. Then a figure appeared from the wings. It was James Dean.

His hair was silver, and he had a clipped mustache. He wore a stylish tuxedo, a carnation in the lapel, but the white tie was askew. He lurched toward the microphone, and the audience gasped.

"Ladies and gen'mun," he began amid a shocked silence. He grasped the statuette and swung it wildly. "I'm very, ver-ee pleased to be here tonight."

The shocked crowd stared in disbelief. This seemed to be the crowning insult of a life of disrespect. Then Mel Brooks, who was seated with his wife, Anne Bancroft, called out, "I get it—the banquet scene from *Giant!*"

The realization spread swiftly, and the industry audience began to laugh, then applaud Jimmy Dean's extraordinary audacity. He played it straight to the end, babbling nonsense and gesturing drunkenly. When he staggered back to the wings, the ovation was tumultuous.

James Dean never made another movie. He retired to the vastness of his New Mexico retreat and shunned all further contact with the film world. Producers sent him scripts, along with contracts worth a million dollars. He didn't even acknowledge them.

He remained out of sight until the summer of 1986. Then the *National Enquirer* carried a front-page headline: JAMES DEAN DYING OF AIDS IN ACTORS' HOME.

Could it be true? The Motion Picture Country Hospital in Woodland Hills would confirm only that James Dean was a patient. No details of his ailment were released. Reporters tried every conceivable means of checking the story; nothing could be confirmed. Every lead came to a dead end.

I was at home one night when the call came. It was a friend at the Motion Picture and Television Fund. He said, "Jimmy Dean wants to see you."

"When?"

"Now. I wouldn't wait."

As I drove on the Ventura Freeway in a driving rainstorm, I thought back to my first interview with Jimmy Dean. It was in early May of 1955, when I met him for the first time at the Griffith Park Planetarium. I watched while Nick Ray directed the rumble scene in *Rebel Without a Cause* between Dean and Corey Allen. Dean had to sign some papers during the lunch break, so I rode with him in the limousine to his lawyer's office and we talked. He was elusive, even distant, but I recognized a rare quality in him.

I interviewed him several times over the years, and while he was never easy to talk to, he was always provocative. And honest. He always spoke his mind, and often got in trouble because of it. As I splashed down the offramp in Woodland Hills, I realized I hadn't seen Dean since the night he won the Oscar, seven years before.

He lay in the hospital bed looking like a miniature James Dean. Recognizing the shock in my face, he cracked, "At least the *Enquirer* got something right—I *am* dying."

I sat in the chair beside the bed, not knowing what to say.

"You still goin' around talkin' to actors?" he asked.

"Yeah, Jimmy. Can't break the habit."

He shook his head disparagingly. Somewhat numbly, I asked him how he was feeling.

"Not bad. They give me so many hypos it's just like my old junkie days. I'm not a charity case, by the way. I'm paying my own way. Besides, I'm leaving 'em a million dollars in my will. Well, why don't you ask me?"

"Ask you what?"

"Do I have AIDS?"

"Do you?"

"No. They tell me it's bone cancer, but I've got another theory."

"What's that?"

"You know I never should have survived that accident in '55. I looked like a broken Tinkertoy. But the gods looked down and said, 'The poor slob hasn't shown what he can do yet—let's put him back together and give him another chance.' Thirty years later, the gods looked down again and said, 'Is that all he can do? Let's drop his option.' And the bones just folded up again."

We talked some more, and then a nurse came into the room to give him another shot and suggest some rest. "There's just one more thing I gotta ask you, Jimmy," I said.

"What?"

"As long as I've known you, you've never given a damn about what anyone wrote or said about you. Why now?"

He was silent for a minute, and I feared he had lost consciousness. Then he spoke.

"If it was only me, I wouldn't care. But I got three kids, half-Indian they are. They're gonna have enough hassle with Jimmy Dean bein' their old man. I don't want to make it any worse for them."

His eyes closed again, and I walked quietly toward the door. As I was leaving, he said, "If you run into Marlon, tell him I said hello."

Five days later, he died at the age of fifty-five.

NATALIE
WOOD

BY MARCIA BORIE

*F*or years, numerous publishers had
been after her. They wanted her
story, the saga of a child performer
turned teenage star, romantic
leading lady, and, ultimately,
character actress. They offered her a
fortune to write about herself as
the glamour girl who had
experienced everything. The book
had to include a recitation of her
romances and marriages, her
triumphs and tragedies, and
particularly, a first-hand account of
her recovery from the traumatic

193

ordeal which followed her miraculous escape from that near-fatal drowning episode.

◈

On the night of her sixtieth birthday, Natalie Wood Wagner, in the presence of a dozen of her dearest Hollywood friends and an equal number of close relatives, decided to make the announcement. Looking fit, trim, and still remarkably beautiful, she stood up at the head of the table and smiled mischievously.

"Thank you for being with me . . . I love your gifts and good wishes . . . you've made me so happy . . . " She paused, then with her innate flair for the dramatic, she continued.

"I feel so great that I've even given myself a present . . . " She reached for the legal-size envelope that had been resting under her napkin. Tearing it open, she withdrew what was obviously a check. "I've accepted an offer to write my autobiography. This is the advance. I'm giving myself the next year off just to sit and write my story. I'm going to tell everything just the way it happened—from my point of view. All of you here tonight will be a part of my book because you are each such an important part of my life. I'm going to include you, and so many others who are no longer with us. Without every one of you, my life would have been so different!"

There was a momentary silence, then a polite burst of applause. You had to hand it to Natalie. Whenever she wanted to take center stage, no one could do it with more authority. As she looked around the room, she could sense that her announcement had stunned those who knew her best—or thought they did.

On each face, Natalie could intuit one common question: "Why?"

In truth, she *had* turned down dozens of lucrative offers to do a book. As one of Hollywood's most popular hyphenates—actress, producer, director, patron of the arts and numerous charities, and millionairess many times over—she needed neither the money nor the notoriety a candid autobiography would bring. Before now, she had always refused. She had said she considered it contrary to her nature to reveal too much of herself. So, for more than fifty years, she had been content to let others write about her. Much of what was written had been true. But a lot was pure Hollywood bullshit. Her press agents had earned their fees. So few people knew what was really on her mind, in her heart. How could they? It had taken her more than half a lifetime to know herself, to accept the real Natasha Gurdin turned Natalie Wood.

Now, for reasons of her own, while she was still mentally sharp, she would relive her life and put it down on paper exactly as *she* saw it. The years of good times and not so good times. The fruitful years mixed with comparatively few barren ones. All the laughter that covered the tears. All the tears that were symptomatic of the frustration and the fear. Surely these, plus the hundreds of hours of psychoanalytical give and take, had equipped her to write something meaningful for others and especially for herself.

Her entire life had been a mixture of fantasy and reality. For years, she had trouble recognizing where one began and the other left off. She was a child of destiny born to win fame and fortune. But destiny demanded repayment. So, after all that had come her way, she had now chosen to share her dreams and her nightmares with anyone who cared to read them. She was determined to create a literary tapestry woven with threads of gold and pastels for the good times, but fused with revealing strands of somber colors symbolizing the price she had paid for being a "chosen one."

She had spent so much of her life seeking privacy without ever really attaining it. Eventually, she realized that she had been fooling herself when, sometimes quite plaintively, she had stated: "I haven't had a private moment since I was six years old . . . let me have some things that only belong to me!"

Now, having lived for sixty years, she knew how really presumptuous she had been; how psyched-out she and so many of her peers had been—believing all of that fairy-tale shit that had become part of their daily reality. How dare they want it all on their own terms! But why had it taken her so long to realize that every joy had its price, every ecstasy and excess its counterpart?

The prospect of public self-examination brought her an inner peace and contentment unlike any she had ever known. Maybe it was because the timing was so perfect. Careerwise, she could afford a year away from the public's eye. She had finished interesting and challenging character leads in two movies which were still unreleased. She had just returned from a triumphant month-long stage tour playing the Grand Duchess in *Anastasia,* receiving some of the best theatrical notices of her career. She considered that vehicle her "lucky play." Sixteen years earlier, she had made her theatrical debut at the Ahmanson Theatre in

Anastasia, only then she had played the *title* role. Scared to death, but determined to try, she had opened in Los Angeles before an audience of her peers—and the reviews had been sensational. It was the beginning of a whole new dimension to her life—a distinguished stage career. Since then, she had done at least one play every other year.

R.J. was happily involved behind the scenes with three projects for his production company. These days, he preferred relaxing on the golf course to the daily grind of the studio. Yet his advice and guidance were sought every step of the way. Occasionally, he appeared in one of his properties, but he preferred producing. He was still a handsome figure of a man, just one year shy of seventy, whose amazing agility on the ski slopes matched his skill on the putting green.

They had been man and wife for twenty-five years—more if you counted the few dozen months of their *first* marriage. Their girls were all grown. Two of them, her stepdaughter, Kate, and their daughter together, Courtney, were married. Her firstborn, Natasha, was still single. But it was that daughter whose name was now sprawled across the world's screens. Natasha was a glittering international star who had already achieved a kind of fame which matched her mother's, and, in one way, even outshone her: Natasha had been voted an Academy Award by her peers. The shiny golden statuette, which had eluded Natalie despite numerous nominations, had gone to Natasha for her second film, ironically, a remake of *Splendor in the Grass.* There was a time when Natalie would have been secretly jealous about that. Instead, she was thrilled to see the Oscar on Natasha's mantelpiece.

But that incident would rate a special chapter in her book. On the night she watched her own daughter receive the award she herself so coveted, she fully grasped the reality of what her own mother, Maria, must have gone through. Maria, who had once wanted to be in the limelight herself, but had been prevented from trying by the circumstances of her life, had become content with her role as "the mother of a star," basking in the reflection of Natalie's glory. Although their lives had been completely different, Natalie had finally felt her own mother's frustrations and then understood what even intensive analysis had failed to fully uncover.

Turning sixty had released so many still-bottled-up feelings inside her. Amazing! Once, she would have had such mixed feelings about aging. She remembered turning forty and dreading the passage of time. Then, after her "miraculous recovery," she thought she had welcomed each passing year as the greatest gift she could ever receive. Now, as she contemplated setting her own thoughts down on paper, she decided to be completely honest with herself—perhaps for the very first time.

Becoming a grandmother also had something to do with her decision to write the book. She wanted it to be a legacy for her precious grandchildren. Katie had two babies, and a few months before her sixtieth birthday, her own "baby," Courtney, had given birth to a son. Before her marriage and motherhood, Courtney had been an active participant in her mother's production company. She helped Natalie find screen and stage properties and had worked to encourage young performers who sought roles in various projects, some of which Natalie had produced and starred in, others she had directed.

Yes, the timing for her autobiography was perfect. R.J. was happy and busy; Natasha was off being a star; Katie and Courtney were wrapped up in their young families. Natalie had the necessary quiet and solitude to work on her manuscript. Although the publisher had given her a list of the very best ghostwriters, she had rejected them. She would do the book herself. Only *she* had felt the elation and the pain that she was now prepared to share.

Natalie armed herself with dozens of yellow legal pads. Each morning, she picked up a pen and began writing nonstop for hours at a time. Each night, she read what she had written— and the pages wound up crumpled and tossed in the wastebasket. How to begin? That is what had her stumped. Dramatically speaking, she wanted a very special opening chapter. She knew enough, having read scripts, novels, plays, to realize that she had to grab her audience—her readers—in those first few opening pages. So far, each time she had started, she began: "I was born in San Francisco, California, on July 20, 1938 . . . "

Well, everybody *knew* she was born. It was what she did with her life that was the important part. Her book needed the proper pacing. There was always time to toss in the biographical facts once she had her readers hooked.

Then it came to her. She would begin Chapter One on Thanksgiving weekend, 1981. Dramatically, that was exciting. Realistically, it was also logical. It was only fitting that she start on that weekend, specifically that special night when she had been given a second chance at life. Then she could go back in time—briefly—then return to November 1981, and on to what had happened since the accident, with perhaps a look into the future—which she knew would provide her with a dramatic ending. She would write exactly what *she* remembered of that November, and not a distillation of all the public conjecture which followed her near-fatal mishap.

"For a very long time, or so it seemed, I was unable to focus . . . unable to zero in on anything that was not a fuzzy blur. The voices around me sounded like bees buzzing incessantly. Suddenly, I sat up in bed, then fell back against the pillow. I kept blinking my eyes until first the room, and then the figures in it, became clearer. I saw a nurse dressed in white seated across the room . . . and R.J. standing next to the bed, his hand holding mine.

"After a few moments, I sat up again. My eyes wide open, I had reentered the state of aliveness. They told me I had been tossing and turning and mumbling incoherently for three days. R.J. leaned down and kissed me and held me in his arms. I started to cry, silently, the tears just falling down my face. I was in pain. I reached up and felt the bandages that covered my head. I shuddered and lay back against the pillows.

"The doctor came in and began to give me something to ease my discomfort. I refused. I needed to know what had happened. I asked for a few minutes alone to talk with my husband.

"I tried to talk, but R.J. kept smothering me with kisses. Then I grabbed hold of his hand and began to speak. I rambled on about how lovely I thought our Thanksgiving dinner had been, how great it was having our family and friends to share such a lovely feast.

"Then I continued, 'But I felt so tired . . . and I couldn't sleep, and that damn dinghy *Valiant* was hitting up against the side of our boat. It kept going slap . . . slap . . . slap . . . I got out of bed . . . reached for my red down jacket. I put on some socks and went up on deck . . . I wanted to secure the dinghy.

"'The rain had stopped. It was so clear and beautiful, but very chilly . . . I went down the steps and reached for the rope and untied *Valiant* . . . I leaned over further to retie it . . . and . . . and . . . suddenly I slipped on the swimming step and lost hold of the rope . . . and I tumbled into the sea . . .'"

She began to sob but insisted on finishing her story. It was as though she *had* to tell it all . . . to articulate the horror and thereby exorcise it.

"'When I fell overboard, I hit my head on *Splendor*'s hull . . . I felt myself being dragged, pulled underwater . . . The damn nightgown was twisted 'round my legs . . . I felt so heavy . . . must have been that down jacket . . . I just kept struggling to get back to the surface . . . it was so dark . . . so scary . . . Then I saw the edge of the dinghy and paddled across to it and hooked my arm over the side.

"'I tried yelling for help . . . I called out to you . . . but my cries were so weak . . . I panicked . . . I don't know how long I was in the water . . . Suddenly I saw the outline of another dinghy heading straight for me . . . I was exhausted, but I managed to call out again . . . and then there was nothingness until just now when I woke up in this hospital bed . . .'"

Natalie found herself choked up with sobs. She set aside the yellow legal tablet and just sat back in the chair until she got control of herself. She had recalled the horror of "that incident" through vivid mind-footage which had remained with her even after more than sixteen years. She shook her head in what was still, for her, disbelief; incredulity over a long-ago night in November 1981, when miraculously she had been given another chance at life.

There was only one problem in beginning her book with that incident. Something had happened that night which no one but R.J. and her doctor knew. Ironically, it had been one of the few deeply personal things which she had managed to keep a secret from the world—until now. Taking up her pen, she started writing again.

"From what I'd said to R.J. when I first woke up in the hospital, he realized that something was terribly wrong. Somehow, I had lost nearly forty-eight hours of memory. He called in my doctor, had me repeat what I had just told him, then the doctor took some tests. He diagnosed me as suffering from what he called a classic case of post-traumatic concussional syndrome. The trauma of falling into the sea, and the sharp blow I'd suffered by hitting my head on the boat's hull, had caused me to lose part of my memory of events that had happened just prior to the accident. He also warned that I might have continued memory lapses for a short period now that I had regained full consciousness.

"In essence, I could remember how I got into the water, but I had totally blanked out any other details of what had happened after the Thanksgiving Day dinner party we had had at our home for family and friends, until the time I found myself on the deck of the *Splendor,* attempting to retie the dinghy.

"Another week's stay in the hospital was followed by ten more days at home. The studio had kept *Brainstorm,* the picture I was filming at the time, on hold. I had only a few key scenes left to shoot. Everyone at MGM was so kind. They assured me that all they wanted was my full recovery. Douglas Trumbull, the producer-director, had a lot of post-production work to do on the special effects which were so integral a part of the film. The delay would not prove too costly.

"Only R.J. and I knew how desperately I needed time before I could return to the studio. Only I knew how hard R.J. worked to help me relearn scenes I had already committed to memory before the accident. Painfully, word by word, he coached me until I was confident I could go back to the set.

"When *Brainstorm* was finished, R.J. and I and the kids packed up and flew off to spend a glorious week together in Switzerland. Christmas had come and gone, but I was determined that our girls would have a snowy week away from home to make up for the time we'd lost during my recuperation. I was so thankful for so many things including the fact that both R.J. and I were *performers.* No one in the family ever knew how hard it had been for me to finish the film. All our daughters cared about was that 'Mommy had been fished from the sea and was well again.'"

◈

Once she had finished a rough draft of the first chapter, Natalie began the slow and, for her, torturous process of giving her book some shape, the proper design. Having written the part which would be most difficult, her near-fatal drowning, she figured the rest would come easily. It didn't. There was still so much of herself to lay bare. It had seemed easy at the time she'd signed the book contract. Now she was having second thoughts.

She decided to abandon plans to go back and start the book at the beginning of her life. Instead, she would spend the next few weeks just jotting down anecdotes, word-impressions of things which had happened to her, people who had made a difference in her life—for better, or for worse. In the process, she would begin opening up, answering questions which she knew her publishers wanted covered, or that she suspected her public wanted revealed on the pages of her life story. In this manner, she hoped, her literary manuscript would fall into place.

It had better! At age sixty, with a signed contract and an advance check of half a million dollars on deposit in her bank account, she sure as hell couldn't admit defeat. Besides, the money was already "spent." For years, both she and R.J. had been contributing heavily to a UCLA building fund for the next wing on the Theatre Arts Department. When she'd signed the book contract, and knew the size her advance would be, she had decided to donate all of it, plus her royalties, to this UCLA project. When she'd communicated this information to the dean at their last building fund committee meeting, she, in turn, had received a surprise. The faculty informed her that they had voted to name the entire wing after her and R.J. Thrilled and grateful, she asked them to keep it a surprise until the ground-breaking ceremonies. It would be a belated twenty-fifth anniversary gift for her husband.

While she had been working on the first chapter of her book, she'd been notified that the ceremonies, marking the turning over of the first spadeful of earth before construction started, were to take place in two weeks. She could hardly wait for R.J.'s expression when he found out the honor they were to receive. As "mere" high school graduates, they were about to join the distinguished list of living donors with a building named for them on one of the world's finest university campuses. In years to come, their children and grandchildren would be proud knowing Natalie Wood and Robert Wagner had left their mark not only on this campus, but on the profession both of them loved and owed so much to—acting. Students for generations in the future could study in beautiful surroundings—because she and R.J. cared.

Natalie went back to work on her book with renewed determination. Her pen fairly flew over the paper as she revealed more intimate truths than she realized herself capable of expressing. No one was spared, least of all herself. She composed passages and paragraphs with a frankness and beauty born of her own "rebirth." Undressing her emotions, she worked with the frenzy of a woman possessed, taking only short breaks for meals and brief visits with her husband, children, and grandchildren.

Natalie came up for air two weeks later as she prepared to go with R.J. and their family to the UCLA ceremonies. The sun was shining brightly as they left the house on yet another occasion when they were to receive the appreciation from a public that had loved them for years.

Members of the Los Angeles City Council, the mayor, numerous civic leaders, hundreds of fans, and the entire UCLA academic community—dressed in ceremonial robes—had come to pay them homage on this special day. Seated on a makeshift platform, the Wagners watched as the dean of the School of Theatre Arts addressed the crowd. Then, summoning them to join him, he handed them the symbolic shovel with which they turned over the first clump of earth. Subsequently, the dean unveiled a huge architectural rendering of the building as it would look upon its completion.

Natalie stood aside, grinning wildly—R.J. stared in amazement as he read the hand-lettered plaque that would be placed on the outside of the edifice: NATALIE WOOD-ROBERT WAGNER THEATRE ARTS WORKSHOP. Sketches of the first floor showed a foyer full of statuary and glass cases in which Natalie's donated collection of pre-Colombian art would be on display. The five-story building, full of classrooms, a library, and a theater in the round, was magnificently etched in the artist's concept of what would, in a year, be a permanent building on the UCLA campus.

Courtney and her husband, and Kate and her family, rushed forward to embrace their parents. Than Natasha came to the front and walked up to the platform. Addressing the dean and the crowd, she said: "When this building opens its doors, I hope you will find room for one more statue. . ." Then, unwrapping a package, she presented her Oscar to the dean requesting that he place it in a case with a plaque dedicating it to her mother. "This Oscar," Natasha said, "which was given to me by my peers, belongs to my mother. It was she who gave me life; she who encouraged me to follow my own dreams. Everything I have accomplished, I owe to her and to my 'special' father, Robert Wagner, who raised me as his own daughter; and also to

Richard Gregson, my biological father, who so generously shared me so I could be raised with my sister Courtney."

There wasn't a dry eye in the house as Natasha Gregson Wagner walked back to her seat after kissing Natalie and R.J.

Back home, the family enjoyed dinner and relived what had been a very special day in all of their lives. The following morning, bright and early, Natalie was back in her den, pen in hand, hard at work on her book. For many more months, as her family left her in peace, Natalie wrote her life story. Finally, when she was finished, she had her secretary begin the job of typing it into the computer. When it was done, she wrapped it in a package and sent it off to New York. No amount of pleading could get her to show anyone in the family what she had written. And her secretary, sworn to secrecy, left on a month's vacation.

Once the manuscript was safely in her publisher's hands, and just before Natalie and R.J. left for a holiday in Italy and the South of France, she made a quick visit to her private physician. After subjecting herself to a battery of tests—agonizing brain scans and other such horrors—she and the doctor had a chat. The diagnosis he had given her some months back had not changed. He had indeed found an inoperable growth and his prognosis of a year—fifteen months at most—still held true. Well, she had used up eleven precious months. It was only a matter of time before the tumor would begin to take its toll.

Once again, the doctor asked Natalie if she was sure she wanted to carry this burden alone. He had kept his word not to tell her husband or daughters. However, fearing for her condition in the following weeks and months, he implored her to allow him to explain exactly what would happen and how she would feel during the final weeks of her illness—he wanted to call in R.J. Once again, Natalie refused. She wanted this final holiday to be "perfect," she explained. Reluctantly, the doctor agreed to keep her secret. After all, it wouldn't be secret too much longer!

Natalie and R.J. and their family and close friends shared a bon voyage dinner. The following morning, the Wagners flew off to Rome and from there motored down to Venice. For seven serene days and nights, they glided by gondola down the canals, walked hand in hand along St. Mark's Square, and in between, Natalie shopped and shopped and shopped.

Each day's packages were carefully labeled with the name of the recipient, until R.J. noticed there were no boxes or bags that seemed to be for Natalie herself. When he questioned his wife, she replied: "I have everything I'll ever need, my darling . . . I'm enjoying buying things for the people I love the most." So, on their last night in Venice, after a sumptuous feast, R.J. presented his wife with a magnificent Bulgari emerald necklace and bracelet.

With tears in her eyes, Natalie took out the jewelry box she had hidden away at the bottom of her luggage. Handing it to R.J., she smiled mischievously. "You've spoiled my timing, darling. I was waiting for just the right moment to give this to you."

Inside, R.J. found a magnificent platinum watch which Natalie had engraved: "To R.J. Thank you for every second of our life together. Love, Nat."

There was another box which held a thin gold I.D. bracelet. Inside were the words: "To the only man I've ever really loved. Remember me, always. Natalie."

That night, they fell asleep wrapped in each other's arms, with a passion that sixty and sixty-nine-year-old people are not given to expressing too often!

The next morning they were off to the South of France to a hideaway villa in St. Paul de Vance. And, six days later, they wound up at the newly restored Hotel Du Cap in Antibes, in a suite with a palatial balcony overlooking the azure Mediterranean Sea. Unbeknownst to Natalie, R.J. had reserved rooms for Kate and Courtney and their husbands, as well as for Natasha and her fiancé, the recently appointed chairman and CEO of England's biggest independent film company. Natalie had laughed when Natasha phoned the news. So, her daughter had fallen for a Brit, too. Well, like mother, like daughter. Only Natalie secretly hoped that Natasha's marriage to *her* Englishman would be much more enduring than the one she had shared with Natasha's father.

During the first week of their stay in Antibes, the Wagners were having breakfast on the terrace when Natalie looked up and saw, to her surprise and delight, her entire collection of daughters, sons-in-law, and one fiancé, trooping into the hotel trailed by numerous bellboys handling dozens of suitcases. Squealing with the sound she used to make as a teenager, Natalie let out a whoop of unrestrained joy. How ever could R.J. have arranged *this* secret—which was so exquisitely timed—when *her* secret, unfortunately, was soon about to be revealed?

The moment the girls were settled, Natalie overwhelmed them all with an impulsive idea. Why not have Natasha's nuptials immediately? Why wait to go home and have a big wedding when everyone they needed was right there? Natasha's fiancé agreed to phone his family and ask them to come at once to Antibes—provided they could find a way around French marriage laws and all of the assorted details that needed to be taken care of.

Everyone got into the spirit of the moment. To skirt certain regulations, it was arranged that the wedding ceremony be conducted on a yacht on the high seas. With each member of the wedding party assigned a different task, everything was settled within four days. Natalie had not stepped foot on a private yacht since "the accident." On the day of Natasha's wedding, she made an exception.

The wedding party assembled on a glorious yacht, *La Victoria*. Natalie couldn't help remembering her own second wedding, also on a yacht, the *Ramblin' Rose*. Katie Wagner had been old enough to be present at the ceremony, but little Natasha Gregson had raced with her tiny baby legs back and forth across the deck so many times, she had fallen asleep when it came time for the actual ceremony. Well, Natalie mused, today Natasha would indeed be awake for *these* nuptials.

The ceremony over, the bridal dinner complete, the toasts drained to the last drops of champagne in the crystal goblets, the bridal party and guests went ashore. Back in Antibes, the wedding party continued, but Natalie begged off and returned to her suite. Insisting that R.J. remain downstairs with their guests, Natalie slowly undressed and prepared for bed.

For the last few days, she had known the end was near. She had muffled severe headaches with medication the doctor had given her. But now, as she could hear the peals of laughter from the open windows of her balcony . . . now the pain was more severe than any she had previously experienced. Frightened but happy, she made her way over to the closet. There, buried deep inside one of her suitcases, was a copy of her manuscript. Carefully, she set it on top of R.J.'s pillow. Then, taking a final sip of water and several more pain pills, she lay down . . . to wait. . . .

When R.J. came in ready to regale his wife with a few more anecdotes about the wedding scene, he found the lights dimmed. Natalie appeared to be sleeping. After getting into pajamas, he wandered over to the bed and found the manuscript on his pillow. Attached to it was a note: "This is for you, my darling, and for the girls. With all my love, Natalie."

He reached over to take her hand . . . and realized there was no pulse. Putting on all of the lights, he raced to kneel by his wife's side. Her eyes were closed . . . and on her lips was just the faintest trace of a smile . . . but she was gone.

With tears falling down his face, Robert Wagner sorrowfully summoned his family. The bride and groom had just been ready to leave on their honeymoon when the call came. Together, holding hands, they stood surrounding her bed. But each, in grief, felt that Natalie had gone peacefully . . . happily. Then they realized why all the haste with the wedding preparations. Natalie had wanted to be present at her first-born's marriage.

Quickly, they each packed and prepared to fly back to America. In his state of sadness, R.J. had just tucked Natalie's manuscript in a suitcase where it remained until after the funeral. When the mourners had come and left . . . when the last family member had gone home—at R.J.'s insistence—he got out the manuscript and walked with it into the den. Sitting down in the chair where Natalie had sat to write her book, R.J. opened the first page and began reading:

DEDICATION

I was born in San Francisco, on July 20, 1938. When I was four, we moved to a little nearby town called Santa Rosa. At that time, my family consisted of my parents, Nicholas and Maria Gurdin, Russian emigrants, and my sister, Olga, who was eight. My name was Natasha.

Shortly after we arrived in Santa Rosa, director Irving Pichel brought a film there on location. Some of the townspeople were hired as extras. My mother, whose maiden name had been Maria Kuleff, had always dreamed of going onstage . . . of performing . . . of standing out in a crowd with a spotlight shining down upon her. Unfortunately, circumstances prevented her dreams from coming true . . . so she decided to live them—through me.

I owe everything that subsequently happened during those next few years to my mother's burning desire to live a life of fame—if only by reflection. There were times growing up when I resented her ambition . . . times when, as a child, working seemed all that my life consisted of . . . but when I grew up and realized the great gift my mother had given me, I learned, eventually, to accept all of the pain that came with my good fortune.

I am one of "the chosen." I have paid a price for my destiny. But no price is too great to have paid for all that has been given me. This book is dedicated first to my mother, without whom Natalie Wood never could have existed . . . To Maria Kuleff Gurdin's memory, I humbly dedicate these pages with joyful thanks for everything she tried to do— even those things I was foolish enough to resent when I was too young to understand.

This book is also dedicated to the only man I have ever truly loved—Robert John Wagner. I saw him first when I was eleven years old—and fell in love with him. He was the person I chose to spend my life with—and I did—with numerous interruptions along the way, which I shall try to explain during the course of writing this manuscript.

The story of my life, I also dedicate to my father, Nicholas Gurdin. He tried his best to be a good father, and I loved him even when I disagreed with many of the old-fashioned ways he had of showing affection. He wanted only the best for me . . . I finally realized that fact when I was a grown woman and had children of my own.

To Natasha and Courtney, children of my flesh and blood, I dedicate this autobiography in the hopes that, as they read it, they will understand my honesty, forgive my transgressions, and know that I have loved them with all of my heart.

To my sisters, Olga and Lana, and to my stepdaughter, Katie, I dedicate this work in the hopes that each of them will understand me better after they have read and digested my innermost feelings.

I dedicate this book to all of the fans who cared for me and supported me and made me a star. I hope I did not *disappoint you in any way. I once felt I only owed you the best performance I could give. Now, I realize, I owe you far more than that . . . I hope you feel you have received it from me.*

To my grandchildren, whom I love and adore, my hope that this story will make you proud . . . and give you courage to be whatever you wish to be. . . . To those grandchildren yet unborn, may you know the same joys with which I have been showered.

Finally, I dedicate this book to little Natasha Gurdin, the child on that street corner in Santa Rosa who learned how to drop an ice-cream cone . . . and cry on cue. You moved to Hollywood, took another name, and became known around the world as Natalie Wood. To you, Natasha, heart of my heart, I pray you feel that, all in all, I have not broken faith with the beauty and innocence of your sweet, blessed soul.

MONTGOMERY
CLIFT

BY PAUL ROSENFIELD

FEBRUARY 1985—HONOLULU

*B*ut why now and why me?"
Montgomery Clift wanted to know.
He was sitting guru-style on the
kitchen floor in the house he never
wanted to leave, trying to figure out
his life. These last twenty years had
seen an incessant invasion of
celebrity privacy, Monty felt, and he
wanted no part of it—this media
hype that had devoured everything.
He did not want to be observed by
People or scrutinized by *Life*. He
certainly didn't want his home
invaded by *Entertainment Tonight*. And

it was costing him his career, or what was left of it. He hadn't worked since 1980—unless you counted the Japanese commercial for which he received a year's income. Now he was being urged to become a spokesman. Monty looked out the window while Nanny peeled potatoes for her Irish stew; he was pummeling her. Nanny was his best friend—for what was it now, twenty-eight years?—so she could take it.

"Why you?" Nanny asked him like she was asking a little boy. "Because, darling, you are the only one."

"The only one left, you mean," said Monty dryly. He was looking not at his friend, but out the window at the grotto that sat at the tip of Diamond Head and belonged—outright, completely, and forever—to him. Only the New York townhouse meant as much to Monty. He looked down at the grotto and said softly to Nanny, "No. Not one actor of my generation, as you'd call it, has had to come out. Not one had to make a case of it. Especially about being bisexual. Even the lisbons, as my mother called lesbians, are discreet. And you know why? Because they have to be. Trust me, honey."

"I do trust you," Nanny said hazily. She had said that very line to Monty maybe fifteen thousand times in the last thirty years. "I do trust you. I do love you, and so on . . . "

"But why do I have to be the first?" Monty wanted to know. The Question Machine, his friends called him. Once on a subject, Monty would not let up. Sometimes for years.

Nanny was silent. She knew Monty had a point. Unlike certain of his peers, Montgomery Clift had not married to keep up appearances. He had not fathered children to boost his ego, or save his masculinity. He had not been arrested (well, almost, but not in America). He had not flaunted and he had not had "beards"—Elizabeth Taylor was nobody's beard; she was his soulmate, and if the publicity people turned them into Hollywood's most enduringly beautiful couple, so what? Monty never employed a publicity person in his life. He had been discreet and without deceit, and he had paid. Nanny knew, Elizabeth knew, Roddy knew, maybe three or four others knew, a secretary or a hairdresser, but nobody else knew, really, what it was like to belong to that very exclusive, terribly restricted club, The Bisexuals.

"Exclusively what and restricted to whom?" as Patrick Dennis would put it. Well, most men simply had a choice to make and a moment to make it. The Club was for men without a choice, men with dual needs. It was said that the wealthiest director in the history of Hollywood belonged, and so did three of the top eleven male box office stars. So did one of the major talk show hosts. But none of this was ever said loudly.

Monty swizzled the mix of grapefruit juice and Campari that he and Nanny consumed by the pitcher. Gracefully, as a gift to her, he put two tumblers on a tray and added a bowl of macadamias. Then he curled his baby finger, a private gesture, and led Nanny toward the jacuzzi. Since Nanny's husband had died two months earlier, she was almost too stoical about things. Or maybe she was just catatonic. The Bluehouse, as Monty dubbed the Hawaii place, would be the perfect spot for Nanny to recharge. She'd loved it as he had, since the early 50s when they did time on the island during the filming of *From Here to Eternity*. Except that they were in their twelfth day, and there were only faint signs of life in her. Not that either of them had anything pressing.

But now this new twist of hers! This sudden need of Nanny's for Monty to go public! Whose idea was it? That's what Monty wondered. Nanny long ago mastered the art of not betraying confidences (a rare art in Hollywood if not Detroit). Even a dozen Campari pitchers would not get her to tell him who put her up to this ridiculous notion. They were playing splish-splash in the hundred-degree water, listening to some piped-in Billie Holiday albums, when Nanny interrupted. She anticipated his question. Or read his mind. As usual.

"It was Danny's idea," she said off-handedly.

Monty was shocked but didn't show it. "Danny?" Nanny's husband, Danny Corwin, was a member of The Club, but he was so forever happily married to Nanny that . . . "Danny?!" This time Monty did sound shocked. His voice took on the whine of his youth.

Nanny raised both her hands to stop him from starting something. "Look—it was practically his—oh, hell, this is going to sound corny—but it was practically his last wish!" Nanny took a deep sip. Since the early 60s, when Monty quit smoking and began serving drinks with straws, they never had drinks together without straws. Monty traveled with boxes of them, long before cocaine made straws a hot number in supermarkets.

"Toward the end, Danny was counseling people," said Nanny. "You know Danny. Chivalry was his third name. Anyway, he was trying to understand the dual thing, the both-ways thing. He was at an age when it no longer plagued him like it does you—forgive me, darling, but it plagues you. Anyway, Danny saw the effects. On younger men."

"I know what Danny saw in younger men," said Monty as if becoming catty on cue. "When it came to younger men,

Danny always went for the baseball bat. He was a major league player, honey."

"Shut up, Monty. You're close to drunk and beyond cruel."

"He had an ebony baseball bat in this very house once."

Nanny waited a moment, until she had his attention. "Who's afraid of Montgomery Clift?" she whispered.

"I am, Nanny, I am."

The two of them laughed in a way only the oldest friends can; it was the laugh of mutual forgiveness.

"The worst part for Danny," she went on, as if nothing had happened, "was that there were no role models. Not a single hero. Gay heroes, yes, sure, but not an openly functional bisexual hero." Nanny giggled at Monty's shenanigans. He was playing "poor me" and splashing himself. "Oh, Monty, of course you're a hero. But, darling, that's just the point. Nobody knows it."

Monty sobered up fast. "Shame on you," he said softly. A wellspring of feelings was in him now, angry feelings. How could Nanny possibly know the pain of being both ways, of aching for a woman the same night a man cradles your head and makes you cry? Even though he knew Nanny did know, through her love for Danny—and for him.

"Fuck your late husband," Monty said in the haughty manner that was his least popular trait. Even the Lunts, who'd been his sponsors, spotted in his haughtiness a pseudo-aristocratic need to be special. It was always tolerated but never easily. "Fuck Danny and fuck you and fuck my being a hero." Now he straightened up and hopped out of the jacuzzi. Suddenly, the haughtiness was gone. "Let's go to the hotel," he said.

It was their one and only ritual: At 5:00 P.M. every day they were in Hawaii, Monty and Nanny snuck into the Kahala Hilton pool to swim. There was an implicit danger to the deed. It was the kind of prank Monty used to play in younger, braver years. In the 40s he and his brother Brooks would gate crash estates in Rhode Island. Later, in the New York years, he and his friend Kev would sneak into some of the swankiest parties on the East Side, timing their entrances perfectly. Almost always they would get away with their pranks.

Monty had to swim. It was his major addiction, and his house had everything but a pool. A membership at the Kahala would have been too serious (not to say expensive). Thus the ritual. So far they'd gotten away with it, but mostly because Nanny was good at playing patrolman.

In the water, Monty would think and usually one of two things would happen: utter depression or utter relaxation. Nanny's idea—that he publicly come out, become the first American male celebrity to admit to bisexuality—was something he wanted to think about. The first bisexual role model. It would get him the cover of *People,* even without a publicist. It might even get him some decent work. Stars had to do things nowadays to maintain stardom; Jane Fonda did it with muscles, Shirley had her spiritual quest. Maybe some savvy sensitive writer would write a role for Monty, his own *Tender Mercies* or *Save the Tiger,* and put him back on the map.

Then he thought again: *Who the fuck am I kidding? I'm nobody's hero! The first half of my life was charmed, and the last half is cursed.*

Actually, the 1970s were the roughest years for Montgomery Clift. The age of the uglies—Pacino, DeNiro, Hoffman—was beyond his pale. Not able to be flagrant, like a Tennessee Williams, or completely closeted, like a Rock Hudson, Monty went out of fashion. Also out of sight and out of mind. In 1969, he'd almost gotten the Jack Nicholson role in *Easy Rider*, and when the movie became a phenomenon, Monty went into a funk that seemed to last a decade. Whereas Nicholson, straight but comfortable with his female side, became what Monty should have become: the first androgynous movie star.

It was in the 1970s when Monty became a therapy junkie, living at Malibu, seeking daily sessions with the hypnotherapist who treated zonked rock stars; seeking primal therapy; seeking EST; seeking solace from generous hostesses like Felicia Karol, the alabaster blonde who used him as an extra man, a prop at dinner parties.

"Don't talk to me about Montgomery Clift," Felicia whispered gravely in late 1986, barely a year after Monty's death. "Don't talk to me about Monty's fabled charm, his style, his patience with complex people. Frankly, Monty bored the pants off people. My husband almost left me because of the nights I devoted to Monty; the nights I sat up until dawn nursing his blues, while Willy slept in the other room solo. This was when Willy was preparing a picture or directing one . . . when a weekend at Trancas really meant relaxing. Unless Monty was around . . . Monty was like Marilyn, he really was. Willy used to say Monty and Marilyn were too talented to live. That they'd mortgaged everything—and I'm not talking money—by the time they were thirty-five. Don't talk to me about Montgomery Clift."

Felicia's husband, the legendary director Willy Karol, reached the same afternoon at his Westwood office, had a

Rashomon-like view of Monty—directly the opposite of his wife's. "Monty walked into a room and lit it, that's all. He could light a room by entering it. Men, women, dogs, everybody responded to Monty. I mean people loved him instantly. You couldn't not. Felicia loved him probably more than she loves me. You know how I know? Because she cooked his favorite dishes. Not for me did Felicia ever cook, trust me. For me the colored cook did the cooking. For Monty, Felicia cooked.

"I think I only regret one thing in terms of Monty. The night I let Felicia sit him next to that doctor, Howard Udell. Howard was sleeping with Janet Freshman for about five minutes, which is why he was at our house to begin with . . . That night he met Monty is one of my few regrets, socially speaking, I mean. Five, six years I think Monty saw him, maybe four, five times a week. The man did Monty no good. None. He didn't do anybody any good. Hell, I think he caused Janet Freshman to have a lobotomy. You sure can't call what she got a facelift."

◈

What follows is a transcript of one of Monty's sessions with Dr. Howard Udell, January 1984:

CLIFT: Tender Mercies? *Who am I kidding? You know the other day some reporter called to read me a quote from Jack Lemmon calling me the best actor of my generation. Ironic, huh? Me, who can't get a job and Jack who never stops working! Jack's a decent fellow—but explain something to me. Lemmon admitted to a drinking problem, yet it doesn't stop him. It's the Irish Virus, so what? Me, I got problems, not so different really, but I got stopped cold. See, what I really want to do is blame bullies like John Huston, but . . .*

DR. UDELL: But you can't blame anyone else. Because that's the curse of intelligence, right? You can't really blame anyone else because you know your life is your responsibility. That's what we discussed—decided—at the last session.

CLIFT: I'll buy that, Hoddie, but if it's true, then what about the TV movie on Freud. What made me fuck up the one chance I had to redo something right? Why did I make myself irresponsible?

DR. UDELL: Maybe to get even?

CLIFT: That's old bullshit. You do know I'm running out of money, don't you? Marty Kraft says I can't afford the apartment in New York anymore. Says I should get a job. Any job. So I said, "Fine, Marty, tell my agent, don't tell me." How's that for taking responsibility? How's that for buck-passing?

DR. UDELL: So it gets passed right back to you. So?

CLIFT: Hod, the last day I actually worked was how many years ago? It was the commercial in Japan, wasn't it? Yeah. Montgomery Clift in Osaka. Not since Marlon Brando in Sayonara, *as Nanny put it. Jesus, this was a Toyota commercial, not a fucking movie. And don't give me the old line about George Scott hawking Chryslers. George Scott is a millionaire with that Connecticut Yankee wife of his. By the*

*way, did that kid I took to Japan with me ever come in for
another session?*

DR. UDELL: No, Monty.

The "kid," Roger Horton, was Monty's partner in a non-
sexual "folie de deux" that probably was the real beginning of
the end. Roger was thirty years younger than Monty, but there
was something almost brotherly about the two of them. Monty's
own brother Brooks even commented on what he called the
"twin soul" quality of the relationship. Roger had an intellectual
brilliance Monty lacked, and a stability. And he cared,
authentically, for Monty and—thank God, as Nanny put it—
they were compatible without being lovers. Since their first
meeting in 1981, at a costuming conference for a movie that
never happened, the two were bound together. Mentor and son
almost. But like everything else in Monty's life, there was a
timespan. When the time had spun, Monty would find himself
disappointed, disillusioned, and "done" with Roger.

"I love Roger emotionally—I love men emotionally—but
I prefer women sexually," Monty told his doctor one day out of
the blue. Monty was wary of his friend not because Roger was
a novelist, but because of his being the catalyst. It was Roger
who originated the idea that Monty should announce his
sexuality. The idea came during one of the long margarita
nights in Roger's Benedict Canyon den. All of a sudden Roger
had become passionate on the subject of Monty's disclosure.

"I don't have a tape recorder on, Monty, and I don't stand
to gain anything. This is for free, and very simple: You can make

a difference. And you know it. You have a continuity in your life now, maybe for the first time. Personally, I think the reason you aren't working is that you haven't been, well, honest. Monty, by taking the risk, by being bold enough to come out of the closet you no longer fit in, you could . . . "

"Save the faggots of the world?" Monty was amused.

His friend Roger, who did not consider himself a faggot, was anything but amused. "Monty, you've built your own torture chamber. How many million other men do you think are bisexual?"

"A hundred million miracles?" Monty replied sarcastically. He moved over to look at the view of the mountains his friend so treasured. They both knew what he was going to say next. "I don't look good enough anymore. I mean to be a spokesman. For anything."

"That's bull, Monty," Roger said harshly. "What did *GQ* call Tom Cruise last month? A straight Montgomery Clift, and almost as timelessly handsome."

"'Enduringly' was the word used, but, Rog, it's no good. The taboo is still so strong. You know it and I know it. We can fantasize otherwise, but the world does not want us living next door."

Roger was almost winded from listening, from beating his and Monty's heads against the wall. But he found himself mysteriously committed to this idea. "Monty, your friends would be behind you. Think about that. And there looks to be a health crisis in this country."

"Here come the journalist's statistics, I'm sure." Monty yawned, for effect.

Roger now sat in front of the fireplace, fiddling with ruler-sized matches, looking at the floor. "This is what I'm thinking," he said to Monty with as much sincerity as he could muster. "It isn't so much the announcement of who or what you are sexually, it's that some of us will finally have a role model, a spokesman, a man of dignity—not to mention style—who can educate, and begin to open other people's eyes."

"Put your dreams away for another day," Monty told his friend as he gathered up his belongings and slung his trademark camera bag over his shoulder. "Write me a script, Rog. Write me a *Tender Mercies* or a *Save the Tiger.*"

"How about a 'Save the Clift?'" Roger smiled knowingly; ten more nights like this and maybe he'd get someplace with his friend. But probably not. They hugged good night anyway.

The next two weeks found Monty thinking a lot about Roger's idea. He quietly—hell, everything he did now was quiet—took himself to Palm Springs, to the house of a friend. There, the nighttime was his true friend, the deep indigo skies clearer than anywhere else. In the desert, Monty could make up his mind. It was the one place he could face his demons. On the fourth day, he called Nanny, to sound her out.

"All you are talking about are some public service announcements." Hers was the voice of sanity. "You are talking about doing commercials, that's all. I do commercials for paper towels. What's the big difference? Monty, honey, make a success of something! It's time."

The line struck a nerve. The new year had crept up with no new possibilities, none, zero, zilch, and Monty was becoming an icon only. Not even summer stock was being offered. And

1985 was for Monty the year he turned 65. It meant any day now, he could count on being one of those "respectable" film actors who get asked to speak at USC Cinema forums. Gradually, his desert tan darkened and his face took on that irresistible, undeniable all-appealing handsomeness—years fell away. One night at a new little bar on Palm Canyon, he ran into Dr. Bruno Bernard (Bruno of Hollywood). Bruno had photographed Monty on his first picture, and he was the last photographer on the set of *The Misfits*. Consequently, the two of them had a history that transcended the years between.

"My boy, you look like a movie star!" the European charmer said with his best charm-boy accent. Bruno was on the brink of celebrating his seventy-fifth birthday at a Hollywood gala. A visit to Switzerland had made him look fifty.

Monty smiled broadly at the old man and the memories they shared. "It's you who looks like a movie star," Monty said softly. "I look like a desert rat!"

Monty bought Bruno another drink, and they recollected how shamelessly he used to preen for Bruno's camera, how savvy he was from the start about his still photos! About how he looked! Now Bruno was over seventy, but it was Monty who was over-the-hill. Forty-five minutes later, when Bruno invited Monty to his house to look at old stills, Monty said yes without even caring if he ever saw a picture of himself again.

"My boy, you were—you are—the crème of my crème," Bruno said lovingly as he began opening boxes of stills marked "1940s late" and "1950s early." "You and Marilyn were my pets, my beauties . . . "

"That's because Elizabeth Taylor favored Johnny Bryson!"

Monty was flattered, and he laughed a little self-consciously. Monty was almost in his cups, but while Bruno liked to reminisce, he didn't much like to listen—he never had. Which meant Monty could say anything and not worry. Bruno was (in the best sense) like the makeup people at the studio in the old days. At four in the morning under hot lights you told them everything and they told nobody. Even today none of them had written a kiss-and-tell book, thank God.

That was the best part of Old Hollywood, Monty thought to himself. The mornings weren't terrifying. There was always somebody to take care of you. Your face, your clothes, there were people to talk to, to trust.

When he left Bruno's ranch house, it was 4:30 in the morning. The old man was a walking encyclopedia of the movie industry—his Racquet Club candids of Tracy and Gable playing chess were worth thousands. In Bruno's kind face Monty saw his youth, his promise. People who possess such promise know its value—they might forget temporarily—but they know what they have.

Monty didn't go to bed that night, preferring instead to wait for the sunrise. When the time was not unrealistic, he phoned Roger, who was in New York to meet with editors. Naturally, he woke Roger. Waking him was like having coffee in the morning. It was a ritual.

"I think I'm ready," Monty said, not even apologizing for the early hour or pausing for a reaction. His voice was nervous but not unsure. "Rog, I think I'm ready. Jane Fonda has exercise and Streisand has Judaism. I've decided a star has to keep his hold on the public no matter what. So how do we orchestrate now?"

"You must be very tan," Roger said groggily. "What you do is fly to New York, like tomorrow. I'll set up meetings for the end of next week with the media wizards. All you do is call Elizabeth."

"Elizabeth?" said Monty, taken aback. "Why Elizabeth?"

"Jesus, Monty, you do live under a rock. No pun intended. Have you read a newspaper in the last century?"

Monty was impatient now. "Roger, what are you talking about?"

"Rock Hudson is in Paris dying of AIDS."

Monty hung up. That night he drove back to Los Angeles. He decided to keep it simple: only a carry-on bag for once in his life. He had booked himself an inside single at the Bergere in a part of Paris where nobody knew anybody. Claire Trevor, a mutual friend, was the only American in Paris who'd been visiting Rock. Monty would ask Claire to help edit his piece. God knows, she was a bright woman, and right-minded. The piece would go from Claire to Roger to *Esquire*—no Nanny, no Dr. Udell—not even Elizabeth would be involved. Monty had written it in a single sitting, after hanging up with Roger. He reread it once but refused to look at it again. It said how Monty felt—about Hollywood, about himself, about his sexuality. When he'd finished it, he breathed differently.

For the first time in his life Montgomery Clift was not ambivalent.

AMELIA
EARHART

BY   ARMAND   DEUTSCH
&   SUSAN   GRANGER

*A*melia Earhart was exhausted. She and her navigator, Fred Noonan, had just left New Guinea on the next leg of her much-publicized effort to become the first woman to circumnavigate the globe along the equator line, covering a staggering 29,595 miles. The daring adventure had already taken her halfway around the globe, capturing front-page attention and affectionate support everywhere she went.

Their July 2, 1937 destination was tiny Howland Island in the vast

Pacific Ocean, some 2,500 miles from New Guinea. Amelia knew full well it was the chanciest leg of the trip. Howland Island was only on her flight plan because the Navy Department had specifically requested that she consider it. They wanted to establish an airfield in this remote outpost, and building one for Amelia Earhart would arouse no suspicions. The Navy would dispatch a ship to the area to guide her. She knew the risks; it was up to her. Amelia was a skilled, highly trained pilot. She had great faith that the Lockheed Corporation had never produced a finer private plane than the small Electra they had custom built for this trip. Noonan was an intrepid navigator, and he repeatedly assured her that, in daylight, with radio assistance, he could find the mere speck of land that was Howland Island. Despite the skepticism of many of her fellow aviators, Amelia elected to follow the route the Navy has suggested.

The flight had started smoothly enough. As she looked down at the endless ocean beneath her, Amelia thought back on the extraordinary career that had brought her to this time and place. Her love, actually, her obsession, with aviation had come upon her early in life. She became the first female passenger to cross the Atlantic Ocean by air, then the first woman to fly solo across the Atlantic, going from Newfoundland to Ireland, and the first woman to solo from Hawaii to California. All this in addition to various continental records. Now she was closing in on her greatest triumph, which, she had already declared to the press, would be her "final record-breaking flight."

Although she had been sitting for twenty hours in the same rigid upright cockpit seat, unable to stretch her limbs, her spirits were high. She began to receive radio calls from the

Navy ship *Itasca,* assigned as her escort. She was "heading for home." For the last several hours, the plane had been buffeted by heavy head winds so they were behind in their flight plan, but it was vital they reach Howland in daylight. The messages from the *Itasca* were coming in loud and clear; they were picking her up perfectly.

All this changed in an instant. The *Itasca* messages suddenly had great gaps and were hopelessly garbled. A dreadful reality hit Amelia: Her radio reception gear was broken. The radiomen aboard the *Itasca* were frantic. Her messages were reaching them, but they quickly realized they were not getting through to her.

She and Noonan were on their own. "When I go," she had often said, "I would like best to go in my plane. Quickly." *But not yet. So much ocean,* she thought, battling panic and despair. They were losing daylight rapidly, and their fast-dwindling gas supply would not permit an endless search for the island.

She sent a frantic Mayday radio message: "We must be circling you but cannot see you. Gas running low." For agonizing minutes she flew onward. Suddenly sputtering, the tiny Electra plummeted toward the water. Amelia knew she should keep the undercarriage retracted, but being out of fuel, she had to pull a dead-stick forced landing. Even over smooth seas, it is difficult to judge a plane's height above the water's surface. If she stalled too high, the impact would kill them both. But these seas were rough with waves of four to six feet. She lowered the flaps and tried to glide smoothly, but the impact was tremendous. In the ditching process, Amelia's head hit the sharp-cornered casing of the instrument panel, momentarily stunning her. Miraculously, she was still alive, but because of the weight of the engines and empty fuel tanks, the Electra was nose down, tail up. Since the cockpit hatch was underwater, she scrambled up the almost vertical slope of the fuel tanks, clutching the life raft and emergency equipment stowed in the fuselage. Gasping, she forced the cabin door open and started to inflate the two-man raft with capsules of carbon dioxide, but the rubber slipped from her hands into the black, undulating sea. With no other choice, she jumped after it, grabbing the raft and continuing the inflation process. "Noonan!" Where was Noonan? Amelia called his name over and over. Water gushed in the air vents in the fuel tanks, and within eight minutes, the Electra sank.

Commander Warner Thompson of the *Itasca* quickly estimated from Amelia's final transmission that she was twenty miles northwest of Howland. In a relatively short time, he spotted her orange kite and green emergency flares. Within moments, she was lifted into the *Itasca*'s lifeboat. There was no trace of Fred Noonan. Upon reaching the ship, Amelia was gently hoisted onto the deck, as members of the crew lined the rail. The medical officer, Captain William Smith, took her pulse. He found it irregular and weak but beating. A cheer went up! Amelia Earhart was alive.

The commander's cabin was transformed into her hospital room, and Amelia drifted between consciousness and unconsciousness. Because of the spartan medical facilities on board, Dr. Smith was limited to the most cursory medical examinations, and Amelia would need detailed tests that he could not possibly make. "I believe she can survive," he told

Commander Thompson, "but we have to get to a top mainland hospital as soon as possible." As the *Itasca* sailed at full speed for Los Angeles, Amelia's home and the nearest mainland port, busy radiomen broadcast full reports of Amelia Earhart's amazing rescue at sea.

During the two-week voyage, Amelia lay as quietly as the rolling ship would permit. It was no problem to make her drink water, since she had a low fever and was constantly thirsty. Food and solid nourishment were another matter. She had to be virtually force-fed.

Somewhat to her surprise, her waking thoughts were mainly of her husband. Dear George! George Putnam had pursued her from the moment they met. Love, even the thought of marriage, had never been a priority. From childhood, her sole obsession had been planes and flying. She lived in a world of men. They were her colleagues. Any relationships had been of the most casual sort. But George's persistence had worn her down. She knew he would love her, help her to finance her flights—a never-ending worry—and manage the time-consuming details of her life. Repeatedly, and again on the day they married, February 7, 1931, she made it perfectly clear that she was fond of him but could promise no more. They had a partnership, she reflected, and it worked well. George would be there to meet her when the *Itasca* docked, and he would make all the hospital arrangements. Amelia cared for her husband more at that moment than she ever had.

Despite her efforts to calm her fears, Amelia thought of the medical examinations looming ahead. Her bruised body tormented her, particularly the throbbing of her left leg.

When the *Itasca* docked at midnight, the press swarmed over the pier. George came to Amelia's stateroom immediately. The sight of him was an enormous relief. She was no longer alone. Amelia managed a wave to the photographers, whose flash cameras captured her being carried off the ship on a stretcher and whisked by ambulance to Good Samaritan Hospital. Despite the hour, Dr. Charles Voss, the chief of staff, greeted her. In record time, she was in a bed and sound asleep.

Early the next morning, Dr. Voss appeared. "I have read Captain Smith's report. I don't need to tell you that the good Lord had his arms around you. A betting man would have put your survival chances at one thousand to one, but you're here and we've got to start rigorous testing immediately. Do you understand?"

Amelia agreed, eager for answers herself. For several days, she was probed and examined "from stem to stern," as Dr. Smith on the *Itasca* had predicted. Dr. Voss had explained that she would not receive direct, individual reports from each doctor. All results would be turned over to him for evaluation.

When the process was completed, Dr. Voss spoke with Amelia and George together. "You're more fortunate than I ever dared to hope. You will need a long period of quiet and recuperation. With physical therapy, I believe even your left leg will recover, although you will have to walk with a cane for a while and the leg may always bother you in bad weather." He paused and continued as gently as he could. "Amelia, our eye doctor did find a slight but incorrectible loss of depth perception. You will live normally, except that you will never be able to drive a car or pilot a plane." As Dr. Voss rose to leave the room, he patted her hand, adding, "Remember, you have lived to tell the tale. You are lucky, Lady Lindy." He was referring to the popular nickname given her due to her uncanny, almost familial resemblance to Charles Lindbergh.

Amelia and George were silent, although tears rolled down her cheeks. They both knew she had been given the nearest thing to a death sentence.

The next morning, George drove Amelia to their Toluca Lake home. They had originally purchased two lots on a golf course and built a smallish, pleasant bungalow. However, George had managed her business affairs well. Her lectures, endorsements, and writing had enabled them to add a handsome addition, consisting of a double study, master bedroom, guest room, and staff quarters. Amelia knew she would be comfortable and cared for, but she had nothing to do from morning to night except work with her physical therapist. For a long period, it didn't matter; she was not physically or mentally prepared for any other activity. She appreciated the affection that surrounded her but lapsed into extended periods of grim silence. Prone to irritation, sometimes George's hovering proved too much, and she had to fight not to express her annoyance.

Amelia sought a second, then a third, opinion about her eyesight, hoping against hope for a reprieve. The results were always the same: Her depth perception was gone. When Amelia left the hospital, George told the press that her doctors had predicted a full recovery. He promised that Amelia would meet with them as soon as she was able. Now he felt the time had come, and she agreed. The press had been in her corner from the start. Of the many questions that bombarded her, two got to the heart of the matter. One reporter asked how difficult it was for her to give up piloting a plane. She answered, "Extremely. It has been the passion of my life. My survival is a miracle, so I remain an optimist. I will never give up hope." Another asked what she considered her greatest achievement. "Not the records," she answered. "Perhaps I've been able to convince some women to broaden their horizons." These responses made headlines.

After the press conference, Amelia seemed to withdraw even further. Always a voracious reader, she turned to books, although she could not bear to look at the aviation journals which in the past had been a staple for her. Instead, she devoured endless detective stories, losing herself in their intricate plots. She also loved movies but only went to them in the early afternoon when attendance was small. Sympathizers made her uncomfortable.

Finally, her hours of physical therapy began to show results. Her appetite increased and her emaciated body began to resemble the trim figure the public remembered. Her state of mind, though, did not keep pace. She worried about what she would do when her strength and health returned. Her doctor, a longtime friend, gave her sound counsel. "Amelia," he said, "you are in the fight of your life. You cannot allow yourself to become habitually depressed. You must try to find an interest that will help you get through this crisis."

This seemed impossible to Amelia but not to the indefatigable George. The next day he said to her, "The doctor says you're well enough to travel. Let's go to New York. The

Mayor has never stopped badgering me about the parade they want to give you. I think it would be a tonic, but more importantly, Fielder Publishers has offered an astounding advance for your autobiography. We can meet with them when we're in the east. You write well, and I think it could be a wonderful project." Amelia agreed, although mustering enthusiasm wasn't easy. What right, she thought, did she have to refuse this man whose only desire was to help and please her?

A week later, they took the train to New York. George had suggested flying, but Amelia was not ready for it, and she enjoyed watching the country roll by. As always, she thought how different it looked at eye level than it did from the sky.

On arriving in New York, they went directly to their hotel. The next morning, a limousine whisked them to City Hall, where, promptly at 11:00 A.M., Mayor LaGuardia greeted Amelia and presented her with the Key to the City and a scroll proclaiming "Amelia Earhart Day." She was escorted to a large white Cadillac convertible that proceeded to Battery Park. Placed at the head of a long line of cars, Amelia perched, in the time-honored tradition, high on the backseat with the mayor and George flanking her on either side.

When the cars pulled out, Amelia was greeted with a deafening roar from the throngs packing the streets and leaning from skyscraper windows. Ticker tape poured down on her. For an instant, she sat frozen, incredulous at being the center of this uniquely New York City experience. In wonderment, she waved back, looking from side to side. *What, she thought, have I done to deserve all this? Failure has never been so richly rewarded. I only wish they were honoring the completion of my flight—and now it can never happen.* But George had been right. The buoyancy and excitement of the crowds, so eager to honor her courage, made her spirits soar. At the parade's conclusion, she thanked the mayor, saying sincerely, "I will never forget this." And she never did.

The following morning, Roger Fielder, president of Fielder Publishers, appeared at their hotel, accompanied by a pleasant-looking young man, Mark Elder, described by Fielder as "brilliant—and the man I hope will be your editor." Fielder told her, "It is our job to imbue you with all the excitement of yesterday's parade. This is a great opportunity for us. Your autobiography will be that rarity in the publishing business—a book that everybody will want."

The total confidence of her publisher and his knowledge of her aviation achievements gave Amelia the extra push she needed to sign the contract. "Now," she told George with a slight frown, "the only thing left is to write the book."

Before leaving for California, she had a long conference with Mark Elder and they hit it off from the start. "You will find that writing a book is hard," he told her. "My job is to help you. I'll make suggestions as I get your material. Those that you like, you'll use. We'll talk on the phone regularly. I'll come to California whenever you need me. Remember, your flying career has fascinated everybody. Our job is to put the reader in your shoes on every page. If we do that, there will never be a dull moment. You and I may have a battle or two along the way, but that's healthy. This is the most exciting assignment I've ever had." His enthusiasm was contagious.

Amelia began the outline of her book on the train home. "Thank goodness I have always kept diaries," she told George.

Her method of work developed quickly. First, she made copious notes from her diaries. Then she did a rough draft, and worked and reworked the material she sent to Mark. Writing made her concentrate, leaving little time for self-pity. George had said it would be a tonic and it was. Mark had predicted that the book would take two years, but in eighteen months, Fielder Publications accepted her final draft.

Amelia's job was done, and she was determined not to sink back into the routine of early-afternoon movies and empty days. So, when an invitation arrived from the White House to a State Dinner honoring the British prime minister, Winston Churchill, Amelia urged George to accept immediately. They speculated that Churchill was coming to the United States to personally report the grim war news to the president, hoping to urge him to join the British against the Nazis.

Amelia was also eager to renew her acquaintance with Eleanor Roosevelt. Several years before, when the first lady had expressed a desire to fly over the Capitol on a clear night, Amelia had called a friend at the Washington airport and arranged for a small plane. The two women, like conspirators, raced from a White House dinner to a waiting car. There were no Secret Service men to impede Mrs. Roosevelt. She refused to have a bodyguard and was resolutely determined to see and do what she wanted. With Amelia, still wearing a long evening dress, as her pilot, the first lady went aloft to admire the lights of the city. Both women relished this secret escapade. At a time when most Americans still thought flying too dangerous, Eleanor Roosevelt delighted in leading the way.

When Amelia and George checked into the Willard Hotel, the manager greeted them, and the staff and guests in the quiet, ornate lobby took note. "She has the aura of a movie star," observed the concierge, who was accustomed to celebrity guests. Returning to the lobby en route to the White House, people commented on how stunning Amelia looked in a high-necked, long-sleeved gown of shimmering green satin. The mirror told her the same thing, but she never believed it. Slacks and boots, she felt, were more her style.

On entering the White House, Amelia and George paused briefly, feeling a moment of awe. To see the president's house was a momentous occasion, but to be a guest for a State Dinner was truly an honor. The White House ushers formed the guests into a line, and as the Marine Corps band broke into the stirring "Hail to the Chief," the president, Mrs. Roosevelt, and Winston Churchill appeared. The guests moved forward, receiving a handshake from each. When Amelia reached the prime minister, he leaned toward her, saying, "I followed your progress, as did everyone on our side of the Atlantic. I breathed a sigh of relief that you were spared. You are a pioneer." Deeply touched by the prime minister's extravagant praise, she murmured her thanks and moved on.

Shortly after dinner, an usher approached her. "Miss Earhart, the prime minister would like to talk to you." Surprised, she was led to a small room where Churchill was holding court, a brandy in one hand and a cigar clamped firmly in his teeth. "My dear, I have an official invitation for you," he began, motioning for her to sit down next to him. "Please come over to our island. You will find we admire you as much as the

Americans. You can perform a unique service. I want you to tour some of our RAF bases and meet the brave young lads who fly in the face of great odds. You would be a morale booster. Perhaps you will catch their spirit and report it to your countrymen." He signaled to an aide. Introducing the two, he said, "This is Major Percy Worthington. Miss Earhart, it will be Major Worthington who will greet you in England. I want you to see a familiar face on your arrival."

Back at the hotel, Amelia told George of this extraordinary invitation. "Do it," he suggested instantly. "Do not underestimate yourself. You have a unique contribution to make." Amelia agreed, realizing that, beginning tonight, her life might once again resonate with purpose. "I'm going," she said, more to herself than to George. "I'm definitely going."

The very next day, she informed Major Worthington, who arranged for Amelia to make the crossing on the *Queen Mary*, which had been reoutfitted for war and was leaving New York in a week. While she was told of the risk of German U-boat and submarine activity, Amelia was certain that the danger could not compare with that of her plane crash and remained undaunted. As instructed, there was no fanfare as Amelia reported to Cunard Pier 90 for departure. Guards patrolled the pier to secure the ship from sabotage, and at night, powerful searchlights played blue-white beams over its hulls and decks. United States intelligence officials had been warned that German agents might take advantage of America's neutrality to plant bombs aboard. The *Queen Mary* sailed in blackout with radio silence.

On board the giant ship, which had been painted a dull gray, the 400 crewmen rattled around the vast spaces designed to hold more than 3,500 people. Amelia had a first-class cabin to herself, if anything could be called first-class on that ship. "We had no carpets, just bare floors, no heating, and the light fixtures were just hanging wires," she wrote in her diary. The most dangerous stretch of the voyage, she was told, was off Ireland, where U-boats congregated to attack heavy traffic funneling into or streaming out of the ports. It was a tense crossing.

Since the Channel route was far too treacherous, the "gray ghost," as the ship was nicknamed, docked at Gourock in Scotland, where Amelia was met, as promised, by Major Worthington, who bore a brief note of welcome from the prime minister. He escorted her to a car with diplomatic plates and they made the long trip to London, which would be her base. Although she had read about the blitz, Amelia was stunned at the change. England was at war, and Americans did not realize the severity of the situation. Food was scarce, petrol scarcer. Skeletons of bombed-out buildings loomed everywhere. Amelia immediately felt the urgency of her visit. If meeting her could boost even one pilot's morale, it was the least she could do. *I could do even more,* she reminded herself. *Churchill wanted me to be a messenger, telling people back home what is really happening in Europe. This is a unique opportunity.*

So Amelia, escorted by Major Worthington, embarked on her task of visiting as many RAF bases as possible. The prime minister had been right. At every base, pilots and crews greeted the famous American flyer eagerly and thanked her for being there. Some of them said, quite pointedly, "Tell your Yanks to come on over. We need them." Each night, Amelia dutifully wrote her detailed observations in a diary, determined to send a report to President Roosevelt that would make a difference.

One hot, humid August afternoon, as Amelia toured the base at Salisbury, she realized she was being observed, almost scrutinized, by a tall, lean Englishman with broad shoulders and a finely chiseled face, distinguished by a cleft in his chin. He quickly came forward to greet Major Worthington. The major murmured an introduction to Lord Michael Howard, which she barely heard. Amelia's unfaltering ease and grace gave way to a vague yet almost pleasurable sense of discomfort under his gaze. She was riveted by his blue eyes, which never for a moment left her face. They shook hands and hers inexplicably trembled. She turned to move on but whirled around again as he murmured, "Dinner tonight?" in a courtly voice as smooth as heirloom silver. "Yes," she said, without a second's hesitation. Her heart was pounding, her face flushed. What was happening?

Dinner at a nearby pub, the Golden Lion, was the beginning, their beginning. It was as if their lives began that night and whatever came before was only a prelude. Michael was utterly, completely charming, a great raconteur, with marvelous manners and a wonderful sense of humor. His calm matched hers. He hated to hurry, as did she. And like her, his concentration was so complete that he could only do one thing at a time. Their hands intertwined naturally. As they left the pub, he gently stroked her soft honey-blonde cropped hair, "like cornsilk," he whispered. Amelia laughed out loud. "Cornsilk is straight, Michael, not curly." His lips stopped her laughter. A fine, warm rain started, but neither of them noticed.

Michael spied an inn, the "Braxton Arms," and indicated the sign to Amelia. She hesitated a moment. She had never done this before. *What about George?* she thought. He was so kind, so unquestioning in his loyalty. But she had never felt like this with George, never eager with desire. Suddenly shivering, she decided she could not, would not leave Michael tonight.

Once in the blessed privacy of their room, Michael slowly untied the red scarf around Amelia's neck and peeled off her white silk blouse, gently kissing every inch of her body. Gingerly, she stepped out of her brown flyer's pants and high-laced boots. She was tall and slim with a boyish figure. Michael gasped; he had never seen anyone so lovely, so incredibly vulnerable. Amelia was instantly his, more completely than she had ever allowed herself to belong to anyone before. Perhaps it was the alacrity of their attraction, perhaps it was the imminent danger of another bombing. Whatever the explanation, Amelia's body and spirit soared on earth for the first time as it had so often when she was in the air. "My God, I'm so incredibly happy," she said aloud, breathless with wonderment, "but, Michael . . ."

"No buts," he silenced her. "We have tonight. I fly tomorrow."

"And then?" she asked with dismay. "I'll be at a base in Romsey."

"You can always go back to London. I'll find a flat for us there," he assured her. "Whenever I stand down, we'll be together."

"Promise?" she implored, tracing the cleft in his chin with her fingertips. "Just the two of us, alone."

"Amelia, I'm yours," he declared seriously, cupping her chin, probing her level gray eyes, "till death—whenever that is."

The next two weeks alternately crawled and flew by. Amelia was plagued by guilt about deceiving George yet frantic when Michael was flying a mission. She startled staid Major Worthington on more than one occasion by demanding to know which RAF squadron was in the air, which had suffered casualties, and which had returned safely, every pilot accounted for.

The Germans were bombing England nightly. London was the principal target, but no location was safe. RAF planes shot down as many Messerschmitts as possible over the Channel, but far too many got through, and casualties were so high that Churchill declared, "Never have so many owed so much to so few."

When Michael and Amelia were together, time unmercifully slipped by. With death never very far away, a few minutes, a few inches, perhaps, it was all the more exciting to be alive. One morning, after they had spent the night clinging to one another, wrapped in a blanket in London's Underground as the eerie, pilotless buzz bombs crashed around them, Michael found a single long-stemmed yellow rose, Amelia's favorite, and had it wrapped in sprigs of rosemary. "Rosemary, that's for remembrance," he explained, quoting Ophelia as she implores Hamlet, "Pray you love, remember." "How can I forget?" Amelia responded.

They both realized that her mission was soon to end. "Michael, I have to go home. I must make sure President Roosevelt gets my report. And there's George . . . he has been so wonderful to me over the years. But, Michael, know this: I thought I had lost the love of my life—flying—but, in you, I have found a new love." Then, Amelia confided to him that she had insisted on taking the train when she traveled between California and New York because she could not bear to fly.

"Amelia, my love," Michael promised her. "I don't know how. I don't know where. But you will fly again—you will fly with me."

Major Worthington escorted Amelia to her homeward voyage and gave her a note of gratitude from the prime minister. This time, Amelia sailed on Cunard's almost empty, untried, and unfinished *Queen Elizabeth,* which, under secret orders and a broadcast barrage of propaganda meant to divert both German and British attention, began a zigzag crossing to New York.

Amelia used the rough crossing to write her report. It was a test of will, since she missed Michael every moment, but she was determined to have it completed so it could be mailed from New York. Morale, she reported, in the RAF and throughout England, was high, despite the destructive and frightening nightly bombings and the possibility of imminent invasion. The British would, as their leader said, "fight to the last man, if necessary." She wrote of the criticism she heard on all sides concerning United States neutrality and the constant urging to "come on in! It's your fight, too." She concluded by respectfully expressing grave doubts that Great Britain could hold out alone indefinitely.

Five days and nineteen hours later, the huge gray liner turned up in the Narrows of the Hudson River. Amelia then boarded a train for California. Alone in her compartment, the impact of how completely her life had changed since she had last crossed the continent hit her with full force. She was hopelessly in love. Nothing in her life had prepared her for the ache that would not leave her. *These are the emotions of a schoolgirl,* she thought wryly, *and I am flying without a compass.*

How little she really knew of Michael. Of war-torn London, she knew more. Casual romances were a way of life. The field was particularly open to RAF pilots. What meant everything to her could mean far less to him. In any event, her marriage to George was, in itself, an insurmountable barrier. Perhaps, she thought, it would be wiser to end it here and forever hold on to her memories.

But it was a course she was unable to follow. She simply could not resist writing. She longed to pour her heart out but knew it would be wrong to give Michael, living in daily danger, a sense of obligation. In the end she wrote a brief note:

> *Michael, dear,*
> *You made London a high point of my life. I will never forget it. I must tell you that returning to the life of a married lady will not be easy.*
> *Please write me so I can know that at least on the day you mail your letters you are alive. I need that. I am going to take a post office box; the number and the address will be on the attached card.*
> *My love,*
> *A.*

Upon her arrival home, she learned from George that her book, *Amelia Earhart: My Story,* was a runaway best-seller. She was in great demand and filled as many requests as possible. It gave her the opportunity to stand publicly against her fellow aviator and national hero, Charles A. Lindbergh, spokesman for the isolation of America. Amelia convincingly expressed her views that the United

States could not stand by but must enter the war against the Nazis. The conflict between Lindy and "Lady Lindy" was fodder for the press. She became a rallying point for entering the conflict.

Lecture fees, endorsement fees, and book royalties poured in. She was becoming wealthy beyond her wildest dreams. Despite George's warm, affectionate guiding of her blossoming career, it all seemed like make-work to her. The high point of her life was visiting the mailbox. She started looking for letters far too soon, since she knew the mails were painfully slow. Each time she saw the empty box, her heart sank. *Life without flying and without Michael,* she thought sadly, *is like living on a salt-free diet. It can be done, but it is dreary.*

Finally, she received a letter. Her heart racing, she opened it on the spot. Michael wrote:

> *London with you was superb. I shall never forget it. I, of course, understand your position. Please do not stop writing. I shall always answer.*
>> *Michael*

Amelia realized he had modeled his letter after her own. More importantly, on the date of the postmark, he was alive and well. She answered the same day. He never failed to respond. The style of their correspondence had been set. She read into his brief notes all she dared and they sustained her.

On December 7, 1941, the United States declared war on Germany as well as Japan. Despite the tragedy of Pearl Harbor, Amelia was thrilled. Her hope for her country's participation had become a reality. She was confident that America's entrance into the conflict would shorten the war and increase Michael's chances for survival.

Almost a year to the day later, George, sitting at his office desk, keeled forward unconscious. Emergency life-saving measures were to no avail. George Putnam, who had meant so much to Amelia in so many ways, had suffered a massive heart attack and was dead. While he had never been her true love, she deeply mourned her husband and friend. She received hundreds of letters of condolence. Everyone George had ever known thought highly of him and praised the unfailing support he had given her.

In the days after George's funeral, Amelia became guilt-ridden as her thoughts turned to Michael. She wanted desperately to write him but could not bring herself to do it. She was free now and it felt to her like begging. The press had thoroughly covered George's death, and she could only hope that the news had appeared in London's newspapers.

Some weeks later, she found a letter in her mailbox. It read:

Amelia, dear,
I read of your loss. Blows of this kind are always difficult and I am sorry. It is, however, in my nature to think of the future.

I chose not to tell you that sometime back I took a little flak in my right leg. Though it is already well on the mend, the RAF sacked me. The whole thing has gotten me a bit down. I implore you, as soon as it is decently possible, please come back. I need you.

Michael

Michael had flown hundreds of missions and been shot down twice before, once over the North Sea, where he was rescued by a trawler, and again when he bailed out of his bullet-riddled Hurricane. He had received numerous medals, a Distinguished Service Order, and two Distinguished Flying Crosses for gallantry. Now he needed her.

Amelia immediately realized that this was a turning point in her life. The decision was hers, and at first it frightened her. His letter had made no mention of marriage.

Years before, she had penned a poem—"Courage."

"Courage is the price that life extracts for granting peace," she wrote. "The soul that knows it not, knows no release from little things." It was the essence of Amelia. She knew she had to join Michael and take her chances with the future. She met with her attorney, instructed him that she might be gone for a long time, and prepared a will.

Arranging permission for a civilian to cross the Atlantic on a Navy warship was virtually impossible, but Amelia would not give up. Finally, her name and fame, and perhaps a discreet suggestion from Mrs. Roosevelt, prevailed. Through a circuitous route, she was able to indicate her arrival information to Michael.

On landing, the first thing Amelia spied was Michael's gaunt but handsome face with its tilted smile. He walked toward her with a slight limp, carrying a mammoth bouquet of yellow roses and sprigs of rosemary. Enveloping her in a hug, he said simply, "Welcome."

"Where do we go from here?" Amelia inquired.

"To Lytton Hall in Wickshire. It has been my home all my life. Now it will be our home."

Amelia's eyes were moist. He had, very casually, proposed to her. *How British,* she thought. "It's a big decision," she said, burying her face in his chest. "I shall have to think about it carefully for at least five minutes."

The corner of Michael's mouth quirked up in a smile, and he bent over to kiss the top of Amelia's head. "I am in a generous mood. I shall give you ten minutes, but I do hope your answer is in the affirmative. It was not my plan to take you back to the Braxton Arms." As he supervised the porter handling her luggage, he added, "In my favor is the fact that on this dock you cannot be out of my sight."

They were, for the most part, silent as they drove through the countryside. Michael said only, "I have dreamed of this every day of my life since you left London. Of course, I never thought it would happen."

"It was the same for me," she replied quietly.

"We're here," Michael announced, veering from an unpaved country road into a long beautiful tree-lined driveway which finally exposed Lytton Hall. Sweeping steps of some fifteen feet led to a massive wooden doorway with glass and leaded panes above. The huge Georgian-type windows commanded a splendid view of a rose garden and the vast fields surrounding the house. A little brook that ran along the far side of the house was sparkling clean with sheep, ewes, and lambs standing on its bank.

The house itself was of old brick, with very high ceilings, and proportions that made one feel smaller when going from room to room. Huge fireplaces were ablaze, giving each room a cozy and definitely welcoming glow.

"This is a virtual palace," Amelia said breathlessly, genuinely stunned. "Is this truly your home?"

"Our home," he corrected her. "I am the ninth generation of Howards to live here. Managing this estate is my business."

Lytton Hall, she would learn, was an immense working farm. Amelia shook her head in bewilderment. *How American,* she thought. She had fallen in love with a man, neither knowing nor caring who he was or where he came from. His lineage was the furthest thing from her mind.

"Tomorrow we will go into Wickshire and be married," he said as a tea tray was brought in by Jerome—the butler who had steadfastly maintained Lytton Hall during Michael's years away at war—along with single-malt whiskey in a decanter with glasses. "I have arranged for our wedding to be at the church vicarage. It is private and will be simple. Also, for the first time in my life, I have hired someone to cope with the press on behalf of my famous bride. It has been agreed that there will be photographers outside the Vicarage but no reporters. A statement of our marriage will be circulated." He grinned. "Not bad for a beginner, huh?" Amelia smiled and nodded. "Not bad at all."

During the simple service, Amelia knew a happiness she had never felt. She realized that this moment was the high point of her life. Newspaper photographs showed Michael and the new Lady Howard beaming with joy leaving the church in a misty rain.

Although American to the core, she developed a kinship to Michael's England from the start. She felt as if a miracle had happened to her. Michael urged her to make any changes to Lytton Hall she desired, but she had no intention of changing the stately manor. She grew used to the absence of closets and, in fact, enjoyed the huge cumbersome wardrobes, although she told Michael she could never understand how American antique dealers were able to sell those cavernous chests for such outrageous prices.

For their first Christmas together, Michael tried to re-create the old, traditional rituals at Lytton Hall. An enormous table was placed in the front hallway and gifts laid out on it. The contents of the boxes reflected the parsimony of war, with both Amelia and Michael giving their own possessions to friends: books, cigarette cases, trinkets, and small pieces of jewelry.

As time passed, Amelia's happiness took deeper root, and her love for Michael grew steadily. She developed a warm friendship with his maternal aunt, Lady Patricia, who occupied a large grace-and-favor apartment at Kensington Palace and yearned for their visits. Despite the exigencies of the war, the Howards enjoyed London, discovering many shared friends, including Amy Phipps Guest, heiress to a Pittsburgh steel fortune and wife of the former British air minister, and Lady Nancy Astor, the former Nancy Langhorne of Virginia, who married Viscount Waldorf Astor and became the first woman to sit as a member of Parliament.

They occasionally visited the chic 400 Club in Leicester Square, the Café de Paris, and the Savoy on the Strand. Writing in her diary, Amelia observed, "Along with the feeling of a certain Allied victory now, it is as if everyone wants to be with everyone else, as if every minute in the present is terribly important, and the future—what will happen after the war—is very vague, very hazy, almost unreal."

But the war did come to an end—at least in Europe. On the morning of May 8, 1945, Amelia and Michael rode their horses through intense, Wagnerian rain to join the entire village of Wickshire to celebrate Germany's unconditional surrender to the Allies in Reims, France. By then, Amelia, dressed in her familiar brown riding breeches, had become a familiar face, impressing those who met her with her natural intelligence, cheerful humor, and quick smile. Women activists were rare in rural England, but she could not change completely. She worked for the reform of local legitimacy laws and other causes. Michael was proud of her, and before too long, the villagers felt the same way. When the young Girl Guides asked her to be their honorary leader, she accepted with pleasure.

The welcome noises of reconstruction reverberated throughout war-ravaged London. Street lamps again illuminated the night and people went out without worrying that a bomb was headed in their direction. Lord and Lady Howard, however, much preferred their life in the country.

Michael's treasured family portraits and collection of pastoral paintings in gilt frames were rehung on the walls, the crystal chandeliers reinstalled, and the fine objets d'art, including Chinese and European porcelains, replaced inside their glass-fronted vitrines. Large boxes filled with the Howard family crystal and china were retrieved from their "hide-outs" and unpacked. Amelia sometimes polished a beautiful "find" with her handkerchief as she uncovered the contents of yet another crate. She chose new fabrics of cream and her favorite brown with coordinated floral designs for the furniture, and, with Michael's enthusiastic approval, supervised converting the former lily pond into a swimming pool. The bracing smell of turpentine and fresh paint was in the air.

On July 4, Independence Day in America, Michael awakened Amelia with the "Star-Spangled Banner" on the gramophone and the news that he had a "surprise" in the works for her.

"What kind of surprise?" she responded eagerly.

"You'll see," he promised. "After breakfast, we'll take the horses. I have something to show you."

Luxuriating in the rising heat of the summer morning, they rode leisurely into a once-deserted pasture where workmen from the village were already in the process of erecting a small rectangular metal structure. "Look familiar to you, Amelia?" Michael teased.

"It looks like a hangar," Amelia answered, a tentative catch in her voice.

"Right you are," he chortled. "That's just what it is. I was able to locate a brand-new aircraft that was never delivered to the RAF. I'm still a damn good pilot, but I've never been much of a navigator. That's your job. As I once told you, we are going to fly together."

Michael had also engaged the services of Freddy Fitzgerald, a crusty former RAF mechanic who dreaded facing mandatory retirement. Amelia and Freddy formed a fast friendship. She spent hours with him, fascinated as he checked out every detail, helped push the plane in and out of the hangar, and lay on the floor as he tinkered with the underbelly.

Boarding the new plane for the first time was an emotional experience for both of them. It was Amelia's first flight since the crash and she did not have a single regret that Michael was at the controls. She was happy to be his navigator.

Their Sunday "air spins," as Michael called them, became the high point of their week. Beneath them stretched Michael's beloved country with its green hills and valleys, lush pastures, and villages clustered around ancient churches.

Later that summer, they flew to Balmoral castle in Scotland at the invitation of King George VI. Amelia wore the same green gown she had worn at the fateful White House dinner honoring Winston Churchill. This time, it was augmented by lovely Chinese jade jewelry that had belonged to Michael's mother. Amelia democratically bobbed her head in greeting, rather than curtsying, which amused Michael immensely. It must have secretly amused the King, too, since he specifically requested that Amelia join the Royal Family as they played charades late into the evening and listened to Scottish reels.

In all of her travels, Amelia Earhart had never imagined the contentment and pleasure she would experience in the months and years that would follow. Amelia and Michael were invited once again to join the Royal Family at Balmoral. As they flew low along the south bank of the River Dee, flanked by the mountains and valleys of Lochnagar, looking to spot the Royal Standard, which flies from a hundred-foot tower when the Monarch is in residence, the plane's single engine inexplicably failed. Amelia and Michael, who had both logged so many dangerous hours in the air, died instantly.

Within hours, radio and newspaper bulletins spread the word. The free world was stunned. England mourned the loss of one of its most acclaimed war heroes and his beloved, even more famous, wife, whom the British had adopted as their own.

On the other side of the Atlantic, Americans simply could not believe that their incomparable "Lady Lindy," who had set so many records and survived a death-defying crash, was gone.

Two days later, Amelia's Los Angeles attorney called a press conference and read her last will and testament. It was simple enough:

Her flying mementoes and correspondence would go to the Smithsonian Institution in Washington, D.C. for public exhibition, and her estate would be used to create a foundation to further the cause of women in the field of aviation.

Finally, she expressed the wish that she be buried on Howland Island. And so it was that Amelia Earhart reached the one destination that had eluded her.

NICOLE BROWN
SIMPSON

BY JENNIE LOUISE FRANKEL

*N*icole Brown Simpson stood on the
balcony of her four-level, Bermuda-
style home overlooking the Mexican
coastline. Her powder-blue silk dress
and matching scarf draped around
her neck, fluttered in the breeze. She
stood tall and strong as she gazed at
the magnificent turquoise-and-
emerald ocean below. Sunset was her
favorite time in Cabo San Lucas, and
tonight's promised to be spectacular.
She was excited. Her husband would
be flying in sometime early this
evening on their private 727 jet.

Nicole owned and maintained six homes around the world and a yacht in the Mediterranean. She and her husband had been flying to Cabo more frequently lately, trying to fill an emptiness in their lives since the kids left home. Soon after Sydney's wedding to the son of a famous Italian clothing designer, Justin had been accepted to the University of Chicago Medical School. And then there was little Michelle . . . Nicole tried not to think about her. But she knew she *must,* in order to complete the final interview with her dearest friend, Faye Resnick, who had been writing a book about what happened *that night* twenty years ago and the events that followed. Nicole found the strength to relive her life in small increments, allowing Faye to sensitively, delicately put everything—at least as much as Nicole chose to divulge—into words, so that the truth would finally be known. It had been a *two-year* undertaking, and tonight would be the final interview.

Nicole looked at her reflection in the half-closed sliding glass door. She didn't look bad for a woman in her fifties. She actually looked quite marvelous. Time had been kind to her. She was still strikingly beautiful, tan, and muscular. She turned heads, even now. Nicole had everything: a loving husband, a wonderful family, a successful career, and more money than she had ever dreamed of. But she would have traded it all not to have lived some of the events that led up to where she was today. She hoped her husband would arrive early enough to share the sunset and a pitcher of margaritas with her dearest friend and business partner, Faye Resnick.

"Faye," Nicole turned and called into the house.

"Faye?" Nicole entered the living room. She stopped suddenly. Pummeling her senses were dozens of lit candles placed about the room. Faye Resnick was standing by the fireplace, lighting the final candles with reverence.

"What are you *doing,* Faye?"

"Lighting candles. Like the old days, when we'd fill the living room with them." Faye smiled.

"Faye," Nicole said firmly, "you know how I feel about candles. They remind me of that night."

"I know."

Nicole took a moment to compose herself. She decided that Faye surely meant no harm. "Besides, I used to light candles in those days to save money on electricity, Faye. That's hardly the case now."

Faye smiled as she handed a margarita to Nicole and lifted her own glass to toast. "I know. Thanks to a lot of hard work by both of us—and going public with our Java house chain—we happen to be two very wealthy women!"

Faye toasted, "Here's to future fortunes!"

"And peace of mind!" added Nicole.

They touched glasses and drank.

"I think there's *another* reason you're lighting these candles, Faye. We've been friends for over twenty years and I can read you like a book."

"Okay, Nicole. I'll admit it. I was hoping the candles would jar you into remembering the night of Ron Goldman's murder."

Nicole became upset. "I told you, I can't remember. It's hopeless. You might as well give up now. That part of the book is simply not going to happen."

"You're *blocking,* Nicole. Just let go!"

Nicole's head was reeling. It made no sense to fill her mind with terrible memories from the past. To Nicole, time was far too precious a gift to spend on anything sad or fearful. After waking up from the coma twenty years ago, she believed every moment of every day was to be savored. She was *grateful* her life had been spared, and sad that Ron Goldman's wasn't. Something about *almost dying* brought Nicole into a whole new appreciation for the miracle of life. And here, in beautiful Mexico, what better godsend than to be sharing precious time with her best friend at her estate, waiting for her man to return; a man who had been taken away from her for too many years. She was happy now, and she wasn't about to waste a moment of her time thinking about anything hurtful.

"Faye, let's get some CDs ready for when he returns." Nicole thumbed through her collection. "We'll play some 'oldies,' Madonna, Prince, ah, yes, Mariah Carey. It's a good thing I have this ancient compact disc player."

Faye laughed. "You're right about that, since they don't even make CDs anymore."

Nicole bent down to pick up a disc and caught her scarf on the corner of an ornate Bustimanti bronze parrot sculpture. "Damn!"

Nicole tried to undo the snag quickly so she could stand up. Off balance, she began to teeter to one side, slightly at first, then lurching. She braced herself on a bureau, instinctively pushing herself into an upright position. In one swift motion her scarf untied and floated languidly to the floor. Nicole faced directly into a mirror. A look of terror came over her face as she found herself staring at the huge, grotesque gash across her neck. Dozens of lit candles reflected ominously in the mirror from various points around the room.

Nicole had gone out of her way to avoid looking at the scars every day for the past twenty years, going so far as to have the mirrors removed from her bathrooms—except for a small fluorescent-lit round mirror she used to apply her makeup. After her morning shower, she would quickly tie matching scarves around her neck. She had scarves custom dyed by Susanna of Beverly Hills to match everything in her wardrobe. She even slept with scarves, making believe the wounds did not exist—on her body or in her memory. Now here they were in bold defiance, demanding recognition. . . . *As hard as she tried, she could not look away.*

Faye rushed to Nicole's side, grabbed her by the shoulders, and shook her. They both faced the mirror. Faye's grip forced Nicole to stay fixated on the ugly image before her. It was a visual intrusion that for years the mere *thought* of made her wretch. "*Think,* Nicole. *Think!*" Faye urged. "You've *got* to. It's the only way you can truly put it behind you."

Some of the memories became stronger over the years. Others faded and died. Nicole had an honest relationship with Faye, but until the interviews for Faye's book began, Nicole preferred not to discuss the past. Faye respected this, but now was determined to get at the truth.

Now Faye was *unrelenting.* This was as close as she had ever been to finding the truth. And she was not about to give up. "*That night,* Nicole. What happened that night?"

Nicole was dazed and expressionless. In the stillness of stunned silence her subconscious—caught off guard—unveiled a flood of uninvited memories: joyous, painful . . . savage . . .

"Say it, Nic! Just say what you're thinking! . . . You can do it. I know you can! You owe yourself the truth, Nic! What is going on in your mind?"

"I . . . I can't."

"You can! That night, Nic . . . think back." Faye picked up one of the lit candles and held it in front of Nicole's face . . . The reflection in the mirror was eerie as shadows flickered across Nicole's face—her scar hidden by the shadow of the light. Slowly, a guttural chuckle came from Nicole's throat, then the beginning of a smile. She was remembering a happy time. She finally spoke, haltingly at first, but the memories started flooding in. Nicole broke her twenty-year, self-imposed silence about that night with one word . . . "Sydney."

Faye's heart quickened. "Sydney? What about her?" Faye seemed to be nearing the truth she'd waited so long to hear.

" . . . Her dance costume . . . Her makeup . . . She was so adorable, Faye. I wish you could have been there. Family . . . elation from the excitement of the night, it was beautiful . . . Sydney was so graceful in her rehearsals. And that night she was so calm and self-assured. I *knew* she was going to be terrific. I was so proud of her . . . so happy to be there, so happy . . ."

Nicole's expression changed. "And then O.J. arrived."

"What about O.J.?"

"He seemed happy, too. At least at first. And I thought to myself, *What right does this man have to be in our lives? What right does he have to be here?*"

"Why, Nicole? Why did you feel that way?"

"I was *angry* with him for threatening to turn me in to the IRS. It would have meant losing my home—the one peaceful, happy home my children had known. And he knew it. He didn't care about me or the children. He just wanted to get even with me for leaving him."

"Go on, Nicole. You're doing good. What else do you remember?"

"I remember I *needed* to talk to you, Faye. But I couldn't reach you. I called the Exodus rehabilitation hospital several times. They told me you were in meetings and therapy. I needed your advice. . . .You see, I knew that after the recital, I was going to tell O.J. he wasn't welcome to celebrate with the family. He didn't deserve to share in our happiness. I suspected he'd show up at Mezzaluna anyway, so we almost went to Toscana. I decided to follow through with my original plans. It seemed easier. I wanted to ask what you thought about *how* I should tell O.J. that it was over. I'd had enough. That night had to be the last of it, Faye. After all, I was carrying another man's child. . . ."

Some time before that fateful night, O.J. had discovered a discarded home pregnancy test in a wastepaper basket in Nicole's home. What he was *doing* there in the first place will never be known. *How* he got into Nicole's home is easier to surmise. The extra key to Nicole's place had been missing for weeks and had never been found. When O.J. reached into the wastepaper basket and picked up the discarded test, there was a brief second when he thought the baby might be his—but that notion soon left his mind. It was replaced by pure anger; a *"How could 'the bitch' do this to me?"* rage pumped through his veins. O.J. couldn't handle Nicole's pregnancies when she was carrying *his* child. It is anyone's guess what was going through his mind when he realized Nicole, his possession, was carrying *another man's child.* His fury progressed from indignation to brutalizing force and uncontrolled violence. He knew the time had come. He would get his revenge.

The night of the dance recital, Nicole told O.J. it was over and that she never wanted to see him again. She was, after all, in love with another man. The "O.J. dance," the craziness, the obsession . . . were over. Or so she thought.

Nicole suspected O.J. would not take the insult easily, but she didn't know of any other way to deal with the situation. She'd tried to explain her feelings too many times before. She'd put up with his denial of the way he treated her as well as his rare promises to be better. She had to make the break and couldn't pretend anymore. . . .

Faye guided Nicole to the couch and they both sat down. Faye handed Nicole another drink. "Please, Nicole, don't stop. You *must* continue. What happened after you arrived at your home? Think, Nicole. . . . What happened after you went to dinner at Mezzaluna?"

Nicole took a deep breath. "When we arrived home, I put Justin and Sydney to bed. They were so tired. Then I lit the candle. . . . I remember you finally called me from Exodus, Faye, and how good it felt to talk with you."

"It was exciting to hear how Sydney's recital went, Nic. And when you told me about your confrontation with O.J., well, I was so proud of you."

"Faye, I felt so strong—like I could handle anything. If the IRS took our house away, so be it. For the first time in my life, I had love. True love. Not a sick, possessive kind of obsession."

Faye continued her probing. "I suspected you were going to have a visitor that night, Nic."

"You were right, Faye. I lit the candles because I was expecting *him*. This was the night I was going to tell him he was the father of my child. The child I was carrying inside of me."

Faye lit a cigarette for Nicole, then one for herself. "Nic, I know how hard this is. Just take your time."

"I knew O.J. would be on a plane that night, so I felt safe. The kids were asleep, and I was still wide awake when my mother called. She had left her glasses, at the restaurant. As it turned out, Ronald Goldman offered to drop them by. I was waiting for him to arrive. I thought I'd make it quick, say hello, get the glasses, and a quick good-bye. You were right, Faye, I was expecting *him* that night. We had been planning this evening for days. I knew O.J. would be out of town. We were both afraid of O.J. But we were so in love, we decided it was worth the risk."

Faye smiled. "I know how much you loved him. Even then."

Nicole's love for O.J. was strong. But her new love was magic. Nicole knew that O.J.'s love was an obsession. He vacillated between love and hatred. O.J. had a pattern. He'd focus on an *imagined injustice,* and Nicole would have hell to pay for his paranoia. This night was no different. Only it was Ron Goldman who would pay the price.

Faye continued to probe. "What happened? *Tell me what happened* when Ron Goldman arrived. Tell me why you went out to greet him on the steps of your home. Can you see it, Nicole? See it . . . feel it. "

Nicole's eyes widened, reliving the entire event as she described it to Faye, moment by moment. "I'm watching out the front window. I want to greet Ron at the gate, before he comes up to the door. The timing is too close, I can't let him stay long. I see Ron walking up to the gate. He has a white envelope in his hand. He's smiling. I open the door and walk out to him. We smile. And then . . . "

"What? Nic, tell me what happened?"

"I only had time to say thank you. The next minute a tall, looming, threateningly dark man appeared. He had a knife in his hand—a big knife. In one silent movement, he stabbed me. Ron tried to protect me, he grabbed for the knife, but the man threw him to the ground and kept stabbing and slashing at him. Blood was gushing, it was everywhere. I was on the ground, paralyzed with fear, unable to move. But I could see what this animal was doing to Ron. In a few moments, Ron lay there in a pool of blood. I thought it was over . . . that the man would leave . . . but it *wasn't* over. For me, it was just the beginning. This hulking, dark figure came back, he stood over me. Oh, no, dear God,

OH, NO! He's holding the blade in his right hand, it's at my throat, he's pressing, harder, deeper . . . Oh, my God . . . "

"Who was that man . . . Nic! TELL ME, WHO WAS HE?"

Nicole continued, "I grabbed at him. He slashed me, over and over and over again. I could feel the blood leaving my body. I put my hands in front of my face, like I'd done so many times before, in an effort to protect myself. I kicked, I tried to scream, but nothing came out. I grabbed the knit cap from his head. It's . . . It's . . . Oh, DEAR GOD. . . . "

Nicole passed out, and Faye got some ice and put it on Nicole's forehead.

◆

Nicole spent two weeks after Ron Goldman's murder lying in a coma. When she awoke, she saw her two sisters, Dominique and Tanya, standing over her hospital bed. They didn't have to tell her that Ron had died, she already knew. No matter how hard she tried, she couldn't remember the details of that night. It was to be months into the trial before little bits and pieces returned for a moment and left as fast as they came. Slowly, painfully, she would be able to remember the events leading up to the tragedy.

She was asked to testify, but she couldn't. She simply didn't have a recollection about who had performed these savage acts. Even the bits and pieces she managed to collect in her daydreams and nightmares didn't reveal a clue as to who had perpetrated this unspeakable butchery.

As the time passed, she refused to watch the trial—the trial where the man she had loved for so many years, the icon, the national hero, OJ. Simpson, stood fighting for his own life. Through the entire trial, she still felt a strange love for this man; the kind of love a woman has for the father of her two children. Could it be that this man's rage was so profound that he took it upon himself to attempt to kill her? Sure, he'd beaten her in the past, but was this man a killer?

Two days before the prosecution's closing arguments, more of that night came to her in a dream. Nicole relived every moment, from the time she walked out of the house to the vicious, rabid attack by a predator who mercilessly stabbed and slashed her and Ronald Goldman, leaving them for dead. The vision got stronger and stronger. She could see her blood spurting all over his face, mixing with the blood of Ron Goldman. She felt his one hand grabbing her hair as the other gruesomely plunged the knife into her body. She could see his eyes, the color of his skin . . .

Could it be? The moment came back to her, that second that seemed to go in slow motion, a moment that was an eternity, when she pulled off his knit cap and looked into his cold-blooded killer eyes . . . the figure hovering over her . . . he . . . he . . . was *smiling*.

The smell of jasmine wafted in from the courtyard as Faye held Nicole, cradled like a baby, in her arms. Soothing her, comforting her, assuring her she was fine and all was well. Nicole sobbed for several minutes, then looked up at Faye and spoke.

"Faye, from the moment I pulled the cap off of his head, I went into shock. After looking into his eyes and witnessing *that* smile, I took one last gasp and blood gushed profusely from so many parts of my body. I slipped into the peaceful, forgiving coma that was to be my only safe haven for the next two weeks. The dreams, the nightmares, all began the moment I regained consciousness. Hard as I tried, it was not my destiny to recall who, what, where, or when . . . The actual crime was so far buried in my psyche, I thought it would never see the light of day. My only concern, my only coherent, *conscious* thought was for the baby. The baby that, to my relief, still grew inside of me."

The miracle of it all, Nicole's baby was still alive. It was no small medical feat for this phenomenon to occur. Every state-of-the-art medical device available was deployed. Monitors, probes, breathing machines, you name it. Not to mention the many, many transfusions. It would be used as a "case study" in emergency room medical treatment lectures, articles, and textbooks for years to come.

The baby was also to be a major topic of discussion by the tabloids. Just *who* was the father? Even at the trial, Robert Shapiro, O.J.'s attorney, tried to get Judge Lance Ito to *order* the necessary genetic tests to determine who the father was. But the Judge realized it would be violating Nicole's civil rights, and he refused to subject her unborn child to the test. He figured she'd been through enough. He didn't order her to testify, either. This was a relief to the defense but a blow to the prosecution. Nicole wanted to help, but she figured, since her memory was so vague, what good would it do? God forbid she help prosecute the wrong man.

Faye had many discussions with Nicole *before* that night, during those terrible times when O.J. stalked Nicole—and Faye was there to witness the acts. But the most troubling times, the most haunting moments for Faye, were hearing

Nicole talk about O.J.'s treatment of her when she was pregnant. How O.J. treated Nicole when she was pregnant with Sydney and Justin was unconscionable. A man who beats a woman is horrible. But while she's pregnant . . . because she's fat? Those must have been difficult secrets for Nicole to keep. Yes, Nicole was indeed strong. She always had been.

"What would you have done if the child had been O.J.'s, Nicole?"

"I would have had another abortion. I could not—would not—have taken the abuse that I knew was in store for me." Nicole reeled, wincing at the thought. "I told myself, 'This is the last time I will allow myself to be beaten by this man.' I told myself, now, everything was different, I now had love; I was carrying a child; and even if the father didn't marry me, I had a future. If I couldn't be strong for myself in the past, I was bound and determined to never let this child know a day of fear from a father who could not control his rage. Sydney and Justin experienced such cruelty and anger in their lives. This child would never know these things. No, for this child, the future did not include knowing the rage of this self-proclaimed Svengali . . . who only knew how to control."

"What happened after you discovered you were pregnant and didn't tell O.J.?"

"Oh, Faye, I *did* tell O.J. That night! It was at Sydney's recital. But the strangest thing, Faye, I could swear, *he already knew*. His reaction didn't fit. He did something very strange. He . . . Faye, I know this is going to sound weird . . . but I swear, I wasn't imagining it . . ." Nicole paused and took a puff of her cigarette.

Faye was anxious. "What did he do, Nic?"

"Faye, we were standing at the back of the auditorium. It was a bit dark, but I swear . . . Faye . . . he . . . "

"Nic, tell me for God's sake! What did he do? What did he say? Did he blow up? Did he get angry? Did he hit you?"

"That's just it. Faye, he didn't do any of those things. Faye . . . I could swear, even in that dimmed light . . . he *smiled*."

"Oh, no, Nic. Are you sure?"

"Yes. He smiled."

For days before that night, Nicole didn't have to endure the relentless telephone calls—O.J. checking up on her every movement. She thought that he had finally faced the reality that she would no longer live in his shadow and be the object of his rage. What Nicole *didn't* know was that this was merely the calm before the storm. It was like a cat, preying on an unsuspecting mouse, slowly but surely boxing the mouse into a corner, touching it, letting it go, holding the tail for a moment, then releasing it. Having a sadistically good time. All the while, knowing with certainty, the mouse would surely . . .

Nicole got that letter from O.J.'s attorney—with veiled threats of turning her in to the IRS. This time O.J. had gone too far. Not only had he gotten away with beating her down, physically and psychologically, but now he was threatening her children—their very lives. The life of her unborn child. This was too much. He had finally gone *too* far.

◈

When Nicole recovered and was allowed to leave the hospital, she was relieved to find out that the IRS, perhaps out of pity, somehow managed to accept an "offer in compromise." She could pay off her tax debt for a fraction of what was owed and keep her home. She no longer got support from O.J. His money was all used up during the trial. Nicole and Faye managed to scrape up the seventy thousand dollars needed to open their first Java International Coffee House. It was an ambitious, almost pretentious name for a little hole-in-the-wall coffee house and espresso bar in Brentwood, but the women had visions and dreams. And besides, like their attorney said, "You'll *grow into* the name. I know you will." And so they did.

One small retail outlet grew to three, and then ten, fifty, a hundred . . . a thousand. Not only did Nicole and Faye have a chain of extremely successful stores around the world, they also came to the point where they bought and owned coffee plantations from Hawaii to Sumatra. Their dream had become an empire.

◈

And as their business grew, so did Sydney, Justin, and Michelle. Nicole was the proud mother of three absolutely beautiful, talented, brilliant children. And through all of her business endeavors, Nicole managed to keep her "values of family" the most important part of her life. In the corporate headquarters of JICH in Beverly Hills, everyone knew that if Nicole's children called, she was to be told, even if it meant putting a business conference with an international consortium on hold. It didn't matter. Her children's needs always came first.

❖

With all her success, Nicole still had her memories. Early in Faye's interviews, they discussed how Nicole dealt with informing the father of her child that their baby had been born.

"When Michelle was born, I sent one simple note to her father. It read, 'We had a baby girl. I've named her Michelle.' He didn't respond, but I could feel in my heart that he was with me in spirit. He told me years later that this was one of the hardest things he'd ever had to do; to keep away from me. His wife had threatened that if he ever got near me, she'd make sure he never saw their children again."

Faye continued to dig deeper. "Tell me about Michelle."

"Michelle was an angel sent from heaven. A little baby girl, born out of love and passion and goodness. How could anything so sweet, so tiny, so perfect represent anything but love. As she grew older, I told her she would someday meet her father. Somehow, I knew in my heart . . . one day, we would be together. And though part of that prediction came true—I *was* to be reunited with her father—Michelle would never know him. She only had her imagination to go on and my descriptions of his kindness and loving attributes . . . and athletic prowess."

For years Nicole couldn't go anywhere without people hounding her. She had always hated publicity, and in an effort to escape the unrelenting reporters, she moved to a complex of architecturally designed replications of French châteaus in Century City. Here, the elegant townhouses were a safe haven for her and the children. Justin, Sydney, and their sister could play in the courtyard or go to friends' houses without having to leave the grounds. It was perfect. Nicole enjoyed sitting outside, behind the house, relaxing, looking at the fountain. Somehow, the cascading water seemed to, if only for that time, wash away some of her most painful memories.

Nicole and Faye took a hand in decorating each new store. They worked with hundreds of little white lights, which became a trademark. Nicole had once seen these lights in an Indian restaurant in New York. They gave each store a feeling of sparkling brightness . . . a place to escape to.

With each passing year, the children became more and more beautiful, more accomplished at each of their particular interests, and more lauded in school and on the athletic field. Along about fifth grade, Sydney changed her interests from dancing to cheerleading and volleyball. She became quite an accomplished jockette, as Nicole called her. She took after her dad. Tall, lean, lovely—poetry in motion. Justin became interested in chemistry. He was always coming up with concoctions in a little laboratory he set up in his bathroom. And Michelle . . .

Nicole continued talking to Faye about Michelle. "What can I say about little Michelle? From the day she was born, she was a treasure in my life. Everybody loved Michelle . . . *everybody*. Michelle was a free spirit. She reminded me of the way I used to be, growing up in Orange County. When she entered a room, she had a presence. She got along with everybody. She had a spirit that was luminescent."

"When did you know? When did you find out?"

Nicole was lost in her description of her precious little girl. "Those who came into contact with her seemed to feel better for the experience. Those ten years I spent with her were a gift. When I got that first call from school, the one where I was asked to come and pick her up because she wasn't feeling well, we all thought she had the flu. I kept her home from school for two weeks and she got better. I canceled that trip to Colombia and Brazil to take care of her. The second time she got sick, she didn't recover as fast as she had before. This time, she had been playing soccer at school, when she fainted. I brought her to three different doctors. None of them could figure out what was wrong."

"Oh, Nic, it was always so sad to me that it took so long for anyone to even suspect."

"That's just it, Faye, she was never sick for any real length of time . . . at least not in the beginning. She got better again and again. The doctors told me they suspected everything from a virus to hepatitis. It wasn't until I took her to the Mayo Clinic in Minnesota that the diagnosis was made. It was here, in a small consultation room, that the unspeakable was spoken. Our precious little girl, this gift of love, had AIDS. If only I hadn't received those blood transfusions when I was in the hospital. Faye, for the first time since the attack, I allowed myself to feel hatred. I thought to myself, *Damn that man. I hope he rots in hell.*"

It took Michelle three years to die. By Nicole's account, those were the worst years of her life. They hurt far more than the scar on her neck or the emotional scars she suffered during her marriage. To watch a child die . . . to mourn that child's death . . . it is something no mother should have to endure. The horror of Nicole's discovering that she had also contracted the disease during those blood transfusions paled in comparison to the grief she experienced during her years of mourning. If only Michelle had lived two years longer. It was then that the cure for AIDS was found. Nicole felt an unexplained guilt that she was allowed to live and her daughter had to die.

Nicole didn't tell Michelle's father for a long time. She waited until they finally met at a charity benefit for the Ronald McDonald House at the Regent Beverly Wilshire Hotel in Beverly Hills. He was there alone. When they looked into each other's eyes, it was as if the last fifteen years had never passed. They were both back together—at least in their minds—sitting on the sofa on South Bundy, talking, laughing, loving. He told Nicole about his children. They talked about his career. When she told him about their daughter, Michelle, he cried. He was sorry for the years he'd missed. He told her his marriage was all but over. He said he needed her. He begged Nicole to forgive him . . . and she did.

It took two more years for him to straighten out his affairs. It was a bitter divorce. His wife said she'd turn the children against him, and somehow she managed to make that threat a reality. The children would never forgive him for leaving their mother. But his love for Nicole was too great. He needed her in his life. He felt a passion unlike anything he'd ever known before. It was an unconditional love. He loved Nicole for herself—the woman she was when he met her and the woman she grew to become.

They were together from that moment on. The children were out of the house, and since Java International Coffee House went public, Nicole had so much more time to spend with her husband. As the CEO of the company, Faye dealt with the day-to-day events, encouraging Nicole to relax and enjoy her life. Faye's child, Francesca, was married and had two children of her own. Francesca put her law degree to good use as the youngest vice president of a Fortune 500 company, her mother and Nicole's golden brainchild, Java International Coffee House.

When Nicole looked into her husband's eyes, memories of the years spent without him faded, and she was once more in the moment, living for the time they had together.

Faye lit a cigarette while Nicole freshened her makeup and adjusted her scarf. The two continued to talk. Nicole was lost in thought about her love for her husband.

"Faye, I love him just as much as I did the first day we met. I can't change the time we've lost. After all, a fool will lose tomorrow, looking back on yesterday."

A car drove up the long road to the house and stopped. A car door slammed. Nicole smiled and ran to the window.

" I think I hear him. Yes, yes, it's him."

A key turned in the lock. . . . The door opened. Nicole rushed to his arms. They embraced. He had a bottle of Cristal champagne in one hand and a large bouquet of yellow roses in the other. They kissed, a slow, tender, passionate kiss. Together they were complete. She could finally let go of the past. The sky was crimson and the silver ocean reflected the moonlit clouds. It seemed as if their daughter, Michelle, was on one of those clouds, looking down on them and smiling. Lost in an embrace, Nicole lovingly whispered his name. "Oh, Marcus . . . "

ARTHUR
ASHE

BY TERRIE MAXINE FRANKEL

"If I ask 'Why me?' about my troubles,
I would have to ask 'Why me?' about my blessings."
—Arthur Ashe, humanitarian, human rights activist, and
first Black tennis player to win Wimbledon

THE YEAR 2021, WASHINGTON, D.C.

*T*he black limousine cruises slowly up Pennsylvania Avenue. Arthur Ashe turns to his wife of forty-four years, Jeanne Moutoussamy-Ashe, and smiles. He's always had an air of dignity about him, even as a child, but today he allows himself to feel emotions he usually fights to keep at bay . . . today he feels a sense of pride and self-satisfaction.

As Arthur adjusts Jeanne's corsage, he reflects, "Why is it that I remember what happened thirty

283

years ago with the accuracy of a SWAT Team, but I can't remember what I had for breakfast?"

"Scrambled eggs and ham," Jeanne says, smiling.

Arthur Ashe lovingly pats Jeanne's hand.

"Well, dear," she consoles, "it's been a very demanding campaign, and you can't be expected to remember everything."

The limo makes its way past The Vietnam War Memorial—a tribute to those who lost their lives over fifty years ago—and the more recent WWIII Memorial, where the granite-etched names and countries represent the millions who died around the world . . . those nameless universal soldiers, whose sacrifices had a profound and far-reaching effect on global politics.

It is a typical January morning in Washington, D.C., eighty degrees and climbing, a weather condition reflective of the global warming trend and the thinning ozone layer. On this twelfth day of January in the year 2021, millions of Americans and citizens of the world are tuning in on their wrist satellite watches to view an event of great magnitude—a ceremony honoring political achievement in its highest form. Today, history will be made.

The limo slowly approaches the Capitol Building and comes to a stop. Secret Service agents open the door. Jeanne Ashe takes the hand of one of the men and is helped out of the car. Arthur Ashe, refusing help, searches for his cane, steadies himself on the arm rest of the open door, and attempting to stand, falls over.

This has happened before. Jeanne instinctively reaches down to give him a hand, but Arthur pushes her away. Despite his protests, the Secret Service people help him to his feet. One of the men returns his cane, and Arthur proceeds to walk toward the Capitol Building, head held high.

Camera flashes go off and autograph seekers are held at bay by guards as Jeanne and Arthur proceed down the red runner. Arthur is dressed in his traditional black Nehru suit and crisp white shirt. Since the style came back into fashion a few years ago, this is his dress of choice. He feels a bit like Nehru, a man of principles, making history against all odds—persecuted, maligned, yet in Arthur's case triumphant in the end, as today's events will attest with the most sacred of affirmations by the American people. Certainly age has been a consideration to the voters. But ultimately, *ideals* have played a more important part in this most coveted of political victories. And now he is preparing mentally for the most important moment of his life.

As Arthur walks, his mind drifts to the election. Victory hasn't come easily. With each state's returns, his and Jeanne's confidence in the outcome had waxed and waned. And it wasn't until the final results were in that the family—whose ancestors descended from a Southern governor and an African slave—felt free to celebrate.

"Excuse me, Mr. and Mrs. Ashe. We'll be taking you to the waiting room until the ceremony is ready to begin." Secret Service people are always polite. They take special courses in protocol.

Upon entering, Jeanne and Arthur scan the room, see two high-backed down-filled tapestry chairs, and slowly make their way toward them. They seem to think alike these days. Arthur makes sure Jeanne is seated comfortably before he sits down—always the gentleman.

"You look wonderful!" Jeanne smiles as she straightens her husband's collar. "I'm so proud of you!"

"And I'm proud of you, Jeanne. You look even more beautiful now than when I married you." Time has been kind to this dedicated wife and mother, whose famed photographic depictions of family life now appear in museums around the world. Jeanne notices a slight change in her husband's demeanor. She watches him closely. She senses he is not feeling well and is afraid.

"Are you all right, darling?"

"Fine, dear. Just a little heartburn," he lies.

Once seated and recognized, curiosity seekers and fans begin to form a line to take audience with the famous pair. As unfamiliar people file past, Arthur thinks he recognizes one of the elderly women now before him. Though vaguely familiar, he's not quite sure who she is until she opens her mouth to speak.

"Remember, Arthur. I once told the press that *I* was more Black than you."

"Why, Billie Jean King! How long has it been?"

"I saw you in the hospital about thirty years ago, but you wouldn't remember, you were in a coma."

"So, you're wrong twice, Billie, my dear lady. You will *never* be Blacker than me, and I remember everything about that hospital stay, including your visit."

Arthur's mind drifts back.

February 7, 1993, New York Hospital. Arthur Ashe, pale and gaunt, is lying in a coma. His heartbeat faint—only detectable by the thin catheter piercing his vein, being threaded up toward his heart. He is dying from pneumocystis carinii pneumonia, a complication of AIDS. Arthur had been infected with the virus via tainted blood transfusions given to him during open heart surgery some years before.

The entire staff of the hospital has a "life wish" for their celebrity patient, and they refuse to give up. They will not *let* him die.

"Get the epinephrine, STAT, his heart has stopped beating!"

The team of nurses and doctors work feverishly. All are wearing masks, gowns, gloves, every precaution taken for an AIDS caregiver in those days—before they realized this virus couldn't be spread that way.

Arthur is fighting for his life. He slips away, his body heaving, struggling to take a breath, his heart unable to pump life-giving oxygen to his necrotizing lungs. His pneumonia has progressed to a point where he is barely alive. His condition is critical, and he's slipping into a coma. He cannot speak, but he is aware of the activity around him.

The desperate resuscitation continues for five minutes, ten minutes, fifteen minutes. Odd. His body feels light. He is floating up, up toward the ceiling! The strange sensation is euphoric. He finds himself looking down at a hospital bed! Peering at a pale lifeless body without a spirit, wondering, *Who can it be?* The body looks strangely familiar and he takes a closer look. It is him! He curiously observes the frenzy of activity over his lifeless frame. One of the doctors wants to give up. Another fights to keep trying. Reluctantly, all rally behind one final push to keep Arthur alive. And all the while, he is aware of everything being said, everything being done, every single movement in the room. But he can't talk . . . he's dead. . . .

His little daughter, Camera, and wife, Jeanne, are now by his bedside, crying, begging . . . praying.

"Don't die now, Daddy! Please don't die! . . . Dear God, *please* don't let my daddy die!"

And with that child's prayer—knowing time is running out—in the moment it takes for one of her little tears to fall, Arthur makes the decision that he *has* to return to his body. He knows that without his being on earth, there is no way for her to fulfill her dreams . . . her destiny.

A nurse cries out, "I'm getting a pulse!"

Once stable, Arthur is immediately hooked up to a heart/lung machine. Six months of plasmaphoresis treatments follow. With each of the two hundred treatments, blood is slowly taken out of one arm and passed through a machine designed to extract certain lymphocytes. The blood is then put through a warming process and redirected back into Arthur's other arm. All of this is in an effort to trap and remove the HIV virus. It is an experimental procedure later found to be worthless. The doctors still don't know why, but during this treatment Arthur regains his strength, enabling him to be deemed a candidate for a heart-lung transplant. The organs are found, the surgery completed, and a long hard road to recovery begins. He is truly a miracle of modern medicine. But he still has AIDS. The AIDS will linger, like an impending death sentence, until a cure is finally found in the year 2001. And though the doctors have no idea what has kept him going—by all accounts of modern medicine, he should have been dead by now—Arthur knows exactly what has kept him alive . . . faith.

Recovery would have been impossible without the love of his family. Jeanne and Camera take great care in their treatment of the person the country is to call "The Miracle Man." And as his strength grows, so does his determination to campaign for a cure for AIDS. Once strong enough to continue, Arthur also campaigns for Haitian rights, and lives to see the return of President Jean-Bertrand Aristide—as well as the two Haitian presidents who follow. Arthur is on the forefront, working tirelessly toward economic reform in Haiti.

Arthur Ashe's brainchild, The Safe Passage Foundation, is incorporated into every public school system in the United States. Millions of children benefit from this innovative program. And the Arthur Ashe Foundation for the Defeat of AIDS, though not entirely responsible for finding the cure, performs exclusionary research that contributes to the discovery of the cure for the disease.

In the years that follow, Arthur and his brother, Johnnie Ashe—an engineer and a retired captain in the Marines—design and build the Ashe Housing Projects. These mini cities revolutionize multi-family housing, and are hailed as "dream" communities by architects, engineers, and city planners. The Ashe Housing Projects become the prototype for "fair housing" communities around the world and stand in testimony to Arthur's famous quote, "I am first and foremost a member of the commonwealth of humanity."

Arthur is jolted into the present.

He feels a hand on his shoulder. Jeanne is shaking him. "Time to wake up now, Arthur. . . . Say good-bye to your friend."

Billie Jean King, realizing Arthur has drifted, shakes his hand, wishes him well, and moves on. Arthur turns to Jeanne and asks, "Where is Camera?"

"I don't know, dear. She should be here soon."

Arthur says hello to his closest friends. Old timers mingle: Governor Andrew Young, Bill Cosby, Andre Agassi, Maya Angelou, Mr. and Mrs. Donald Dell, and former president of the United States Newt Gingrich. And there are the somewhat younger well-wishers, including Nadia Comaneci, presently ambassador to the Republic of United Slavic Countries, and the upper echelon of the Safe Passage Foundation. Of course there's Arthur's brother, Johnnie, as well as many other attendees too numerous to mention.

As the line continues forming, Arthur senses someone is in the room; a man within whose blood flows the same drive and determination as in his own. This man could be his brother; *is* his brother in the commonwealth of humanity. As he approaches, Arthur tries to peer through the crowd. The man of color walks with a limp, his face down, making sure not to fall while supporting himself with a hardwood cane fashioned with a green malachite handle. Arthur doesn't have to see the face to know who it is . . . Jesse Jackson.

As Jackson comes closer, Arthur stares into his deep brown eyes. He has white hair now; they both do. Hell, all of his friends do. They share the same wearied walk, the deep lines in the face—battle scars from the past. There is a history here.

Arthur is looking at Jesse, but his mind drifts once again to the past . . .

◆

"Get off of the tennis court, nigger!"

Richmond, Virginia in the late 1940s is a place of deeply ingrained segregation. Blacks and whites have different bathrooms and different schools, and while growing up, Arthur is forced to sit in the back of the public bus.

At seven, Arthur is no match for the thirteen-year-old boys who blatantly stake claim to the tennis courts. To these boys Arthur is fair game for their threatening antics of racial superiority.

The bully takes the racket from Arthur's hand and lunges in a threatening manner. But Arthur stands strong. He can take whatever they have to give. He won't run, he won't cower—he's going to hold on to his self-respect. The bully soon realizes Arthur isn't going to go home crying, so the racket is relinquished. Arthur picks up his tennis balls and slowly, calmly heads home.

This is a turning point for Arthur. The wounds of prejudice cut deep. The scars will toughen him. It is on this day he makes the decision that whatever it takes, by whatever means he can find in his being, he will fight the battle against injustice and racism.

◆

Arthur finds himself saying out loud, "I kept my self-respect!"

Jesse Jackson says, "We all did, Arthur, we all did."

"Tomorrow, at the Lincoln Memorial, there's going to be a rally, Arthur. I want you to attend." Arthur thinks about how many causes he's marched for, protested for. He's always felt that protesting is one of the most invigorating things he's ever done. It makes him feel alive . . . with a purpose.

"What's the cause, Jesse?"

"It's for de-socializing medicine. You know what a big issue it is these days. The doctors are overworked and underpaid."

Arthur nods in agreement and adds, "Look what happened in England. Socialized medicine bankrupt the country."

"Then I can count on you, Arthur?"

"Of course. What time?"

"Tomorrow, noon. I'll have someone from the World Rainbow Coalition pick you up."

"I've got my own transportation. I'll see you there."

It is obvious that Jesse is pleased. He has a gleam in his eye. He hugs Arthur and moves on to Jeanne.

A young Hispanic in his early teens, who has been waiting patiently in line, now stands before Arthur.

"Wasn't that Jesse Jackson?" the young man asks.

Arthur responds as he extends his arm to shake the young man's hand.

"Yes." Arthur is still lost in thought as he continues. "Jesse Jackson always said I wasn't arrogant enough. Maybe . . . but I did get things done."

"Boy, I'll say, Mr. Ashe. We're studying the 'Ashe, One World, One People, Freedom Act' in school right now."

"Splendid!"

Arthur feels a pain in his chest. He doesn't want to alarm anybody, so he suffers silently. The only indication of his discomfort is his right hand clutching his cane. The young man continues. "Can I ask a favor, Mr. Ashe?"

"Certainly."

"Would you sign my tennis ball?"

"Of course."

The boy digs deep into his pocket and pulls out a tennis ball and a felt-tipped pen.

Arthur takes the ball and pen in his hand, looks at the ball, and once again recollects times gone by. Memories of a friend who passed away many years ago flood his mind.

Richmond Virginia, 1950. Little Arthur looks up wide-eyed at his hero and mentor, Ronald Charity, a part-time black tennis teacher who has befriended him.

"Practice, practice, practice, Arthur. Hit five hundred balls and then hit five hundred more."

Arthur says out loud, "I hit a *thousand* balls a day, and then a *thousand* more."

The young man, still waiting for Arthur to sign the ball, says, "Wow! That's a lot!"

"That's the only way to get good. Practice, practice, practice!" Arthur looks at the boy. "You are a smart young man.

Tell me, what is your name?"

He answers proudly, "My name is Paco Gonzales."

The name touches a tender part of Arthur's heart. "You have the same last name as a man I admired growing up. A hero of mine. He was a great tennis player. His name was Pancho Gonzales."

The boy becomes visibly excited, his grin turning to a huge, very proud smile.

"That's my great-grandfather!"

Arthur affectionately pulls the young man toward him and gives him a hug.

Two Secret Service men approach. "Ten minutes to the Inauguration."

Arthur looks at the young boy and tosses the signed tennis ball up in the air. The boy happily catches the prize and walks off.

Hurriedly, a presidential aide approaches. "Mr. Ashe, one of our speechwriters has taken the liberty of preparing a few words for you to say." As the aide hands the piece of paper over, Arthur becomes agitated and pushes it away.

"I write my own speeches. I AM A WRITER! Haven't you ever heard of my book, *Days of Grace?*" It was on the *New York Times* bestsellers list. And *Nights of Grace,* the sequel, was in the top ten for six months! . . . I know *exactly* what to sssaaayyyy suhhh . . . uh . . . I'll . . . ugh!!" Arthur cannot finish his words. His speech is slurred, his mind races . . . *Rush . . . pain . . . PILLS! PILLS . . . got to get . . . need pills.*

Jeanne searches desperately through her purse, pulls out a pill box, and fumbles to open it. "Water! Someone get water!"

Jeanne is handed a glass of water by a Secret Service man. She pops the pills into her husband's mouth and holds the water to his lips. Arthur is dazed. He swallows.

"Is he all right?" someone asks.

"He'll be fine in a minute. He's been through this before." Jeanne sighs.

Arthur waves them off. "I'm fine, just fine!" He knows he can't become ill now. He has waited too long for this moment. He convinces everyone he's all right.

Just then, Arthur hears the whir of a nuclear-chip-powered wheel chair approaching. His heart races, and he turns to the direction of the sound. Gazing at the icon before him, he is overjoyed. Leaning on his cane, he bends over to embrace his most cherished friend and colleague.

"Nelson."

"Arthur."

Tears come to Arthur's eyes. It has been several years since he has seen his dear friend. Nelson looks frail and weak—which is to be expected of a man his age. Since the average life expectancy these days is ninety-five years, Mandela is pushing the limit and quite fortunate to still be alive. Doctors believe that the starvation diet he experienced in jail contributed to his longevity.

Nelson speaks in barely a whisper. "The doctors advised me not to come, but nothing could keep me from being here."

Arthur glows. "It means so much to me for you to be here today . . ." Arthur's voice trails off. He is getting emotional, another trait that seems to come more often with age.

Nelson Mandela queries, "Remember when we first met, Arthur?"

"It was so long ago, Nelson."

"It was here in the United States, after my release from prison in South Africa."

Arthur thinks a moment and responds, "Now I remember. They gave you a ticker tape parade down Wall Street."

Mandela smiles. "That was a truly memorable time for me, Arthur. You were the first person I wanted to meet when I came to America. And I can remember when I first heard of *you*. I was still in prison when you first visited South Africa. Word of your visit spread through the country—and the prison as well. We heard of a man, a *Black* man, who *insisted* on being treated as a human being—which for us at the time was unheard of. You would not accept being restricted. Arthur, you were a hero to us all!"

Arthur remembers the visit. "And you, Nelson, had been a hero to me. I wanted to visit you in prison, but I was not allowed to."

"I read your three-volume work, *A Hard Road to Glory*, about Black American athletes, over and over while I was in jail."

Arthur gets philosophical. "Our lives were similar— though thousands of miles separated us—like seeds laying dormant in the frozen earth, waiting for our season to come."

"And look at us now, Arthur. We are like old palm trees whose fronds have fallen."

"But we've planted a thousand seeds, and they are growing, Nelson, they are growing. And they shall continue to grow, long after we die."

A reporter notices the two legends talking. She directs her cameraman to follow her over to the far side of the room and requests an interview with Mr. Mandela. He agrees.

"Tell me, Mr. Mandela, how do you feel about the recent renaming of your country to The United Townships of Mandela?"

"The honor is something I humbly accept. But believe me, the true miracle is not in the name of my country, it is that my country has risen from the depths of poverty and chaos to become an elite world economic power. But we have not forgotten our brothers in other African nations. And until the entire world knows no hunger or prejudice, we will continue on our journey. Now, if you will excuse me. I have a front-row space reserved to observe this most exciting event!" The wheel chair whirs off.

"Where's Camera?" Arthur is concerned.

"There! She's coming up the the runway now!" Jeanne beams with pride.

Arthur looks over to see their daughter, Camera. Dressed in a pink wool suit with black velvet trim, a small black hat, and white gloves, she walks proudly with her husband, Jaquime, and two daughters, Jeanne and Star. Throngs of people surround her as she looks over, gives her father a loving wink, and continues holding audience with the well-wishers. Arthur notices his granddaughter holding a doll—a blonde curly haired doll that once belonged to his daughter.

Curiously, Arthur says out loud, "Blonde doll . . . blonde doll . . . "

Arthur drifts again . . .

❖

August 30, 1992—National Tennis Center in Flushing Meadows, New York. Almost thirty years ago, the day before the U.S. Open. The event is for the Arthur Ashe

Foundation for the Defeat of AIDS. It is a beautiful, sun-filled day. Many celebrities, including McEnroe, Graf, Navratilova, and ten thousand fans show up. CBS is televising the event, live. How can this beautiful day possibly turn into a racial issue?

Arthur and Jeanne's good friends Marjory and Stan Smith have purchased identical blonde dolls, one for their daughter, Austin, the other for Camera. Camera is playing with her doll and it is obvious the television camera is focusing on this little Black girl playing with a blonde doll.

Arthur turns to his wife and whispers, "Jeanne, we've got to do something about Camera playing with a white doll. I can just hear my Black brothers telling me I was corrupting my daughter with ideas of white superiority."

It is a sad day. Arthur and Jeanne are torn between what the black community might say about their daughter innocently playing with a white doll and letting their daughter continue to play.

Sadly, Arthur remembers how he resolved the problem as he speaks out loud.

"I asked my wife to take the doll away!"

"I didn't quite understand you, Mr. Ashe." The Secret Service man is standing over Arthur.

"He's just thinking out loud," Jeanne explains to the baffled man. "He does that sometimes. "

"What did you say, Jeanne?"

"Nothing, dear."

"We're ready to seat you on the stage now, Mr. and Mrs. Ashe."

The Secret Service agents escort Arthur and Jeanne outside to a platform set up on the Capitol lawn. They both walk slowly to the stage and are directed to their seats. Arthur helps Jeanne to her chair and then sits down. Jeanne and Arthur look at each other—a silent, knowing look, one born of years of growing together, of shared experiences, of a lifetime of loving each other. They proudly look over to their daughter, Camera.

With her husband and children by her side, Camera steps up to the chief justice of the Supreme Court. She puts her left hand on a bible and raises her right hand in the air, and the Inaugural ceremony of the 50th president of the United States of America begins. . . .

And in President Camera Ashe-Brown's acceptance speech this day—after thanking the people of the United States, her election campaign manager, and especially her parents, Arthur and Jeanne Moutoussamy-Ashe—she closes with the following statement: "At the impressionable age of seven, my parents brought me to a tennis benefit for the Arthur Ashe Foundation for the Defeat of AIDS. My father instructed my mother to take a white doll away from me, for fear of reprisal from the Black community. And on *that* day, I decided I wanted to become president of the United States, to make sure that my daughter, and my daughter's daughter, would never have to be aware of the difference in the color of people's skin, as my father and his father and his father's father before him."

Camera reaches over and takes her daughter Star's hand and the blonde-haired doll she has been clutching, holds them up in the air, and says, "And as an American, I am proud to say . . . that day has come!"

EPILOGUE: Camera Ashe-Brown was not only the first African American to hold this office, but also the youngest president in the history of the United States of America. President Ashe-Brown sponsored legislation to help people of all color. Jeanne Ashe died during the third year of her daughter's first term of office. Arthur Ashe never made the Jesse Jackson march at the Lincoln Memorial. He died the evening of the Inaugural Ball.

GARLAND

BY RICHARD HACK

*T*here was an unnatural silence
about the place. Ordinarily, the
large room in Westminster
Hospital's south wing would be
pulsing with the sound of doctors
and nurses attending to the
medical facility's biggest ward. The
sophisticated medical equipment
would beat out a background
theme as some of Great Britain's
finest doctors treated deadbeats
and dilettantes alike, in the kind of
classless society created by
socialized medicine.

In the dim light which stole by the heavy drawn curtains, the ward took on an eerie quality. With the exception of a single large bed on one side, surrounded by several machines quietly keeping vigil over a solitary patient, the room was void of any signs of life.

The silence was the worst, however; and made all the more out of place when one considered that the frail, tiny woman curled up in one corner of the oversized bed was a legendary singer—Judy Garland.

◆

June 21, 1969. When Mickey Deans turned on the television to watch "The Royal Family," a documentary about the reigning monarch and her clan, and wrapped his arms around his wife of six months, he had little thought of illness. True, his own throat had been sore for several days, and Dr. Traherne had sent over some penicillin. But it was more an irritation than cause for concern.

Even when Judy excused herself, pointing to her throat, he laughingly said, "You, too. Now we both have the flu."

Later in bed, he would feel the coolness of her legs press against his back. And as he fell into a heavy sleep, she was softly humming some new tunes they had rehearsed earlier in the day. There was certainly no hint of the suffering to come.

By 11:00 A.M., the sun had long since risen past the bedroom windows of the cottage they were renting in Cadogan Place. "A real charmer," they had called it when singer Johnnie Ray found it for them after Judy's opening at London's Talk of the Town nightclub. It had been a five-week run and the critics were less than kind, pointing out that she looked "gaunt" and "haggard." But the Cadogan Place cottage more than compensated for any harsh words.

Hardly large enough to be called a house, the place was comfortable, like a favorite easy chair, and proper despite an occasional frayed edge. Lately, the cottage had taken on the sounds of construction as a new dressing room was being added to the master bedroom to make it easier for Judy to apply her makeup before shows. This was home, and both Judy and Mickey demonstrated it with every loving touch.

Mickey didn't hear the birds chirping outside the bedroom window that morning, or the dogs barking down the street. The incessant ringing of the telephone finally pulled him from his deep sleep. Stubbornly, he awoke, pushing aside a dream that imagined Judy wildly twirling in a field of daisies, dressed all in white and laughing as if it were the happiest day of her life. Groping for the phone, Mickey noticed Judy was no longer in bed.

Struggling to wipe the last cobwebs of sleep from his mind, he recognized the tipsy voice of Judy's old friend Charlie Cochran on the line from Los Angeles.

"Madame Gumm, if you please," Charlie requested, referring to Judy by her real last name.

"Madame Gumm has already arisen." Mickey laughed, responding in a pretentious British accent. "I'll have Madame phone you back momentarily," he quipped. And with that, he hung up and slowly rose to find his wife.

Moving past the mini-construction site on the far side of the room, Mickey knocked on the locked bathroom door.

Silence. Again he knocked, calling her name and twisting the knob as if a little encouragement might spring it open.

Suddenly possessed by a chill of panic, Mickey climbed out of the window of the partially completed dressing room and walked hurriedly across the roof, clutching his pajama bottoms against the summer wind. Peering in through the bathroom window, he saw Judy sitting on the commode, her hands pressed tightly against her temples, silently screaming out in pain.

Mickey crashed through the window, scattering bottles and toothbrushes across the room, his heart beating in an audible spasm. As he reached Judy, her eyes began to roll back in her head, and as her shoulders went limp, she collapsed in his arms.

Trembling at the sight of what he presumed was death, Mickey held Judy tightly as if to squeeze life back into her body. "Oh, my God! Hold on, baby. Hold on," he found himself saying as he quickly picked her up and struggled to get her out of the bathroom.

The moments felt like hours after he laid her gently on the bed. Fumbling with the phone to call the doctor; the agility of the attendants as they carried her to the ambulance; rushing through endless corridors until she slipped out of sight past the emergency room door; the look on the administrator's face when he asked her name and heard: "Judy Garland Deans."

They had rushed into the mews cottage with such authority that Mickey hadn't once questioned their well-rehearsed procedure. The quick use of oxygen, the strapping onto the stretcher. Then the breakneck ride through the streets of London, past the House of Parliament, as the siren screamed its piercing blast, echoing in his head until he thought it would burst.

He waited for what seemed like an eternity, though actually it had been slightly over an hour since the horror began. Only then, after endless pacing in an empty hallway, did Mickey walk outside for some air. A battery of press was already waiting to pounce on any tidbit of information.

He told them he knew nothing, that he couldn't speak. Still, the flashbulbs lighted the hospital entrance with the intensity of fireworks. And then he saw it. An extra edition of the *Daily Sun* was pushed in his face, with the bold headline: JUDY GARLAND CLINGS TO LIFE AFTER SUICIDE ATTEMPT.

Nausea overwhelmed him. Half-walking, half-stumbling back into Westminster, Mickey demanded answers to questions he was afraid to ask. "Yes, she has taken a toxic overdose of Seconal," the doctors said. "Apparently not intentional," they added, as if to reassure his doubts.

The drug was one of Judy's old standbys—the magic elixir that had put her to sleep nightly since her early days at MGM. *But how? Why?* Mickey thought, knowing full well that he had control of all her pills and doled them out with pharmaceutical precision no matter how Judy might beg for more.

"We've pumped her stomach, Mr. Deans, and found only traces. But there's been an enormous buildup of the drug in her body over the years. It's placed an enormous strain on her entire system. Unfortunately, your wife has suffered a massive stroke to the left side of the brain," explained Dr. Holmby, the hospital's chief neurosurgeon, walking as he spoke. "And X rays indicate a further aneurysm," he continued.

"Aneurysm?" Mickey questioned.

"It's a weakness in the artery wall inside the brain that

continues to expand like a balloon until it eventually explodes with such force that it damages the surrounding tissues," Dr. Holmby explained.

He pointed to an X ray, pinpointing a tiny white spot at the union of the internal carotid and posterior communicating arteries. It meant little to Mickey, other than the knowledge that his wife would surely die if the doctors didn't operate; and would most probably die if they tried.

After giving his permission, the long wait began. Two hours stretched into three, then four. During intermittent breaks, he tried telephoning Liza Minnelli—Judy's daughter in New York—but could only get her service. He tried contacting Sid Luft, Judy's ex-husband and father of her two other children, but there was no answer.

And then he remembered Charlie Cochran in Los Angeles, still waiting for Judy's return call. Charlie was an old friend. Perhaps he could track down the rest of the family.

"Charlie, Judy's been hurt," was all he could say when he finally had the operator complete the call. "We don't know much more. Find Liza and tell her to come right away."

If the family had been slow to hear the news, London was buzzing with it. Bad news always travels that way, it seems. Crowds began to gather outside the hospital. Several hundred fans, some clutching Garland record albums, were keeping a vigil alongside curiosity seekers who were satisfied merely to stare at her corner window on the third floor.

When they finally wheeled her out of the operating room, it had been eight hours since Mickey had last seen Judy. Only a small portion of her famous face was visible. The rest was wrapped in bandages that made it appear three times its normal size.

Dr. Holmby was smiling as he followed her out, nodding his head yes as Mickey asked the unspoken.

"I know now why they call her a trouper," the doctor said. "We've removed several blood clots from her brain, and clamped off the aneurysm. Now comes the hard part," he added, patting Mickey on the back. "The waiting." Doctors have their standard phrases. That was one.

Judy had fallen into a coma, and for the next several weeks her condition would remain critical. She was kept secluded in her specially prepared room at the Westminster, placed in the remodeled ward to buffer her from normal hospital traffic and the chance intrusion of a fan.

Liza had flown in from vacationing in the Hamptons and, together with Mickey, kept a vigil. Judy's postoperative coma refused to break, imprisoning her in some dark and distant trap of time that pulled her ever deeper despite their pleas for her to wake.

Every day at least a dozen bouquets of flowers and hundreds of letters of cheer arrived at Westminster. While the flowers went to various wards around the complex, Mickey carefully read every card and letter, knowing that if anything would make Judy respond, it would be the fans she had always refused to let down.

One month and a day after the stroke, on one of those balmy summer Sundays that London surprises herself with so infrequently, Liza opened the curtains in Judy's room to watch some newborn birds in a tree outside. Their mother was obviously out foraging for food, and her little brood was creating the most noisy fuss, shrilly chirping for her return.

As much to soothe herself as the babies, Liza began to sing softly, "Somewhere over the rainbow, blue birds fly. Birds fly over the rainbow, why then . . . "

"Oh, why can't I," joined a voice from across the room.

Liza turned with a start to find Judy awake and staring. After thirty-one days of silence, Garland sang! At the moment she had more the look of a scared, wide-eyed waif than a superstar, and it was difficult to tell who was more surprised.

"Mama! Oh, Mama!" Liza screamed, running to her side. She fought the overwhelming desire to squeeze her mother but couldn't help clutching her hand in excitement.

Then just as suddenly her incredible joy turned to fear. "Mama, Mama, it's Liza," she pleaded.

Judy, seemingly awake and alert, showed no sign of recognition; she didn't utter another sound. The tubes running from her nose and throat coupled with an unblinking stare did little to alleviate Liza's anxiety. And then, just as quickly as the moment came, it ended. Judy once again drifted off to sleep.

Each successive day, however, brought more movement from "Madame Gumm." She began to wake with regularity now, moving her eyes, holding up her left hand to wave weakly, and eventually managing her slightly twisted smile. Yet it was a silent smile, masking speechless suffering.

Occasionally, she broke through that silence and started quietly humming and singing her favorite songs—"Swanee" and "Chicago" among them—not always remembering all the words, but then she never did. That part of the Garland charm remained.

Though it was obvious from her singing that her legendary voice and speech mechanism weren't impaired by the stroke, she was still unable to talk. By some ironic quirk of nature, it seems that the section of the brain which is the storehouse for song lyrics and music has nothing to do with spontaneous speech or word recognition.

In addition, the stroke had left her right side paralyzed from the neck down, but the doctors felt confident that the muscles could be restored. Judy soon learned to eat and drink with her left hand, and within several days the doctors brought in a team of physical therapists to begin retraining her limbs.

Earlier, Mickey had wanted her flown back to the United States for treatment. When Judy found herself in emotional trouble or needed help with her various drug problems in the past, it was always to Peter Bent Brigham Hospital where she fled. She felt comfortable in the well-known facility in Boston, associated with the Harvard Medical School. But Judy's doctors at Westminster were giving her excellent care, and equally as important, no one had mentioned paying any bills—money always being a concern in Garland's life.

Every day the local papers would carry a report on her condition—not always the most accurate, of course. While the hospital would issue weekly updates, it wasn't often enough for the local tabloids, which reported headlines like JUDY GARLAND NEVER TO WALK AGAIN or GARLAND IN DRUG-INDUCED STUPOR AFTER STROKE.

Not to be outdone, the U.S. newspapers provided continuing reports, as well—slightly less dramatic, but nevertheless just as misleading. It was, after all, a journalist's dream—the image of the long-suffering Garland putting up the fight for her life, once again triumphant. And readers as well as reporters were seemingly insatiable in their search for the smallest tidbit of news.

In reality, much of her days were spent in frustration, trying to relearn the simplest of motions. She had been equipped with a hip and leg brace, which she dragged around like the heavy weight it was, occasionally keeping time to her humming by lurching herself around the room with the aid of a walker.

Although she had managed to put on a little weight, her body was still so frail that the clumsy metal and the matron-like shoe to which it was attached seemed grotesquely out of proportion to the rest of her figure. Her shapely legs, always a source of pride to Judy no matter how the rest of her body might have fluctuated in weight, now were her greatest embarrassment. And she took great pains to make sure they were covered at all times.

Several days before Judy was scheduled to leave Westminster, it became more and more obvious that she was shaking loose the shackles chaining the spoken word inside her mind. At first, she began to just utter sounds—nothing intelligible, more grunts than words.

Frowns poured across her brow as she strained to release the images piling one atop the other. But it was by accident that the cherished moment happened.

One of her least favorite sessions was a test the doctors did for sensitivity by gently tickling her right sole with a needle. The frustration at knowing she *should* feel something and yet didn't would eat away inside her for hours afterward.

This day, however, the needle caused her foot to twitch and receive a healthy jab in the process. "OUCH!" came out of her mouth with such force that several nurses from across the hall came to investigate.

It wasn't much, but there was a standing ovation as sincere as any Judy Garland had ever received.

Leaving the hospital on August 15 proved a challenge both in agility and patience. Since word of the pending departure had leaked out in the press, it had been decided to stage an exit which would satisfy the fans, but be the least taxing to Judy.

Barricades had been erected along the hospital's south side, across from the delivery dock to the administration building. The raised concrete area for receiving supplies offered the perfect protected showcase for the convalescing star.

As Judy was wheeled down the corridor toward the exit, the cheers from the waiting crowd echoed in intensity. Though both Mickey and Liza had been against it, Dr. Holmby felt that a positive, visual demonstration of love from Judy's fans might be the best therapy for the recovering performer. He was wrong.

Nearly a thousand fans were scattered across the side lawn of Westminster, and when Judy finally came into view, the resulting outcry took on odious dimensions. The few bobbies on duty were helpless to stop the push of fans trying to gain a closer glimpse of their cherished idol.

Judy was rushed into the waiting ambulance with her nurse, with Mickey and Liza just barely able to escape the throng. As the ambulance inched its way through the crowd, Judy sobbed uncontrollably. It was the first time since her stroke she had cried, her mind opened to release her suffering in the silence of her tears.

Back at their mews cottage, another group of fans were waiting. Fortunately, their next-door neighbor, Richard Harris, who had spent the previous evening drinking on a pub crawl, had little time to put up with what he called "a collection of elderly women and wimpish men playing recordings of Judy Garland singing 'Over the Rainbow' on their portable tape decks." He promptly called the local constable, who dispatched some men to clear the area.

Once inside, Judy was immediately placed in bed, and quite promptly fell into the deep sleep only exhaustion can bring. Ironically, while the stroke had left her speech impaired, her body paralyzed, and her mind a prison for memory, it had freed her from an even more tormenting hell: her addiction to drugs.

It was a story Judy loved to tell. Ever since her earliest days at MGM, she was given pills to pep up and pills to calm down. Everyone did it, she said. But while everyone else was taking a little white pill that mixed Benzedrine with phenobarbital to lose weight and gain energy, Judy found herself taking more and more of the drug to feel normal. Without it, she felt depressed, confused, and anxious. So much so that when the little white pill turned to a little yellow pill (after the addition of Amytal Sodium), MGM's brightest star was a full-fledged addict.

Nembutals (she called them her "Yellows") and Thorazine came next, followed by "Reds," or Seconals, to numb her to sleep. By day it was Ritalin to put her back on her feet. And while her drug abuse was the stuff of legend, doctors feared that any determined attempt at eliminating the pills would kill her.

Yet the body has a way of protecting itself, and after Judy's stroke, surgery, and subsequent coma, any withdrawal she suffered from a lifetime of drug abuse was absorbed in the process of recuperation.

Still, the next several months of therapy would be the hardest that Judy had ever had to endure. On Dr. Holmby's recommendation, a speech therapist was hired from a place called St. Aloysius Parish, while a physiotherapist was dispatched on loan from Westminster, and together they set out to rebuild a star who had spent the majority of her life tearing herself down.

Despite the seemingly insurmountable odds, Liza was convinced that her mother could make a complete recovery. She kept reminding herself that, after all, less than ten years before, Patricia Neal had had a series of strokes, far worse than Judy's, and had gone on to have a child and perform again.

And Judy herself seemed up to the challenge. Twice a day, she would play word games, using giant cue cards as prompts. Knowing that her song lyrics were still clear in her mind made it easier. Words like "rainbow" and "trolley" and "wizard" were flashed for her recognition. Yet the progress was frustratingly slow. Words discovered one day were lost again the next.

Depression is the worst enemy of any recovery from a serious illness, and both Mickey and Liza made it a point to pull Judy away from it whenever possible. Evenings were spent around the piano in singalongs. And with each passing day, the darkness inside Judy's mind was broken with gentle fragments of light.

Since there wasn't really enough room in their small cottage for long-term guests, Liza rented a flat in nearby Mayfair that belonged to Alfred Lunt, the famed American actor. Although he rarely visited the place, he and wife Lynn Fontanne kept it for those "rare moments when England's legitimate theater is in flower."

Soon Judy was making excursions over to the "Lunt Dump" as she called it, and clearly enjoying her moments out of the house. Physically, her condition had improved so well that during the six months since she had left the hospital, she had regained almost all mobility in her right arm, and was hobbling around quite freely despite her brace.

Not that there weren't occasional setbacks. Out of frustration, she would bang her left fist on tables, screaming profanity without the slightest stammer. Throwing ashtrays at walls was also very popular, but doomed, however, to extinction when the ashtray supply diminished.

For a while she also began locking herself in her room where she would remain sometimes as long as a day without stirring. Her therapist soon learned these spells came and went in patterns, a throwback to her days as the pampered star. Gradually, they decreased in number as her body increased in strength.

Like the calm which follows a storm, Judy eventually accepted her situation, and even began to develop an interest in needlepoint, samples of which began appearing with regularity around the house in the form of cushions and pillows and plaques that read "There's No Place Like Home." Perhaps only someone who had spent the majority of his or her life in hotels on the road could appreciate how important Judy's home life became to her.

As her speech improved, her curiosity was aimed more at kitchen utensils than show business. The marvel of Teflon-coated cookware alone enchanted her for several days. In fact, for a period of time, the only food being served in the house was fried eggs "à là Gumm," cooked to demonstrate how they slipped effortlessly from the pan.

While visitors were carefully paced, both in number and time, Judy was most comfortable in the company of her closest friends. And no amount of convincing would pry her into the public. Mickey had long since given up trying to get Judy to accept dinner invitations. "Not yet, Mickey. So-o-on," she would say, dropping the subject.

One topic which couldn't be put off much longer was money. While Judy's medical expenses at Westminster had been paid through an arrangement with the Screen Actors Guild, the cost of therapy and living expenses was fast depleting what savings they had. Judy, of course, had a history of money problems.

Despite having earned an estimated $14 million for MGM, another $3 million in record deals, plus an amount the IRS once estimated at $6.5 million in concert tours since 1951, Judy Garland spent most of her life in debt. Her mother, her agents, and her husbands had seen to that, not to mention managers who left her owing $200,000 in back taxes.

She had no jewelry or artwork to hock. In fact, other than her clothes, her scrapbooks, a photograph of herself with John F. Kennedy, and a couple of pairs of favorite earrings, her memories were her only possessions. And half of those were now lost.

"I can always sing for my supper," she had quipped in the past. Now that option was no longer hers. Still unable to concentrate for extended periods of time, and not yet totally rehabilitated, it could be years before another performance might be possible.

Several months before her stroke, however, Mickey had been in negotiations to open up a chain of Judy Garland Cinemas. The syndicate of businessmen who had originally been approached to fund the project had backed out, afraid of her reputation for no-shows and irresponsibility.

Now things were different. Judy's illness and spirited recovery had created such worldwide sympathy that the press had built her up into a saint of suffering. It was an image that fit the Garland mold, and one she knew how to play to the hilt.

The syndicate was now eager to reopen negotiations, but that meant Mickey would have to fly to New York and leave Judy for the first time in over a year. Just weeks earlier, Liza had also left London, to return to Hollywood to discuss the film version of the Broadway hit *Cabaret* with producer Cy Feuer.

John Kander and Fred Ebb, who wrote the music and lyrics, had insisted that Liza meet Cy, so convinced were they that she would be the perfect performer to recreate the role of Sally Bowles.

For Judy, the news was just as exciting, and she would not listen to any talk of Liza staying in London to "take care of Mama." For Mickey to leave was another story. The two had grown closer as Judy improved, and the doctors became worried that an extended separation might slow her progress.

As apprehensive as Judy was over the thought of being left behind, it was obvious she was hardly in shape to make the trip herself, and she knew how desperately they needed the money that a string of mini-theatres could bring. After much deliberation and cajoling, it was decided that Mickey would travel to New York "for several weeks, no more," he promised.

September 6, 1970. The day before he was scheduled to leave, Judy arranged with several of their closest friends—agent Philip Roberge, Reverend Peter Delaney, her two therapists who were now like members of the family, and a neighbor, Michael Nelson—to surprise Mickey with what she called a "going away but hurry back" party, aimed at calming her spirits as much as buoying his.

Judy insisted on doing all the cooking, which meant that while the guests began to arrive at seven o'clock, dinner was still in a state of raw ingredients by nine. Finally, Philip took over frying some hamburgers, while Judy instructed him on the use of Teflon pans.

The highlight of the night was to have been a chocolate cake Judy had ordered from a nearby bakery owned by a Chinese couple named Pan and Foo. They had somehow managed to misspell Bon Voyage, writing instead Bob Voyage, prompting everyone to kid Judy about her mysterious beau. However, it was Mickey who stole the spotlight with a surprise all his own.

With everyone assembled in the living room around the fire, he handed Judy a small trunk tied with a huge yellow ribbon and a card that said, "To warm your feet while I'm gone. Love, Mickey."

Like a child at Christmas, Judy struggled to tear the ribbon from the trunk, yanking with all her regained strength. Not able to bear it another second, she reached for her needlepoint scissors and snipped the bow.

As the lid of the trunk popped open, out jumped a tiny Maltese puppy with a tag that announced his name was "Toto." Amid the "oohs" and "aahs" of everyone in the group, Judy hugged the small moppet of fur, tears streaming down her face. "I lo-ve yo-u, Mickey," she stuttered, throwing him a kiss. "I love you, too, hon," he silently mouthed in response.

That night, Toto took up his position at the foot of the bed and became the new ruler of the roost. If Mickey had bought a lucky charm, it couldn't have worked better magic than that puppy. Whenever he would call from New York, and ask about Judy's progress, she would always answer with "Today, Toto and I planted a bed of flowers near the back door; or Toto and I walked out for the mail."

And it was Toto who came to the rescue when Mickey said he had to stay in the States a while longer, something about another offer from a theater chain in Los Angeles. Judy merely rocked herself to sleep, holding her dog and thanking God that at least something hadn't deserted her.

With the exception of a couple of weekend trips back to London, and a few days vacation at Christmas, Mickey had been away for nearly five months. Five months to the day, in fact, when London was hit by one of its worse storms in decades. TV newscasts had warned of its arrival, and Judy was terrified.

It was a phobia left over from childhood when a freak storm had hit Grand Rapids. Judy's mother, Ethel Gumm, became so hysterical by the force of the storm that she took her three small girls down into the basement of their house and locked them there all night. It was a horrifying experience which haunted her still.

As the winds began to pick up, Judy huddled on the sofa with Toto, clutching the dog and flinching with every groan of the old cottage. The afternoon sun, normally peeking through the leaded windows in the dining room, long since abandoned its post, disappearing instead behind dark, ominous clouds.

The first trickle of rain began to fall just after four o'clock. Judy turned on the television set to block out the sound, picked up a stack of magazines that seemed to be piled in every corner of the living room, and tried to catch up on old reading.

Any serious thought of ridding her mind of anxiety fled with the first crash of thunder. It shook the very ground at Cadogan Place, just as the lightning that followed lit up the countryside for miles around.

Grabbing Toto and half-running, half-stumbling to the bedroom, Judy buffered her ears with pillows as she pulled herself into bed. *Jesus Christ,* she thought to herself. *This is Dorothy and Toto going over the fucking rainbow.*

For the first time in months, she longed for some pills. Tuinals, Nembutals. Anything! For years she had supplies better than the neighborhood pharmacy. Now when she *really* needed them, she thought, there's not one in the house. God, how she wished to just blot out the fear.

A raging clap of thunder that could only have meant the heavens had just broken in two sent Toto leaping from the bed.

"Toto! Toto, yo-u come ba-ck here this minute," Judy screamed.

She stopped at the bedroom door, screaming to an empty house, her voice absorbed by the violence of the storm.

"Damn you, Toto!"

Struggling to control her fear, she removed her brace.

"Wi-th my luck, you'd at-tract lightning," she muttered to the heap of metal as she tossed it on the floor, half-laughing at the thought. "Toto, when I fi-nd you," she screamed as she limped through the house, shaking her fist as she went, "you are going to be-e one sad puppy.

"When you're smiling, when you're smiling, the whole world smiles with you," Judy began to sing softly to herself as she made her way from room to room.

With each successive crash of lightning, her voice got louder. The great Judy Garland, giving a concert for one. Or, make that two. Before she reached the end of the song, there was Toto cowering in the corner of the fireplace. Until the rain stopped early the next morning, they didn't budge from the spot.

As emotionally upsetting as the storm had been, it proved to be a turning point in Judy's recovery. No longer did she feel unable to care for herself. No longer was there that barrier of self-doubt that spells the difference between hope and despair. For the very first time, Judy shared the belief that there would be an end to her illness. And her brace was packed away forever.

◈

April 20, 1971. Mickey's arrival back in London was turned into an occasion. Judy surprised him at the airport. Disguised in a blonde wig and Krishna robe, she not only didn't attract attention, she found people actually were avoiding her.

Her limp was now more a stiffness in her stride, an ever-so-slight arc of her leg as if perhaps her right shoe were heavier than her left; something more sensed than noticed.

Keeping pace with her growing confidence was an equally growing ego. She was beginning to feel like a star again, taking great pains with her hair and makeup, and selecting her wardrobe with an unerring eye. And she was able to make the slight stammer remaining in her speech sound enchanting.

"Hello there, good lo-oking." She winked at Mickey as she put her arm in his and led him to their waiting car. "Ne-ed a lift?"

The radiance she projected was filled with an optimism about the future, a future in which Mickey had already staked a large claim.

The car hadn't yet reached their mews cottage when Mickey told her the news. "I've closed the theater deal, hon. We'll be rich."

"No! Yo-ou closed it?" Judy shouted. "Why-hy didn't you tell me?" she asked, jabbing him in the side, laughing.

"I wanted to see your face, luv," he said. "The people at Cinerama came through, and if all goes as planned, there will be two dozen Judy Garland Cinemas across the country within two years and a dozen more the year after that. And to launch the project," he said, pulling her close, "they've decided to convert their flagship theater in Hollywood into the first of the chain. It's all been arranged, luv. They're opening it on New Year's Eve, and they want you to perform," he added.

"Wh-a-t," Judy said, able to understand but unwilling to comprehend. "Pe-erform?" she repeated in disbelief.

"You can do it, hon," he said, patting her hand. And those were the last words shared between them until they reached Cadogan Place.

Mickey had spent over seven months in difficult negotiations to complete the deal with Cinerama, and the only thing remaining to bring it to fruition was Judy's cooperation. Yet it was the one thing he couldn't possibly guarantee.

"No-oo more performing," Judy said as she slowly closed the front door behind her. "I can't do it. It's be-en nearly two years since I've sung be-fo-ore an audience. Mickey, don't ask me to do it. Not yet," she pleaded.

She wanted to please. She had *always* wanted to please. But this was too much for even Mickey to expect.

"What, you're never going to sing again?" asked Mickey, walking away from her.

"Mic-ckey," she begged, holding out her hand.

"Listen, Judy, this deal is worth a lot of money to you. Over a million dollars next year alone. It's the kind of stability that you have said over and *over* was missing from your life. And now that I've arranged for Judy Garland, singer, to become Judy Garland, businesswoman, all you can say is 'Mic-ckey'?"

"What do you wa-nt me to-o do," she screamed back. "Limp on stage, stutter out 'Over the Rainbow' and be laughed all the way back to London? Make a fool of *yourself,* not me!" she added, stomping out of the room as best she could.

"If that's what it takes, yes!" he yelled, chasing after her and grabbing her firmly by the shoulders. Spinning her around, Mickey felt his grip press into the flesh of her arms. His eyes narrowed to form catlike slits as his temper flared. "You want to feel sorry for yourself, and remain an invalid, fine! Act like a baby all you want, but don't expect me to keep holding the bottle."

"Let me go. You're hurting me!" she screamed, pulling herself free.

"Let you go? I'll let you go, all right, baby." With a single swipe of his arm, he sent a flower vase and their wedding picture flying off the piano and across the room, before slamming out of the house.

Only Judy's gentle sobs broke the deadly silence that remained.

Two days passed, then a week. And Judy heard nothing from Mickey. She refused to continue her therapy. She had her first cigarette in months, and was eating so little that she soon began to look gaunt and pasty once again. Finally, for consolation, she called Liza in Hollywood and was shaken when Mickey answered the phone.

"Mic-ckey?" she said, not believing her ears.

"Judy Garland, isn't it?" he kidded. "The famous sing-er," he added, stretching out the word.

"I've missed you, baby," she cooed in the receiver.

"Enough to come to California?" he asked.

"Enough to come to Cali-forni-a and sing," she replied.

"You mean that?" Mickey said incredulously.

"What more can they do that they haven't already done?" She laughed. "Just be there to push me onstage."

And he would.

Just under three months were left before the New Year's Eve show. And much work lay ahead. Because Judy had regained much of her lost weight and was a rather shapely 110 pounds, new costumes were ordered. Bob Mackie, the young protégé of Ray Aghayan, was called and designed three new outfits—all of which, he was told, would show off Judy's legs. Mickey wanted everyone to see what shape she was in.

He called every shot, approved every move, becoming more assertive with each passing day. A hard, dictatorial quality began to spike Mickey's mood, yet if Judy noticed, she tolerated it in silence.

Vocal coach Bob Easton was working with Judy twice a week, while Mort Lindsay was hired to reorchestrate her old numbers. The folks at Cinerama felt that what her audience of fans would want to hear were their favorites, and Judy agreed. At this point, just walking and talking was enough of a chore without learning new material as well.

Cinerama had decided that since there would be only a single show, tickets would be priced at $1,000 apiece with a two-ticket maximum. Judy would receive half of the gross, with the remainder going to drug abuse foundations. As excited as she was over the prospect of that kind of a windfall, she secretly wondered whether any would sell. She had little need to worry. Within two hours after the 1200 seats went on sale, the SOLD OUT sign was posted.

By Thanksgiving, it was a rejuvenated Judy who celebrated the holiday with her children, Charlie Cochran, ex-husband Sid Luft, and Mickey. After a feast of turkey with all the traditional trimmings, the family gathered around the piano for a holiday singathon.

At last, I've found happiness, Judy thought to herself.

The mood was not to last, however. As December began and the long shadows of winter crept across their lawn in Brentwood, Judy became more quick-tempered and less tolerant of Mickey's increasingly foul moods. With Christmas still weeks away, she wanted New Year's Eve to come and go quickly.

The reality of having to perform again colored every thought. Despite the fact that rehearsals were going well, Judy started to have doubts about her ability to face an audience.

It wasn't a fear relating to her stroke. Only the smallest trace of a limp was visible in her walk, and her speech had returned so close to normal that days would go by without a single slip.

This was a fear that had tugged at her all her life. She was a full-fledged fraud, her mind told her. Without talent, without appeal. And lucky beyond belief to have kidded folks this long.

When the thought gripped her, no one or nothing could snap it loose. Yet, just as quickly, she was back onstage, chatting with the familiar stagehands and joking about "the old days."

For Christmas, she gave her crew and orchestra small silver pill boxes, engraved "Love always, Judy."

"They're empty! They're empty!" she kidded as they unwrapped their gifts. But her laughter was hiding an awful secret.

Days earlier, she had left rehearsal early and made a surprise visit to her old friend, Dr. Max Zimmerman. It was Dr. Zimmerman who had helped her regulate her drug intake in the early 60s, and she felt that he alone might understand her need for them now.

Mickey prayed a lot those last few days, but never more than on the night of December 31, 1971. Judy seemed nervous and unusually quiet all the way to the theater. Mickey chalked it off to stage fright and was at his charming best in an effort to keep the mood light.

Judy had decided to put her makeup on herself and just have it touched up before going onstage. Dressed in a white sequined dress, her hair freshly done by Vidal Sassoon, she looked more radiant than Mickey had ever seen her, far younger than her forty-nine years. And she held Mickey's hand like a child, silently playing with the ends of his fingers.

At the theater, all was bedlam. Sunset Boulevard had been closed for several hours, and traffic was backed up for blocks. A red carpet had been rolled out in front for arriving guests, and bleachers had been erected across the street for fans to cheer the lucky few who gained entrance.

Despite being the dead of winter, it was a beautiful night in Hollywood, the kind that finds the Santa Ana winds blowing from the east, enchanting all with their warmth.

All except Judy. Her dressing room was filled with flowers and telegrams of congratulations. She immediately ordered them taken away, grabbing a bottle of Scotch off a tray as the room was cleared.

"But, hon, what's the matter?" Mickey asked gently, not wanting to upset her more.

"Get out!" she screamed, hitting him around the shoulders as he stumbled backward toward the door.

As her dressing room door slammed shut and locked, the crowd assembled outside heard gentle sobbing from the star inside. Mickey moved quickly to assure everyone it was only a small tantrum.

"A little stage fright," he said, laughing.

If he found something funny about the situation, nobody else did. Too many times in the past had they seen this scenario played out. And every time, it ended the same. No show.

Mickey went down to the audience to welcome his guests—Liza, her husband, Peter, Lorna and Joey Luft with their father, Sid, and Charlie Cochran, who had flown in from New York.

All was in place. The newly remodeled theater had replaced every seat and installed all new carpeting in preparation for the night. The circular walls had new fabric draped to provide ear-perfect acoustics.

Mickey felt his palms perspiring as he shook hands with the president of Cinerama and his wife, a Judy Garland fan from the 40s who had originally convinced her husband that he should sign the deal. He tried to look calm as he excused himself to check once more on his wife.

What he found was a hysterical stage manager.

"She says she won't go on, Mr. Deans," he blurted out, his voice rising with each word. "She says she won't sing."

"Oh, God." Mickey sighed, realizing his worst fears had been realized.

He tried banging on her door, but she refused to come out. He tried compliments, bribes, threats. Nothing worked.

"She says she has Ritalins, Mr. Deans," the stage manager confessed.

"Don't believe her, it's a bluff," Mickey responded confidently, slamming his fists into her dressing room door, screaming, "No more drugs!" loud enough that he felt certain the entire audience could hear.

At that point he didn't care. The important thing was that *Judy* heard and listened. He told the stage manager to start the overture exactly on time at 10:00 P.M., and returned to his seat next to Liza.

Seated directly in front of them, Mickey noticed Dr. Zimmerman and exchanged a surprised hello.

"Thanks again for the seats, Mickey," he said, shaking hands. "Judy really didn't have to go to all this trouble. I would have been happy to help her at any time, you know that." He smiled.

"Help her?" Mickey questioned.

"Yes, you know. The Ritalins. She said she wasn't taking them anymore, of course. But, just having a bottle to hold in her purse would help her get through this. A security blanket, she said. You know."

"Yes," said Mickey, the sweat beginning to bead more intensely across his brow.

The house lights began to dim as Mickey dropped into his seat. With his heart pounding, he squeezed Liza's hand and said a silent prayer. At the first sounds of the overture from the Mort Lindsay Orchestra, the entire audience was on its feet, applauding in a display of affection that Hollywood would always remember.

As it ended, the silver and blue-beaded curtain was slowly raised. In the center of an empty stage, a single spotlight cut a piercing wedge of brilliance. Silence, except for a rush of breath as the entire audience inhaled in expectation.

And then she was there. Stepping into the spotlight— sparkling, shimmering like the legend she created.

Her voice that night prompted many to remember earlier triumphs at the Palace and Carnegie Hall. It was full and driven from the very depth of her tiny body to fill the stage, the theater, and out into the street.

For twenty-two songs, she spun her magic, removing any doubt that Judy Garland was home to stay. By the time midnight arrived and the audience joined in to sing "Auld Lang Syne," tears poured from every eye in the house. The paroxysm of emotion felt that night moved the packed theater to pandemonium.

And that applause continues still. She had conquered drugs, depression, paranoia, divorce, and a paralyzing stroke, and with each passing year her legend would grow. She became an inspiration to a drug- and disease-torn nation that victory needs only the courage to grasp it.

The months following her triumph found her marriage to Mickey Deans failing. As her confidence grew, his seemed to shrink in direct proportion. They had simply outgrown one another, Judy had said as she handed him the unopened bottle of Ritalin and said a last good-bye.

And any thoughts of longing to go over the rainbow were packed away forever. Judy Garland had at last discovered that she *was* the rainbow all the time.

MARILYN BECK, the author of *Marilyn Beck's Hollywood* and *Only Make Believe*, is a syndicated columnist. Beck is currently featured weekly on E! Entertainment's "The Gossip Show."

The late MARCIA BORIE worked as a reporter for the entertainment trade paper *The Hollywood Reporter*.

ARMAND DEUTSCH is a former MGM film producer in the golden age of Hollywood, was chairman of a successful venture capital firm. Frequently published, his most recent book is *Me and Bogie—and Other Friends and Acquaintances from a Life in Hollywood and Beyond*.

JENNIE LOUISE FRANKEL is a professional screenwriter, composer, and producer.

TERRIE MAXINE FRANKEL, co-founder of the *Producer's Guild of America Magazine*, is co-author of *Tales from the Casting Couch*.

SUSAN GRANGER is a nationally syndicated movie and drama critic for CRN Radio Network and can be seen on American Movie Classic Cable TV.

RICHARD HACK was the television editor and critic for the entertainment trade paper *The Hollywood Reporter*. His other books include *Next to Hughes, Jackson Family Values, Richard Hack's Complete Home Video Companion for Parents,* and *Memories of Madison County*. He lives in Maui, Hawaii, and Beverly Hills, California.

ORLANDO RAMIREZ's work has appeared in the *San Diego Reader* and the *San Diego Union-Tribune*. He is a columnist for the Copley News Service and currently writes for the *Riverside Press-Enterprise*.

The late PAUL ROSENFIELD covered Hollywood for the *Los Angeles Times* from 1969 to 1990 and later worked as a contributing editor for *Vanity Fair*.

VERNON SCOTT has been writing a daily column on Hollywood for United Press International for forty-five years. He wrote extensively for *Ladies Home Journal, McCall's,* and *Good Housekeeping* for thirty years and is the author of two books with Jill Ireland, *Life Wish* and *Life Lines*.

BOB THOMAS has covered Hollywood for the Associated Press for more than half a century, and is the author of thirty books including biographies of Walt Disney, Fred Astaire, Joan Crawford. He is also the host and interviewer for cable television's "Hollywood Stars."

LES WHITTEN is a former investigative reporter who worked with Jack Anderson, *The Washington Post*, and many others. His work includes extensive coverage of the Kennedy era. He is the author of fifteen books, including nine novels.